DEADLY SYNDROME

DEADLY SYNDROME

Arline Todd

DEADLY SYNDROME

"The White House" photo © Ryan Beiler/Dreamstime
"Helicopter" photo © Igor Dolgov/Dreamstime
"Alpine Ski Slopes" photo © Antoine Beyeler/Dreamstime
Cover design by Arline Todd

ISBN-13: 978-1484044872
ISBN-10: 1484044878

Printed in USA.

Dedication

To my daughter, Diane Marie Todd, whose image graces the cover of this book. She is the mother *par excellence* of my four precious grandchildren as well as a busy, successful executive in the business world. And yet she manages to make time for me, especially when it is sorely needed.

Acknowledgments

Many thanks to my sister Sandra Miller for her support and encouragement during the preparation of this book. I know it was difficult for her to take time away from her commitment as Altrusa governor of District Eleven. Thanks also to my sister Linda Hagerty for her generous assistance with the typing and retyping involved with the manuscript, even though she objected to the fate of certain characters.

My gratitude to my fellow book club members—all avid readers, authors, or reviewers—for their advice and their good wishes during the creation of this book, especially Juliet Burns (a.k.a. Jillian Burns), Debrah Huston Coward, Kelley Hartsell, and Yvonne Jocks (a.k.a.) Evelyn Vaughn.

As a former active member of Altrusa International Inc., I want to acknowledge the generosity of its members who work hard at the community level to promote the spread of literacy on a worldwide basis. Altrusa is the first service organization to adopt a program to stamp out illiteracy. If you would like to join, volunteer, or just learn more about Altrusa International, go to www.altrusa.com.

And finally, sincere thanks to my daughter Diane for her help, for her unwavering confidence in my writing, and for letting me use her picture on the cover of this book, despite her inclination against it.

Prologue

RESA MYLES STARED at the pair of pantyhose she had just pulled out from under the couch pillow. They were not hers. Why were they here in Steve's apartment? A feeling of apprehension settled over her heart and her pulse raced. What was going on? Her mind started making all kinds of excuses, but somewhere deep inside she knew the truth.

She stood up as Steve Sheldon came back into the room, drinks in hand. Her throat was tight and she couldn't keep the trembling from her voice as she held up the hosiery. "Who left these here?"

He frowned and glanced at the pantyhose, then sat down on the couch and put their drinks on the coffee table. "I don't know."

"You don't know! They were on your couch, stuffed behind your throw pillow. And they're not mine."

"Are you sure?"

"Yes."

"Then, obviously someone left them here. I don't know who it was."

Stunned, Resa sank back onto the couch next to Steve. "Are you saying different women have been here and you don't know which one left her stockings behind?"

Steve sighed and ran his fingers through his dark hair, then took a large swallow from his drink. The look on his ruggedly handsome face was a mixture of guilt and anger. "Yes."

Resa buried her face in both hands, smothering a small moan. "You're sleeping with other women."

"It's no big deal—just recreational sex. They don't mean anything. You're the only one I really care about. I love you. You know that."

"Then why?" Bewildered, she locked her gaze on his gray-blue eyes.

Steve rubbed his forehead. "I want to keep things light. No commitments. I'm not going through that hell again."

His messy divorce. She understood his fears, but he went too far. He'd lied to her. And she had made it easy for him by not questioning his movements. As a CIA agent, Steve was often secretive about late meetings and sudden trips he had to take. She was never sure whether he was in the country or not. . . . But there must have been so many lies.

She felt her eyes filling with tears and blinked them back. She believed with all her heart that lies were the death of a relationship. When she spoke, the words came out choked with pain. "I won't be part of some harem."

Steve plunked his drink back onto the coffee table, his hand unsteady. "You're not. They don't mean anything. These relationships aren't important. They're casual. It just helps me feel free. I don't want to be tied down. What can I say?"

Resa stood, walked over to the fireplace, and leaned her head on the mantle. She was cold. Earlier, Steve had kindled a fire, and she welcomed the warmth soaking into her trembling body. The pungent odor of the burning logs stung her nose.

She heard Steve rise and walk toward her. She kept her back to him.

"What do you want, Resa? Tell me."

She was silent for a moment, the hurt still too deep.

"I want this not to have happened," she whispered and turned to face him.

"I'm sorry. I never meant to hurt you. I do love you." He put his arms around her.

"I can't live with this."

"You're breaking off with me?" He stepped back.

"Yes, I guess I am. I won't pay the penalty for your ex-wife's behavior." Her trembling eased off and an odd feeling of numbness, of unreality flooded through her.

He turned away and sat back on the couch, elbows on knees, and looked up at her with a frown. "That's not what I want, but maybe it's for the best."

"How can you say that?" Did she mean so little to him? How could he be so callous? She felt a prick of resentment stir to life amidst the hurt.

He shrugged. "Big things are happening for you right now—the presidential appointment. You'll be kept running."

Resa almost winced. Yes, she'd be busy. The president had put her in charge of his new Control of Cancer Agency. As the key molecular biologist on the program, she would spearhead a major international push to cure cancer. It was an honor. Her career was soaring.

However, her personal life sucked.

But she was not in the wrong here. He was. She turned to him and her voice was hard. "If you decide to grow up, give me a call."

It was over.

She grabbed her purse and walked toward the door without giving him a chance to reply.

Dazed, Steve caught his breath as he watched her tall, slender form move with the liquid grace he knew so well. He buried his face in his hands as the door closed behind her.

"Damn, what the hell have I done?"

He pictured the hurt in her dark blue eyes, and saw again in his mind the tremble in her fingers as she brushed back the thick, dark chestnut curls that fell to her shoulders. Deep down he had known one day Resa would find out about the others. What he didn't expect was the wrenching pain he felt at hurting her, losing her.

He loved her, but he knew love didn't last. He had made a major effort to keep the love he felt for Resa manageable. Light and casual. He would enjoy loving her and when it was over, he'd let her go.

So why the hell did it hurt so much? Why did he feel an almost unbearable loss? Why was her beautiful heart-shaped face with its fine features locked in his mind?

I'll get over it, he told himself.

But he wasn't sure he believed that.

Chapter 1

Three Years Later, Washington, D.C.

RESA MYLES STEPPED into the Oval Office and smiled, determined to mask the hint of trepidation she felt at this unscheduled meeting with the president. "Good afternoon, Mr. President."

President Matthew Harland rose and came around the desk to shake Resa's extended hand with a firm, practiced grip. He guided her away from the large mahogany desk, which was flanked by the flags of office and dominated the room, toward a comfortable grouping of couches and chairs.

"Sit down, Dr. Myles. Relax. I know you're probably a little tired from the early flight. How are things at the Stanford Center?" Harland was taking glasses from a tall, polished cabinet. Resa knew that Harland prided himself on remembering what particular drink each of his regular visitors preferred; he enjoyed playing the role of host and chose to ignore the tradition that callers at the White House remain standing while the president stood. She had been told that Harland was at times secretly amused at the disconcerted looks from visitors who, new to his routine, found themselves being seated and personally served by the president.

"Thank you, Mr. President." Resa had seated herself on the roomy couch and placed her briefcase on a small coffee table. "Things are going quite well, sir. I have some of the most recent data with me, but you may have seen it already on the CCA network," she commented, referring to the secure computer network linking the worldwide cancer research centers that were funded under the Control of Cancer Agency.

Watching the president, Resa reflected that she had never seen him make an awkward gesture. Harland was a big man, but he moved gracefully, as if he were under the eye of a television camera. In a man of his build it gave the impression of controlled strength.

"Yes, I've seen it." Harland handed Resa a drink and sat opposite her. "Scotch and a little water," he said, nodding toward the drink Resa held.

Resa murmured her thanks. Usually they met later in the day; she wasn't a lunchtime drinker and would have preferred coffee, but she gestured with the glass, sipped her drink, and waited for the president to get around to the real reason for the meeting. Her uneasiness was confirmed when she had been whisked through the Chief of Staff David Blair's office, for usually she would have had at least an hour to kill, either talking to Blair or checking on the latest computer output on the network at the nearby CCA Computer Center, while the president—often behind schedule because of unplanned meetings—caught up on his regular appointments.

Harland smiled, and then said with quiet pride, "I'm activating Project Immunity." He paused to let the full import of his statement be realized. "I'll give the public announcement this evening in a special television appearance to the country. The directors of the other research centers will be notified through CCA channels, but I wanted to give you the news in person, because your group led the development of the Stanford vaccine."

Resa was stunned. Her heart slammed into high gear at Harland's words. She was speechless. She was sure that she had heard correctly, but still could not accept it. For a moment, she was no longer in the room: she was at a press conference held a few months ago at the Stanford Cancer Research Center in California.

"Dr. Myles, could you give us an estimate of how much longer it will be before the Stanford vaccine is released?" The standard question had come from one of the reporters. And she had given her stock reply, hiding the quick annoyance that had welled up within her.

"Gentlemen, the Stanford vaccine is not a wonder drug; it is a virus, a live virus. To be specific, it is a benign, synthetic virus that acts on the human genome." More than once Resa had cause to regret the layman's penchant for labels that tended to obscure meanings. The users too rarely remembered the real nature of what they were discussing.

"I'll admit that so far the tests have been successful and we are encouraged, even optimistic, but we must be certain of the exact action of the virus on human cells. The synthetic virus is unique in that it penetrates directly into the nucleus of the cell where it counteracts the action of the cancer virus. I would estimate at least another year of careful testing under controlled laboratory conditions before it can be released to the general public."

Harland's voice jolted her back to the reality of the present. "Well, Dr. Myles. No comment?" His tone held a touch of disappointment. Apparently, in his eyes she had not been mindful of the significance of the moment.

Resa realized that he had expected her to be pleased by his announcement. "Yes, I have a comment." She took a deep breath. "We're not ready, sir. The vaccine hasn't been completely tested yet.

You can't activate Project Immunity."

Harland brushed aside Resa's objections with an impatient wave of his hand. "I can, and I have. You're being overcautious. Either that or you're not being realistic. I've had a team of medical advisors studying the data from all twenty research centers since the CCA was formed. Did you think I'd just pour billions into the project without any control over it? That vaccine has been tested more thoroughly than anything ever developed in the past. Look at the polio vaccine and way back to diphtheria, smallpox . . ." His voice trailed off as he exhausted his meager store of medical history. He shook his head in irritation.

Judging from the expression on Harland's face, Resa decided it was obvious that this meeting was not going according to his plan. She controlled her growing anger, but grimaced inwardly. Harland didn't know what he was talking about. His premise was wrong because he was trying to compare things that were just not comparable. Medical advisors—hell! They were idiots! Harland should fire the whole bunch.

"Nothing, I repeat, nothing we've ever developed before has an action like the Stanford vaccine," she averred. "Mr. President, we are recoding the nucleic acid in human cells that has been disrupted by a cancer virus; we are modifying the basic molecule that controls life. And I, for one, am not satisfied that we know enough about exactly what effect the synthetic virus has on the entire DNA molecule." She spoke slowly, distinctly, as if she could force understanding with carefully chosen words.

Harland started to speak and then hesitated. He seemed suddenly uneasy. Resa could tell that her strong opposition to his releasing the vaccine disconcerted him.

"Have you had any indications that it's not safe?" Harland asked quietly. "Something that's not in the reports?"

Resa sighed and admitted, "No, sir, I haven't."

Harland relaxed, the uneasiness gone as if it had never existed, once more smiling, confident. "Well, Resa, I think it's just the suddenness of the news that's throwing you. I would have asked for your opinion much earlier, even your assistance in the planning for the immunizations, but I didn't want to keep you away from the laboratory." He smiled and rose. "After all, that's where you're needed most."

The president went to his desk, pressed the intercom and asked his secretary to summon his Chief of Staff, David Blair.

"Resa, I want you to review the computer analyses yourself and talk to the advisory staff, if you wish. Blair will escort you around. Then, if you find anything concrete that we've missed, that you feel is dangerous, we can go over the matter again. I think you'll be pleased and surprised at the careful data correlation. Our entire test data are there as well as the foreign information supplied to us under the international agreements for joint research."

The door opened and Blair stepped into the Oval Office. The smile on Blair's face as he came into the room to grip Resa's outstretched hand was genuine. There was a rapport between them that Resa, more than once, had wished she could establish with the president. Blair was short, stocky, and gray-haired and seemed unassuming, until one noticed the lively intelligence in his hazel eyes. The man moved and thought with the facile alertness born of a superior intellect. At every important White House meeting, David Blair was there in the background, alert for any flaw in logic, never swayed by emotional, heated discussions.

"Good to see you, Resa," was his hearty greeting. "How is sunny California?"

"Raining." Resa gave him a rueful grin.

Blair laughed. "I still think you're better off than we are here. The heaviest snow in years." He waved in the general direction of the window.

She forced a smile. "You won't get an argument from me."

"Dave." Harland waved him over. "Would you escort Dr. Myles down to the CCA offices? She's going to look through the test data."

"Yes, sir. It will be my pleasure." Blair smiled and gestured for

Resa to precede him.

Resa walked in silence beside Blair to an elevator that took them down several levels. Then they walked down a long corridor toward the Data Processing area. Her thoughts churned; she felt numb. She resented being used like some pawn on a chessboard, manipulated according to someone else's plan.

Blair, with his usual tact, had taken one look at the grim set to Resa's jaw and remained quiet. Obviously, he was waiting for her to choose her own time to speak.

They reached the door and Resa shrugged. "Let's get it over with," she said in a resigned voice. She knew what to expect: the same data her group at Stanford had been sending through the computer link for the past three years, multiplied by about fifty.

Even without looking at it, she thought bitterly, I know there damn well will be no dangerous facts—as Harland had phrased it.

A low buzz of conversation and the clicking of computer keyboards greeted them as Resa followed Blair past the banks of computer equipment to a small, glass-enclosed office that shut out most of the noise, yet permitted the occupant a view of the entire room. Blair took a thick folder from the drawer of a filing cabinet and placed it on the desk in front of her.

"There is a precedent you know. In 1976 President Gerald Ford made the decision to immunize all 220 million Americans against the Swine Flu to prevent a possible plague. His mass inoculation program had a price tag of $135 million."

Resa raised one eyebrow. "I'm familiar with it. That program was a fiasco. In the fall of 1976, the serums were ready and America's public health bureaucracy had thousands of doctors, nurses, technicians, and paramedics ready to give out the shots across the whole country. Just about every school, clinic, and even firehouse was pulled into service. And right away there were serious side effects—from heart attacks to neurological problems, including the debilitating Guillain-Barre syndrome.

Hundreds of Americans were killed or seriously injured by the inoculations the government gave them to stave off the flu virus."

Blair nodded. "Yes, that did force the government to suspend the program after having inoculated some 40 million people. But, Resa, even though you, and others, call it a fiasco, some medical historians named it the finest hour of America's public health bureaucracy. Officials had a very real fear of a plague that would kill millions."

"Well, Dave, for that matter there are historians who suggested that President Ford's desire to win the presidential office on his own played a big part in his decision to launch the program."

"I do admire your tenacity." He smiled at her and then tapped the folder he had set in front of her. "It's all yours. Take your time and look it over. I'll get some coffee for us and then we can talk."

Resa nodded her thanks and turned her attention to the folder. The label on the front read: "Final Analysis: Cancer Vaccine Laboratory Tests." She swore to herself, her anger briefly rekindled, and started poring over the material.

It was as expected. Nothing new, but everything neatly packaged. The statistical probabilities that no untoward action was latent in the serum were impressive—until one stopped to consider the relatively limited data and testing on which the probabilities were based.

Christ, they've even included confidence coefficients to indicate the probabilities that their statements in different areas of the analysis are correct—

The simple random sample of test volunteers in Category D—i.e., original medical prognosis incurable—is sufficiently large to construct a confidence interval to measure the magnitude of the sampling error. A confidence coefficient of .996 indicates the probability that the procedure will lead to correct interval estimates is 99.6. A normal distribution can be assumed for the population of—

Finally, Resa shoved the papers aside and took a sip of the hot coffee Blair had placed beside her on the desk. She leaned back in the chair and regarded Blair somberly.

"Dave, this has hit me like a ton of bricks. I still feel like I'm in a mild state of shock. Will you tell me how the hell a bunch of politicians can make a medical decision of this magnitude?"

"I'll try. To be honest, Resa, I wasn't expecting you to oppose Harland's decision." Blair smiled, but his eyes had a worried look. "To complicate the matter even further, there are some things that will have to stay off the record." He paused and tapped a button that closed the blinds over the room's glass partitions.

Resa nodded her acceptance. She had a high-level security clearance and understood that what Blair was going to tell her would have to be kept confidential.

"The most significant item is that the CIA reports the Russians are doing a secret build-up of supplies of the Stanford vaccine. Under the joint international research program, they were supplied with samples of the vaccine when it had first been synthesized, and now they're stockpiling it."

Resa caught her breath in shock. "Oh, my God," she murmured.

"The decision Harland has made is not new. I've known about it for some time, but couldn't say anything to you until he gave the go ahead."

Resa hid her surprise and just nodded. Blair's loyalty to the presidential office was almost legendary in political circles. He had served as chief of staff to the two presidents before Harland and disregarded political party ties or personal gain. He was the rarity on the political scene—an honest man and a truthful one, but not a naïve one. There were rumors that on occasion he would present his advice in two parts: what action would be best for the president, and what action would be best for the country.

Blair continued. "The initial steps to prepare for mass immunization were taken about six months ago. It was kept quiet for two reasons. One, because the human trials had not yet been completed on any but critical cancer cases, and something may have come up that would mean canceling the immunization program. You can imagine the furor that would result.

"Secondly, for political reasons. Harland has alienated a number of important congressional factions with the billions he has poured into the CCA. Our foreign aid has been drastically reduced, the Mars probe program has almost been halted, plus the cuts in federal aid for education, welfare, and so on.

"He needs the good will that should result from an announcement that the hoped-for mass immunization program of the cure/preventive vaccine is ready and will go into effect immediately. And so he had to take action to have large quantities of the vaccine synthesized in advance and gamble that the tests would continue to be successful. He's very grateful to you, Resa, for your part in developing and proving the serum."

A glib reply was on the tip of Resa's tongue, but she held it back. She nodded acknowledgment and waited for Blair to finish.

"I know you see the research as exclusive to the scientific domain," Blair said gently, "but there are these other ramifications. Harland has been ruthless in providing funds for the program. But it's an election year. Now he has to reap what political benefits he can from the investment. Especially before some foreign power beats him to the punch."

Resa considered his words carefully. "I see the points you're making, and I know what it has cost Harland to back the CCA, but from a researcher's point of view I still cannot condone mass immunization at this time."

Blair looked at her sharply. "It's damned important politically that the vaccine is released now rather than six months or a year from now, but if the vaccine isn't safe, I know he wouldn't do it."

"That's my problem. I don't know of anything wrong with it. Harland asked the same question a little differently. But I don't think it's ready. We've gone through the different stages in the research and development so fast it has made me uneasy. We don't know exactly what is happening inside the cell when the synthesized virus penetrates it. It seems to act as we have hypothesized, but we don't know for certain. Call it intuition or cold feet. Something inside me keeps thinking—too fast, too fast. And it's been like that since the program started."

Blair studied her for a moment and then put his hand lightly on hers. "Isn't it possible that you may never know exactly what happens? Aren't there other drugs, other treatments, which work but are not fully understood?"

"Well, yes."

"Then—"

"All right, Dave. I can't change my mind, but I will stop arguing the point. There's really nothing I can do about it anyway, is there?"

"No. Not at this point. Not without some solid facts."

"When is Harland making the announcement?"

"This evening, at about seven o'clock your time." Blair looked at his watch. "Are you planning on catching an earlier plane or would you like to stay for a while and join me for dinner?"

"Let me take a rain check on the dinner. I think it would be better if I take an earlier plane and get back to Stanford so I'll be there when the announcement is made. Is it all right if I give my own staff a little advance warning?"

"Yes, I think so. Do you want to call them? They may all be gone by the time you get back to the Center."

"That's a good idea. I'll have my secretary set up a meeting for six o'clock. That will give us an hour before the announcement." She rose. "Now I think I'd better hurry."

"I'll take care of changing your flight. You'll have less trouble that way. By the time you get to the airport, your new reservations will be waiting."

Resa shook hands with Blair warmly. "Thanks for the background information, Dave. It's safe with me. I appreciate your trying to help."

"No problem. I'll escort you out."

Blair used the intercom on the desk to request a car to stand by, and they walked back to the side entrance.

On their way she and Blair spoke, as if by mutual consent, about lighter, more trivial matters. The walk was short. "Thank you, Dave. Let's keep in touch."

"I'll make a point of it, Resa." Blair shook her hand briefly. "Travel safe."

As Resa had expected, when she passed through the exit into the softly falling snow, she was joined unobtrusively by a nondescript man who gave her a short nod, murmured, "This way, Dr. Myles," and steered her to a car waiting at the curb. Suppressing a smile, Resa dutifully followed the man's lead, stepped into the car, and settled herself on the leather cushions. The special agents who had conducted her to her frequent conferences with the president over the last three years rotated on some unknown schedule. But to Resa, they all seemed so much alike that it didn't matter which one she drew. Without fail, they were ordinary men and women, neatly dressed, with the average looks that blended well in a crowd, all polite but distant, all avoiding conversation when a nod or gesture would do.

The brief drive to the airport was, as usual, a quiet one. And, at this time of the year, she decided, not a scenic one. The park-like beauty of the nation's capital was bleak in these winter months, and even the snow that shrouded the city seemed grayed and dull. The sun, pale gold veiled by somber clouds, shone on streets that were wet with churned and melted ice; near the curbs, mounds of dirty snow turning to slush were piled between the parked cars.

Resa's thoughts were preoccupied as she went through the familiar routine of checking in at the terminal and boarding the plane. How to handle the inevitable questions from her staff, from her colleagues, from the reporters? Underlying the discussions with Blair and Harland had been a request for her cooperation, for a united front, and yet, in all honesty, she could not give them that. But she couldn't go overboard in the opposite direction either, at least not without cutting her own throat.

Instinctively, she knew that she would be eased out of the program if she fought Harland too vigorously over the issue.

How different things were now from the auspicious beginning years ago when she had isolated the first human cancer virus. The achievement had come years before expected and had seemed to touch off a euphoric frenzy in a world grown weary of bad news. The medical community was stunned, the world was jubilant, but the politicians were shrewd. They carefully assessed the reaction of the people. For everyone seemed to have, at least to some degree, that hidden dread of cancer, not to be faced, not to be thought about—it couldn't happen to them.

Her brother-in-law, Paul Linder, had called it right. Resa remembered Paul's serious face and the dry tone of his comment. "The world would revere the researcher who found a cure for cancer . . . and some of that reverence is bound to rub off on those who helped. . . ."

Harland had been newly elected president then. He had seized the initiative and backed an all-out, vigorous, and expensive attack on what he euphemistically and inaccurately called the nation's number one health problem. (He had managed beautifully to ignore heart disease.) Overnight, he had created the CCA, the Control of Cancer Agency, and pressed hard for cooperation in the United Nations. Enthused delegates consulted their governments and then voted unanimously to sign an agreement for joint international cancer research.

All the delegates expressed their respective nations' confidence that the scientists of the world would achieve success . . . for brotherhood among nations . . . for the benefit of all mankind . . . etc.

And now Harland wielded the results of those years of research like a political weapon. Her thoughts churning, Resa wrestled during the entire trip with the problem and with the future problems she could see developing.

Eventually, her eyes fastened on the clouds outside the window, a solid expanse of roiling white that seemed to flow endlessly toward some distant horizon. The bright sunlight glowed on small wisps of cloud that rose in delicate curls and turned and shifted in a constant graceful motion as the plane raced the setting sun across the country.

CNN—BREAKING NEWS
LIVE FROM WASHINGTON CORRESPONDENT
ALICE ROBERTA JENNINGS

"Today, the White House announced that President Harland will make a special announcement to the nation from the Assembly Chamber of the United Nations Building. His speech will be carried live by all major networks and beamed abroad via satellite. No details on the exact nature of the special announcement were available.

"When asked if a crisis had occurred, a White House spokesperson said that was definitely not the case. He stated that the news is of a positive nature, but refused to elaborate further. The president's speech is scheduled for 10:00 p.m. Eastern time."

Chapter 2

Moscow, the Russian Federation

THE DARKNESS OF a cloudy night lay over the city. A heavy snow was falling, and the large flakes were whipped into whorls and eddies by a rising wind. For the four men meeting in a secluded room, the night and the snow and the wind were friends, a shield against curious eyes that might glance behind the stone wall, and wonder. Inside the room, closed windows and heavy damask drapes cut off the sounds of the storm.

Here, for the moment, Moscow was forgotten.

The men sat in comfortable armchairs in front of a small ornate fireplace in which logs burned slowly, casting a flickering muted light over the room and its occupants. A small table lamp held back the dark shadows from the far corners of the room and extended the small circle of light around the group. The soft glow of wood-paneled walls, the polished mahogany of the furniture, the rich dark colors of the furnishings receded into the background.

These four men were the real rulers of the Russian Federation. President Aleksandr Ivanovich Vassilov, the chief of state, was speaking; the others listened intently, for it was Vassilov who dominated the meeting. It was Vassilov who had put Russia on a sound economical footing; Vassilov who had reinstated the KGB in all but name.

Decades ago, Mikhail Gorbachev had dissolved the Soviet Union's Committee for State Security, the KGB, along with the USSR in late 1991, but most of the KGB's assets and activities were continued through several separate organizations.

Vassilov had taken control of the two most powerful of those organizations—the Foreign Intelligence Service or SVR and the Federal Security Service or FSB.

While outwardly remaining a proponent of Gorbachev's *glasnost*, known in the western world as openness, Vassilov's pursuit of power was relentless and often secretive. He knew how to use power, and often did so ruthlessly. His was the pragmatic mind that evaluated all efforts in terms of concrete results, his the cold logic that justified any means to achieve those results.

When he spoke, his voice was flat, cool, emotionless. "It's essential that we verify this detail. We can cover everything that's happened so far. But if there's any leak of this, we'll face more than just worldwide censure." Vassilov broke off as the door to the room opened.

A SHORT, THIN man in his late sixties moved hesitantly into the circle of light, urged forward by the stolid guard accompanying him. The guard motioned to a straight-backed chair and the man sank onto it gratefully, for his legs were trembling and his heart was thudding painfully in his chest. Pale and beaded with sweat, he looked uncertainly at the four men facing him; he had recognized them instantly. His eyes met the cold, intense gaze of Vassilov and slid quickly away.

The room was quiet. No one spoke. Only the low crackle of the fire and the rattle of an occasional gust of snow-laden wind on the panes broke the silence. The man dabbed his brow and wiped his hands on a folded handkerchief and tried to relax his taut muscles. The trapped bird in his chest still struggled against the ribs of its cage.

Vassilov's cool, disciplined voice broke the silence. "You are Dr. Aleksei Dimitrov, Director of Pathology at the Obninsk Psychiatric Institute?"

Dimitrov moistened his lips. "Yes," he whispered.

"Tell us why you were arrested, doctor." The cold, quiet voice went on.

"I—" Dimitrov moistened his lips again, his voice quavered.

"Speak up." The merciless voice sharpened slightly.

"Some—some of my patients . . . died. The others—I don't know what will happen. I was trying to help them. Please believe me," he pleaded. "I thought it was safe. I never would have given them anything if I had known what would happen. I was trying to help them. I was trying to cure them." His voice broke and he buried his face in his hands. The same questions, over and over and over. What did they want from him? It was too much. He needed rest, food, quiet.

Grigori Vasilievich Keldysk, head of the FSB, leaned forward and spoke gently, soothingly, as one would speak to a child. "Sit down, doctor. We want to help you. We just want you to tell us what happened once again, in your own words."

He motioned to the guard who waited in the dark background. "Water."

Dimitrov accepted the glass held out to him by the guard, and for the first time since his arrest, felt a rising hope. "Thank you," he whispered.

VASSILOV ONLY HALF-LISTENED as Keldysk patiently drew the story from the old man. The Federal Security Service, the FSB, had carefully documented Dimitrov's theories and his subsequent experimentation. The doctor believed that a virus similar to cancer viruses caused certain mental illnesses. He had developed his theory by analyzing autopsy results of mentally ill patients. He found that a significant number of deaths of those mentally ill patients were caused by cancer, much more than deaths from cancer in the general population. He theorized that something about the cancers that killed these patients had also caused them to become mentally ill.

And his theory could have some validity, thought Vassilov.

Dimitrov had tried to cure some of the patients at the psychiatric institute by giving them the promising cancer cure/preventive vaccine being tested on critical cancer patients under the joint international research program, the same vaccine that was being stockpiled secretly in a dozen different laboratories under Vassilov's own orders.

Now he needed confirmation of only one fact from the doctor, and Vassilov was content to let the shrewd, but patient, Keldysk handle the doctor.

It did not take long. The door closed softly behind Dimitrov and the guard.

"An excellent interrogation," commented Igor Valentinovich Ustinov, director of the SVR, the Foreign Intelligence Service.

Keldysk nodded and said quietly, "No one at the psychiatric institute knew what Dimitrov was giving his patients. Only a technician at the Cancer Research Center is involved. Dimitrov bribed him to steal a supply of the experimental vaccine from the research laboratory. It was the Stanford vaccine."

"Have the technician arrested." Vassilov poured a small brandy and settled himself comfortably back in the armchair while Keldysk telephoned low-voiced instructions. The fourth man in the room, Premier Nikolai Mikailovich Kolchak, the head of government, studied the sheaf of papers on the table before him.

Vassilov sipped his drink slowly, his eyes thoughtful, his mind wandering over the events that had shaped this moment. The fragments of information gathered by the FSB over the past six months began to fit together. A pattern was forming, and his mind leaped beyond the rudimentary pattern and contemplated the final result. The vaccine both he and the Americans were stockpiling was lethal to healthy, noncancerous people. And no one outside this room knew this fact.

"Eventually, everyone will know." Premier Kolchak spoke for the first time. He was in his late fifties, short, thickset, with muscles flaccid. He shifted his bulk in the chair and continued. "After all, it's only a matter of time until the cancer research institutes broaden their test programs to include healthy people. We could be the first to issue a warning."

Kolchak's voice pulled Vassilov's thoughts back to the present "What will we do?" Kolchak asked.

Vassilov slowly gathered the loose papers from the table. "We do nothing," he said quietly, just the hint of a smile on his face.

It was a measure of the confidence he had in his own power that he did not even glance at the other three men to ascertain their approval, their disapproval. And they knew from the finality in his voice that the meeting was over, for Vassilov never confided the full scope of his plans to anyone.

The three men left. Once more the room was quiet, and Vassilov sat alone watching the fire. The tiny flames licked around the logs and flared briefly, lighting his dark, intense features that were now relieved by a half-smile.

He felt a stir of excitement. He felt for a moment the almost omniscient power of one who could influence events to come, could mark the future by either choosing to act or choosing not to act. It was an awareness that here was the shaping of a critical event—cause and effect. Here, the inexorable building of a series of events, the formation of intricate patterns culminating in a critical decision point.

And the decision was his.

RUSSIAN FEDERATION NEWS AGENCY

OBNINSK — Dr. *Aleksei Dimitrov, 64, Director of Pathology at the Obninsk Psychiatric Institute was killed early today in a fire that destroyed the entire pathology wing of the clinic. The fire was reported at 5:15 a.m. when smoke drifting to the upper floors in the building alerted a night watchman. Three units of the local fire department responded to the alarm and prevented the fire from spreading to patient-occupied wings of the clinic.*

Hospital officials state that Dr. Dimitrov frequently worked late at night on private research projects. This fire is thought to have started from a faulty heater in the doctor's office. He is survived by a daughter, Olga Karnev, who resides in Moscow with her husband and two children.

Chapter 3

Palo Alto, California

THE HELICOPTER, LIKE a ponderous bird, settled slowly onto the landing deck on the roof of the Stanford Cancer Research Center at the Stanford University campus. A cold, damp wind blew—it came from over the Pacific Ocean some sixteen miles distant from the campus beyond the foothills of the Santa Cruz Mountains. The light was fading fast, and the heliport atop the ten-story building was lit with bright floodlights.

Resa crouched a little under the slowly revolving blades of the helicopter as she went quickly to the roof elevator, the wind whipping her overcoat against her knees and threatening to pull the briefcase out of her hand.

Her office suite was on the top floor of the building, and as she entered the outer office she was surprised to see her secretary, Marge Bryson, still there behind her desk: fresh, alert, iron-gray hair nearly in place, not a wrinkle in her severely tailored suit.

"Marge! You didn't have to stay."

Marge ignored the comment and followed Resa into her office. "Did you have dinner on the plane?" Marge took the overcoat from the chair on which Resa had tossed it and hung it neatly in a small closet.

"No. I wasn't hungry when they served what passes for dinner," she replied. "Have all the arrangements been made for the meeting?"

Resa sat down behind her oversize walnut desk, unpacking the papers from her briefcase, papers that hadn't even been looked at by the president.

"Yes, everything's been arranged." The older woman looked at Resa's face with open disapproval. "You look tired and pale. You have time for dinner before the meeting, and the Center cafeteria is still open. Do you want to go down there, or shall I have a tray sent up?"

She was persistent, and Resa knew from the tone of her voice that the wisest thing for her to do was acquiesce gracefully. Mrs. Margaret Bryson was the best secretary, watchdog, and right arm she had ever had, but sometimes the woman took on the aspects of a marine drill sergeant.

"A tray please. Anything will do. A snack is fine."

Marge nodded and started for the door.

"Oh, Marge, please hold any calls or visitors, will you. I need to get a few notes together for the conference."

"Will do." The door shut softly behind her.

Resa started sorting the papers out. She was glad that her secretary had stayed late. One of the benefits of being single was the freedom of not having to consider anyone else in her comings and goings, but one of the drawbacks was that there was never anyone waiting when she returned from a trip.

Well, that wasn't entirely the case. Her beautiful cat, Isis, would definitely be waiting. Luckily, Isis liked the cleaning woman, Elena, who looked after the routine housekeeping chores for Resa. And when Resa had to travel, Elena looked after Isis as well.

That's where I'd like to be right now, she thought. Home. Sitting in front of a cozy fire with Isis purring on my lap.

"Later," she said aloud, and skimmed quickly through the e-mail that had accumulated during the day. Nothing here that wouldn't wait, she decided, and turned her attention to the notes she had started on the plane.

The best approach would be the objective one. Give them the facts only, and leave plenty of time for a question-and-answer session before the television broadcast. Her personal misgivings would be best saved for a private discussion with a few of the senior researchers on the staff. The click of her keyboard sounded loud in the quiet room; for a while it was the only sound.

Just as she finished the notes, Marge came in with a tray. She placed it on a small table in front of the couch in the conference area of the office and motioned for Resa to sit down.

"Eat it now while it's hot." Marge placed a sheet of paper beside the tray. "This message came in on the direct link for you from David Blair in Washington."

Resa scanned the paper quickly. After completion of the Stanford vaccine tests, the CCA research was to be oriented toward genetics, mainly the study of disease carried in genes within the DNA molecule. Federal subsidies would continue.

That's a relief, she thought. No cutbacks for the present, at least. But maybe it's more of a bribe to keep her in line. The iron hand in the velvet glove? No, Blair wouldn't play that game, Resa decided. But she wasn't too sure President Harland wouldn't.

She lifted the cover off the tray of food, and despite the weight on her mind, chuckled at Marge's idea of a snack: roast chicken, whipped potatoes and gravy, green beans, salad, and even pie to go with the coffee. But it did smell good and she suddenly realized she was very hungry.

She ate quickly, gathered her notes, and left the office. On her way out she stopped to give some additional instructions to Marge.

"Would you call my sister, Catherine, in Los Gatos and give her a message for me? Tell her to watch the president's broadcast tonight at seven o'clock and that she is *not* to rush out tomorrow and do anything about it. Be sure she sees that Paul is informed, too. Tell her I'll call her tomorrow and explain more fully."

"Yes, doctor," she said, puzzled.

Resa smiled ruefully. "It will make more sense shortly, Marge."

THE STAFF LOUNGE was centrally located on the second floor of the building. It was a large room decorated in bright, vivid colors with a thick carpet and comfortable chairs and sofas interspersed with small end tables and large coffee tables for the sofas. A long table held a large coffee urn, stacks of cups and saucers, and wide platters piled high with sandwiches. On one wall, shelves reached from floor to ceiling and were liberally stocked with books and magazines. On another wall, placed high for easy viewing, was a large television screen.

The hum of conversation died down as Resa entered the room. Obviously, they've been speculating about the reason for the meeting, Resa surmised, as she faced the group and motioned for them to sit down.

"I'm sorry to call all of you in here at such an inconvenient hour, but it was unavoidable. This will be a brief announcement because I want to be finished in time to hear the president's speech at seven. I'm sure all of you will want to watch it as well."

This cryptic comment had their attention now and the background noise of clattering dishes and low-voiced questions and answers ceased.

"As you all know, when the president created the Control of Cancer Agency, it was set up to be independent of the National Institutes of Health and responsible directly to the president himself. Our Research Center here at Stanford was the first to be supported under the CCA program, and we know first-hand what the virtually unlimited funds have enabled us to accomplish in a remarkably short time. There have been some drawbacks," she paused and grinned.

"Directly proportional," called a voice in a rueful tone.

Resa waited for the short burst of laughter to subside and then went on in a more serious tone.

"We've hit another drawback of sorts, a serious one. The president—on the basis of data from the CCA research centers—has decided to activate Project Immunity."

A startled silence followed her statement and then there was a torrent of exclamations and questions. Resa held up both hands for quiet.

"Doctor, with the Stanford vaccine?"

"Yes, with the Stanford vaccine." This set off another burst of noise.

Resa signaled again for quiet. "The decision was made by the president himself, based on computer analyses of test data and on the recommendation of his medical advisory board." And they do exactly what Harland wants. "I was not consulted, merely informed in advance; today, in fact, much as I'm informing you now.

"When? I don't know the exact details. I imagine the president will be giving more information in his speech tonight." Resa continued to answer the additional questions for a few minutes. "Well that's all I wanted to say. We have about thirty minutes to kick the thing around. Would someone get the color adjusted on that set so it'll be ready?"

Resa circulated through the group—answering questions, expanding explanations—with one eye on the screen. When she saw the presidential seal that presaged the special program, she moved off to one side of the room to watch.

On the screen was an outside view of the U.N. General Assembly Building, with its unusual flat gray dome projecting from its roof. The screen dissolved into an interior view of the assembly chamber. The galleries and the seats usually reserved for delegates were packed with people. The camera planned slowly over the crowd toward the dais with its green-carpeted steps leading to two landings.

The lectern, sheathed in dark marble, at which the delegates usually stood, was on the lower landing; tonight it was empty and the camera closed in farther up and behind it to the second landing. Here, behind a desk shaped like a judge's bench and finished in oyster-white marble sat President Matthew Harland, his strong blunt features composed, smile dignified. Rising behind the president was a gilt panel on which was fixed a bronze disk bearing the UN emblem—a global map of the world, in white.

The noise from the crowded chamber quieted: the president began to speak.

"Ladies and gentlemen . . . fellow Americans. I come to you this evening with a message of great importance that will affect the lives of people everywhere." He paused and smiled.

That smile, Resa thought, probably lowered the blood pressures that had shot up at his opening statement. She had been startled herself: she had not expected Harland to leap right into it that way.

"In past decades our Nation has achieved great advances in science and technology. Tonight, I am here to tell you that we have once again achieved a great breakthrough—this time in the field of medicine.

"As president of the United States, and in my capacity as director of the Control of Cancer Agency, I have activated Project Immunity. Cancer—the Nation's most dreaded health problem—has been defeated." His voice was strong, deep, vibrant.

"As I speak to you now, supplies of the serum are being flown to points of distribution all over the country. The Red Cross, Civil Defense Units, and local health agencies are being alerted to receive and distribute the serum."

Again he paused, this time to let the thunderous applause that greeted his words subside. "In addition, ample stocks of the serum have been made available to the World Health Organization. At this very moment, military aircraft are flying supplies to designated foreign areas. . . ."

Resa noticed that Mark Ashton, one of the senior members on her staff, was making his way toward her. Resa went to meet him, and they moved to an unoccupied corner of the room. She studied the face of the older man. Ashton's usually benign expression was grim. His white hair was rumpled: he had a habit of running his fingers through it when he was annoyed or angry.

"Resa, the Stanford vaccine isn't ready to be used on a large scale. I'm all for expanding the test program, but not mass immunizations. What did you say to them in Washington?"

"That and more," Resa replied dryly. "I tried to talk some sense into them, but this"—she nodded toward the screen—"is political maneuvering." She went on to explain in detail what had occurred in Washington, but withheld the confidential information that Blair had shared with her. Occasionally, she glanced over at the screen, but the president had essentially completed this key announcement in the opening of his speech and was well into the finer details of activating Project Immunity. The staff had broken up into small groups to discuss the announcement, unable to concentrate on the more mundane—to them—details of the president's speech.

Ashton, mollified by Resa's careful explanations, finally drifted off to another part of the room and was engaged in a heated discussion. Resa heard a few isolated phrases and knew they would be at this verbal dissection of the situation for another hour at least. But she had had enough of talk, of speculation, of argument, for one day and slipped quietly into the hall.

She took the elevator back to the top floor, and on an impulse walked past her office suite—now in darkness—and entered a room at the far end of the hall. Here, in a bank along one wall, was the computerized equipment with which the photomicrographs taken by the electron microscope were viewed and analyzed.

Resa went to the console and activated the large screen on the panel before her, then keyed in specific instructions.

On the glowing screen an image, called from the memory banks of the mainframe computer, took form: It was the first cancer virus she had isolated and identified; the virus causing rhabdomyosarcoma, a rare cancer (and usually fatal) that attacked the voluntary muscles of the body. Its shape was an icosahedron, of twenty faces, each of which was covered with protein particles that formed a protective shell around the lethal strand of nucleic acid inside.

She stared intently at the glowing structure.

The face of the enemy.

It was difficult, even for her, to believe that in this form the virus was harmless; that it, or viruses like it, were in her own body, quiescent, helpless. For it was only after a virus invaded a cell that it was deadly.

Resa could picture the process in her mind. The virus plunging viciously into a cell, shedding its protective protein coating as it entered, its single strand of RNA penetrating directly into the cell nucleus. Here, in the heart of the cell, the intruder would take over the cell's DNA and order the wild cell division that could eventually destroy the body.

There were more than a hundred such viruses causing as many different forms of cancer, but they all had two things in common. All caused the wild growth of cells; all had a terrifying tendency to spread uncontrolled throughout the body. These two factors made the viruses lethal; and these two factors held the key that had led to the development of the vaccine.

It had seemed so simple on the surface, so obvious, so logical. Maybe that would account for her misgivings. Had it been too simple? Had they missed something? She thought back to the early development stages of the synthetic virus. The nucleic acid in every different cancer virus had been analyzed to identify the chemical bonding codes of each individual virus. Out of the millions of possible combinations, computers had sorted out the particular codes that were common factors present in all of the viruses. Among these common factors had to be the ones that controlled the lethal action of wild cell growth and uncontrolled spreading. From there the next step had been to synthesize a benign virus to inhibit only that particular portion of the nucleic code in the cancer viruses that was malignant.

Resa turned a switch and the screen went blank. This was accomplishing nothing. Tomorrow I'll have another check run on the bonding codes, she thought as she left the Center and crossed the parking lot. She turned her car toward her home in the Palo Alto foothills overlooking the Stanford University campus.

She really didn't expect the results of the check to show any differences in the bonding codes, but the thought, for some reason, was a comforting one and she left the Center easier in mind than she had been all day.

RADIO STATION KGSH (Palo Alto, California) —

"This is Mariah Mauney live with an important update: The cancer immunizations in the Palo Alto-Stanford area are scheduled for 8:00 a.m. tomorrow. Medical teams have been assigned to every outpatient clinic, fire station, church, school, and library in the local area. The addresses of these locations are listed in your telephone directory, but will also be broadcast at the end of this announcement.

"The major firms in the area will have special clinics set up on their premises and employees should report to work as usual. Inoculation teams will be present at every school to administer the serum to students.

"Medical officials have stated that children under six years of age will not be given inoculations, and they advise that pregnant women consult their physicians before taking the vaccine."

Chapter 4

Obninsk, The Russian Federation

HEAVY SNOWS WERE still sweeping across the Russian Federation, and tonight at Obninsk, some 35 miles southwest of Moscow, the storm unleashed its full fury on a small military convoy of covered trucks. Sergeant Andrei Aleksandrovich Lobachevski, the lead driver, swore under his breath as the gusting wind threatened to push his truck off the narrow road. On the windshield, the wet snow seemed to form ice the instant it landed, before the struggling wipers had a chance to clear it. Eyes narrowed, he squinted at the small circle on the window where the hot air from the defrosters hit with full force, giving him at least a blurred view of the road. His headlights were almost useless in the heavy snow.

Ahead, in the distance, he could see faint lights and the dim outlines of the buildings at the Obninsk Psychiatric Institute, set back on low hills and surrounded by a high fence. As he approached the main entrance, a guard swung the heavy gate open, and Andrei's headlights picked up a motorcycle escort just inside the gate who signaled that he would lead the way.

Andrei put the truck in low gear and followed slowly behind the dim figure. He looked toward the complex of buildings on the hillside and repressed a shiver that was not from the cold.

He had always felt a strong distaste for the mental cases. During his tour with the military he had seen quite a few of them. They were so damned unpredictable. But he knew there was more to his uneasiness than mere personal distaste.

The mental hospitals were surrounded with an aura of dread, for the psychiatrists held unique positions in the Russian hierarchy. They could control a young person's entry to an academic institution, they could forbid the ordinary tourist a trip abroad, they could even rule on a man's suitability for employment. Here, health officers committed the dissenters and the outspoken intellectuals for emergency treatment because of their abnormal behavior.

Technically, the courts could not sentence a man to prison or to a labor camp unless he had violated the criminal code, but the psychiatrists' power was harsh and arbitrary. It was a common punishment for dissenters to be confined to a mental hospital that was in reality little more than a prison. And once a man had this mark on his record, it stayed with him for the rest of his life, a dark specter on which doors closed and the faces of friends turned aside.

The motorcycle escort led the convoy around to the back of one of the buildings where a squad of men, heavily clothed against the storm, swung their flashlights and waved their arms to direct the parking of the trucks. Andrei climbed out of his truck jerkily, his muscles stiff from clenching the wheel in the cold cab. For this I have given up a night with Natalia, he thought bitterly as he moved to join one of the other drivers, Vasily Yurievich Bunin, a friend who had moved off closer to the building to gain some shelter from the icy wind.

The two men were part of a detail that had been called in that evening for a special assignment. They knew their trucks had been hurriedly refitted to accommodate litters, but they knew nothing else about the identity of their passengers. Only Andrei, in charge of the detail, knew the destination of the convoy. The other drivers had been instructed to follow him.

A pair of large double-doors opened at the back of the building, and attendants began carrying litters down the ramp to the waiting trucks. The figures on the litters lay still, covered from head to toe with heavy blankets held in place by wide straps. Occasionally, a muffled groan could be heard from one of the figures, but for the most part the operation was carried out quietly, with only the low-voiced directions of the military health officials and the crunching of heavy boots in the snow to mar the windy silence.

Andrei took out a pack of cigarettes and turned to his friend. "Have one, Vasily Yurievich."

"Ah, you're too good to me, Andrei Aleksandrovich." He took the cigarette. "Thank you, my friend."

Heads close together to shield their faces from the wind, they lit their cigarettes.

"A bad night," Vasily murmured.

"Yes." Andrei nodded. He stood quietly watching the procession of litters pass back and forth beside them.

"Where do we take them from here?"

Vasily's question was in disregard to the orders they had received, but Vasily was a friend. . . . Anyway, what does it matter now, Andrei thought, I don't know much more than the other drivers do about what's going on.

"A train is waiting. . . . It's on a siding just this side of Moscow." He shrugged. "That's all I know." And that was all he wanted to know. He never questioned his orders, never commented on them, never speculated about them. His success in the military was the result of obedient and efficient performance. And he knew it.

The last truck was almost loaded. Andrei turned to go, but then stopped as his eye caught sight of the litter passing down the ramp. The slight figure took up only half the length of the stretcher; the form was very small, like that of a child.

But there should be no children here at Obninsk.

At the bottom of the ramp, one of the attendants carrying the litter slipped on the snow that had been hard packed by the tramping boots passing back and forth and fell to his knees, jerking his end of the litter sideways. The small figure fell forward, the buckle holding the upper strap in place snapped open, and as Andrei sprang to help, a gust of wind tore the blanket from the tiny form. It was a child, a little girl.

Andrei stared in disbelief. He felt Vasily grab his arm and heard his friend's muffled curse. Most of the skin was gone from the child's face. It looked as if the skin had been rubbed from it with coarse sandpaper; her face was red and swollen and covered with sores oozing fluid. Her hair was matted in places to the reddened flesh and there were small trickles of blood around her cracked lips.

The attendant quickly pulled the blanket back in place and buckled the strap. Brusquely, he motioned the two drivers toward the trucks.

Andrei turned and went slowly back to his truck. Behind him he heard Vasily's footsteps and his low-voiced call as he passed by.

"*Do svidaniya*, Andrei Aleksandrovich."

Once again, truck doors slammed shut and cold motors were coaxed into life. The motorcycle escort pulled out first, with the convoy forming up behind them, following dutifully until they dropped off at the main gate and waved the trucks on through.

His face set, Andrei drove as fast as he dared through the storm, with hands gripped hard on the wheel. He tried to put the child out of his mind, but her face seemed etched in his memory.

He tried to concentrate on holding the truck steady on the snow-covered road. He thought of his own physical discomfort in the icy cab, the cramps in taut muscles, the pain beginning to swell behind eyes tired from straining to see the road.

He thought of the vacation he planned to take in the summer. He thought of Natalia. He thought of her soft skin, her hot nakedness against him, her generous breasts that would cradle his head. And his mind kept turning back to the horror he had seen. He wanted it out of his mind. He wanted it not to have happened.

"Damn those bastards," he muttered savagely. "Why didn't they keep that blanket tied down over the kid?"

RUSSIAN FEDERATION NEWS AGENCY

MOSCOW—Two railroad cars carrying patients from the Obninsk Psychiatric Institute who were being relocated to a new facility north of Moscow derailed while passing over the Altovskya gorge.

The cars broke through the wooden sides of the railroad bridge's siding and plummeted into the rocky gorge. Military troops overseeing rescue attempts were greatly hampered by heavy winds and snow.

No survivors were found.

Chapter 5

Palo Alto, California

IT WAS COLD, penetrating and insidious. Resa could feel it numbing the muscles in her limbs as she strained to pull herself up to the crossbar at her head. Beneath her she could feel the rung on which she crouched begin to tremble under her weight; above her, the massive double spiral that held the crossbars soared upward out of sight. She was trapped in the spiral: clinging, groping, reaching, climbing desperately to the safety that she knew intuitively was at its summit, while beneath her the structure crumbled and fell away.

All around her others—some were people she knew—struggled silently in their own giant spirals. Occasionally someone would fall, twisting grotesquely amid shattered rungs into the emptiness below, and the sight would spur her to more frantic efforts to reach safety. She wanted to shout to them, but couldn't: the deadly cold was almost paralyzing her.

She willed her hand to grope upward and felt the rungs sway and begin to break up beneath her. Panic overwhelmed her; she lunged for any kind of a grip on the spiral ladder, and missed.

She was falling, falling, endlessly falling. . . .

Resa awoke suddenly, startled. It took her a few moments to free her mind from the nightmare struggle and adjust to the familiar surroundings of her bedroom. Her gaze picked out the sharp outline of the walnut chest and cabinets lining the far wall, the comfortable chintz chair in the corner, the dark fireplace, the closed drapes covering the wall window, all dimly lit now by the meager light that precedes full dawn. With a heavy sigh, she turned and groped for the alarm clock on the bedside table and felt a flash of annoyance at being awakened a full hour earlier than necessary.

Why the nightmare?

In those first moments of waking, her precise mind had noted the distorted but obvious similarity between the giant double spiral in her dream and the double helix structure of the nucleic acid molecule, DNA. Sure, she was against Harland's handling of the project and worried about the effect of the vaccine on the master molecule, but that didn't warrant such a frenzied outburst from her subconscious. . . . She shrugged philosophically, content to let the questions drop for the present. She had more important things to do than analyze her dreams.

Another full day was starting. She thought about the extra things she wanted to squeeze into it as she went into her compact, well-equipped kitchen to start breakfast. Isis was immediately under her feet.

"Hello, pretty girl," she said to the cat and bent down to stroke her fluffy, pale gray fur.

Isis raised one paw and patted her leg, and then fixed her with a stare from her leaf-green eyes.

"I know, I know. You're hungry."

Resa fixed a plate for the cat, her mind still on work problems.

The bonding codes. It wouldn't take much computer time to check them out. She'd let one of the staff handle it. Her sister, Catherine, had to be called. And hell, how to get out of a press conference? She didn't look forward to straddling the fence on the immunization program issue. And some of those reporters were too damned sharp to fool. And she certainly wasn't going to endorse the program either.

While the coffee percolated, she showered, examining her image in the bathroom mirror with that slightly critical air of one aware of the growing number of years passing. She had a leisurely breakfast and was relaxing in the warmth of the sunlight streaming through the window, enjoying the aroma from her second cup of coffee when the telephone rang.

It was Catherine, her bright exuberant voice rushing over the words as if impatient that there wasn't a quicker way to convey meanings.

"Resa, dear, I couldn't wait for you to call. What's happened? We watched the broadcast. I almost called you late last night but Paul said to wait. And this morning the radio has been giving out instructions. . . ."

"Is Paul there?" Resa asked quickly.

"Yes. He hasn't left for work yet. Do you want to talk to him?"

"Tell him to get on the extension." She heard the click of the phone and Paul Linder's deep unhurried voice.

"Good morning, Resa. Problems?"

"In a way," Resa replied. "Look you two, don't rush out to get those shots. Wait a while. You won't develop a terminal carcinoma suddenly in the next month or so. I think it best to be cautious. I may be wrong, but I don't like the way this program has been rushed along. Personally, I'm not satisfied that we know enough about the vaccine to use it on a mass scale. That's it—nothing concrete, just my own misgivings."

"Oh, Resa," came Catherine's voice, sympathetic, protective. "Did you tell them, big sister?"

"Did I!" She laughed. "It fell flat. I'll tell you about it next time I see you."

"Isn't that tonight?" Paul asked.

"Yes!" Catherine put in quickly. "I've invited Steve Sheldon to the dinner party, and you're supposed to come. Do you remember him?"

Did she remember him? Resa remembered all too well. She had spent a lot of time during the past three years trying to forget him, but he was wedged firmly in her mind. Steve was an old school friend of Paul's. And she had never told Catherine and Paul exactly why she and Steve had split.

Steve was with the CIA, and Resa had found it difficult to cope with his frequently abrupt absences and the secretive nature of his work. She knew her sister thought that was why she broke off her relationship with Steve. But what had really finished them was the other women he had been seeing. She had had no desire to be part of his harem, and even though it had torn her apart, she had broken off with him when she found out there were others. Even now, she felt a sharp twinge of pain at the memory of how she had found out that he had been lying to her.

"It's on my calendar. I'll be there. What time was it?" She had forgotten about the party, but Marge would have reminded her of it today.

"Come around seven. Just bring yourself."

"And don't worry," Paul added. "We'll wait out this immunization thing with you."

Resa put the phone down and grinned as she imagined the ironclad instructions Paul would quietly issue to her impulsive younger sister.

She gathered her briefcase and coat, gave Isis a warm hug, glanced at the breakfast dishes, decided to break her own rule and let them wait, and left for the Research Center. Steve Sheldon was on her mind. She missed him, damn it. Even after all this time, the mention of his name brought back heated memories that turned her knees weak. She eased her car in the wide half-circle around the Stanford campus and firmly put Steve Sheldon out of her mind.

She took little notice of the countryside on these daily drives, for the landscape bore the same shades of green and brown, muted, static, that only a year without seasons could produce. Beyond the campus, the hills were lost in a smoggy haze that defied the strong rays of the sun. It was only after a hard rain with a strong wind that the air was clean enough to see them clearly.

She slowed down to avoid students crossing the drive haphazardly on the way to early classes, taking their own special shortcuts across the grassy plots and through dead-end streets.

On her left, Hoover Tower stood tall and graceful, rising above the towering eucalyptus trees bordering the drive, and up ahead she could see the tall, gleaming bulk of the Research Center dominating the 50-acre plot on which it had been built. The campus was a mixture of the old and the new: the soaring, modern research buildings side-by-side with the age-mellowed, rectilinear stone buildings. Serene and graceful, the Romanesque buildings were joined by covered arcades formed of successive half-circle arches that were supported by short columns with decorated capitals. The campus was steeped in history, for some of the buildings dated back to the 1890's, and she enjoyed the feeling of permanence, of continuance, of stability that the juxtaposition of the very old and the very new engendered.

She drove past the large CCA sign to her reserved space in the parking lot and was surprised at the amount of activity at the adjacent Stanford Medical Center. The parking lots there were full, and long lines of people encircled the group of buildings. There was quite a mixture of humanity in the line-up: men in business suits, briefcases in hand and overcoats draped carelessly over arm or shoulder; women in colorful casual slacks and jackets, some with their hair wound in outsize curlers; men in rough work clothes; career women, smart, sleek, and elaborately coifed; children, tired of waiting in line and excited by the change in daily routine, scooted in and out among the lines of people, shouting to each other as they improvised games. And all in all, the crowd looked happy, there were many smiles and much good-natured chatting going on.

Thank God, they're all for the outpatient clinics, Resa thought, relieved that the Research Center would not be coping with the mass invasion and concerned that there was such a large immediate response to Harland's Project Immunity.

She left the car and walked briskly through the Research Center's lobby to the elevators. There was more activity than usual here, too. Resa could feel a tense excitement in the air that reminded her a little of the atmosphere on a holiday eve; the low-pitched speakers paged personnel and announced conferences continuously, and people moved through the crowded lobby with a jaunty air. There were greetings from all sides as soon as she had entered, but her purposeful stride discouraged more than the briefest exchanges.

At her office, Resa gave instructions to Marge and then checked her appointment calendar on the computer. She shook her head. "No press conferences, Marge. See to it, will you? If you have to give out a statement from me, tell them 'no comment.'" That good old standby wouldn't deter the press for long, but at least she'd gain a small breathing space, a little more time to decide just what she was going to say.

Marge nodded and added the extra note on her pad.

"You have a priority call, doctor. Thurston was put on the critical list early this morning, and Dr. Martinson asked if you would stop by."

"Tell him I'm on my way." Resa put on a white lab coat over her suit and left for the Medical wing, reviewing in her mind the case history of the patient.

Thurston had been referred to the Center about two weeks ago with a diagnosis of advanced primary carcinoma of the liver and secondary anemia. The prognosis was fatal; the duration a few months. The condition was relatively rare because most cancers of the liver were secondary, resulting from a primary growth that was usually in the stomach or colon. Resa had thought the man had a fair chance of surviving—with massive doses of the vaccine to stop the cancerous growth. Liver function tests had shown that the disease was well advanced, but liver cells—unlike the heart or brain—did regenerate. He had a chance. But now something had obviously gone wrong.

She saw Dr. Martinson waiting in front of the nurses' station, a young man, chart in hand, fidgeting with his stethoscope as he tried to assume a cool, unconcerned detachment. "He's in 407." Martinson joined Resa and the two continued down the corridor. He let down then and the words came out in a quick rush.

"I think he's terminal, Dr. Myles. Probably too much liver damage before we got the vaccine into him. That's the hell of it. In the liver the onset is so insidious, the symptoms so vague that he put off getting to his doctor—" He broke off as they entered the patient's room.

Resa went directly to the bedside. The patient's vital signs were being monitored and displayed on a screen above the bed. A duplicate remote display screen was located at the nurses' station where warnings would flash when critical levels were reached. She studied the tracings on the screen for a few moments and then looked at the patient.

Thurston was comatose. The jaundice of his skin was pronounced, his muscles were flaccid, his skin loosely wrinkled from loss of flesh, his breathing shallow, harsh and labored. Resa checked the flow of oxygen to the mask on Thurston's face and used a penlight to examine his eyes. She shook her head, and murmured, "Sluggish response." Then she looked at the intravenous taped in place on the patient's thin arm to be sure the needle had not slipped out of the vein, allowing the solution to infiltrate surrounding tissue, before she folded back the sheet to begin her examination. She was anxious to see if there had been any change in the size of the growth.

Percussion showed the dull area still the same, still occupying the greater portion of the epigastrium, extending beyond the median line and pushing the diaphragm upward. She palpated Thurston's abdomen and under her fingers could feel distinctly the irregular nodules projecting from the enlarged portion of the liver that extended below the free border of the ribs.

Martinson saw her concern. "I found no increase in the growth."

Resa nodded in agreement and completed the examination. She motioned toward the door, always conscious of the fact that hearing was the last sense to go in a dying patient. She didn't want to say inadvertently anything hurtful to add to the patient's burden.

She read the current notes and lab results on Thurston's chart carefully. "The growth has been controlled," she said quietly, "however, I don't think he'll make it. He started to pull out of it last week, but I believe you're right—we were too late starting him on the vaccine." The two walked slowly back toward the nurses' station as they talked.

"There's nothing else we can do for him but make sure he's not in any pain," she said to Martinson. "You'll notify his family?"

Martinson nodded. "They're here." He gestured toward a small waiting room at the end of the corridor.

She didn't envy the young doctor that chore. Resa handed back the chart. "I want you to take a biopsy of his liver so we can get a complete microscopy work-up done right away. When I stop by the EM lab later today, I'll tell Mac what I want done with the specimen."

IT WAS LATE in the afternoon by the time Resa was able to get to the EM lab. First, her daily rounds of the research areas had run late, and then what was supposed to have been a brief conference with Mark Ashton had lasted for two hours. Like a pendulum, Ashton had swung from harsh disapproval to excited agreement with the president's immunization plans. The persuasive powers of the news media and the adulation of the general public had won out over medical caution. "The Stanford vaccine has secured its place in history as the greatest cure man has yet achieved," Ashton had said.

Dispassionately, Resa finally suggested that Ashton act as liaison for the Center with the press and other media, and had left the older man in a state of glowing approval.

The red light outside the double lab doors was lit, indicating that the electron microscope was being used, so Resa closed the outer door carefully before opening the inner door to the lab itself.

She stepped inside the darkened room and paused by the door to let her eyes adjust. She could see the dim form of the researcher standing in front of the electron microscope, head bent over the eyepiece, hands held high adjusting the long column of the microscope to sharpen his view. Only the glow from red and green signal lights and the florescent shine through the porthole lit the room.

The man straightened and turned. "I've been expecting you, Resa," said Dr. James MacBride, better known as Mac by almost everyone at the Center.

"Well, I'm about four hours later than I thought I'd be. But you know how it goes."

"Especially now?"

"Yes, especially now." She studied her friend's sober face: dark eyes and gray hair, ruddy complexion, small-boned but strong, even features. Mac, her mentor and a family friend for as long as she could remember, was a strange combination of quicksilver and patience; he had a hot temper when aroused, but almost unbelievable self-control before he reached that boiling point.

He was the father figure she and Catherine had had after their parents were killed in a car accident when the girls were in their teens. They called him Uncle Mac, even though he was not a blood relative. It was an honorary term, started when their parents were still alive. Mac had steered Resa toward molecular biology, and she would always be grateful for that. Despite the current problems, it was a field she loved.

"What do you think of all this, Mac?"

"Not much," was the terse reply. "I don't know the rules of the game the bigwigs are playing, and I don't want to play anyway. They should all take a closer look at what they're playing with." He motioned to the eyepiece on the electron microscope. "I think we still have a lot to learn about the vaccine: benign or not, it's still a virus, and they're tricky devils."

"That's about how I feel, Mac, but I can't do a damn thing about it."

"Aye, I know . . . I hear all the news. It filters down to me right quick enough." He smiled. "Coffee?"

"Yes, coffee sounds good."

They went to a break room adjacent to the laboratory, which served as a combination dressing room and lounge for the lab personnel.

"Before I forget, Mac. The lab will be getting a liver specimen on a patient named Thurston that I want you to keep an eye on. Martinson is doing a stat biopsy It's a terminal case. He's been on the vaccine for about two weeks, and I'm especially interested in some good micrographs of the nuclei. I thought there'd be enough regeneration in the liver cells, but it doesn't look that way."

"Will do—I'll let you know as soon as they're ready." Mac poured two cups of coffee with his usual brisk, efficient movements and handed one to Resa who had sprawled out on the nearest lounge with a sigh of relief.

"I think I'm aging rapidly."

Mac scowled. "I told you a month ago what you needed—a good solid week up at the cabin. No telephones, no doorbells, no people—well, not too many—but plenty of fresh clean air, snow, mountains, and peace and quiet."

"Let's make it soon," Resa said, remembering their last trip to Mac's mountain cabin on the north shore of Lake Tahoe. It had been a good vacation. Paul and Catherine had gone with them. They had had their choice of half a dozen nearby ski areas that could be reached quickly by a short drive, and after each day of hard skiing, they enjoyed a good dinner and their choice of the many *après* ski parties held both at the ski resorts and at private lodges.

And, maybe best of all, there were the quiet evenings in Mac's cabin with hot-buttered rum in front of a roaring fire, while outside the wind and snow blew through the tall trees, accentuating the warm refuge of the spacious cabin. Isis liked to stay inside the cabin, but did foray outside briefly to test the snow. Her high-stepping antics had everyone laughing.

"Well, you have your key if you can get away before I have a chance to get some time off." Mac patted her shoulder.

Resa grinned at him. "I'll give it some serious thought, Uncle Mac," She glanced at her watch. "Say, you are coming to the dinner party, aren't you?"

"I wouldn't miss it for the world. And it's tonight so we both better get a move on."

It was almost five-thirty. Most of the day staff had already left and the corridors had that after-hours' emptiness. Only on the patient-occupied floors would the bustle of activity continue.

The two parted, gathered their belongings, and then rejoined each other getting on the elevator, exchanging a few comments on what they would find at Catherine's latest dinner party. She had a flair for rounding up what she called "different, but interesting" guests. The chances were very good that no two people would share the same occupation, for this was to be one of her "well-rounded" parties.

"See you in a few hours." Resa parted with Mac at the parking lot entrance.

She drove out of the now almost-empty lot and went quickly through the winding campus roads to the main highway, where she encountered chaos. Traffic was almost at a standstill. By itself, that was not unusual, for thousands were trying to get home during these peak traffic hours, but today they seemed to be enjoying the congestion. After a few moments, the reason why became clear.

In every open space—shopping centers, parking lots, gas stations, bank lots, school yards—large drive-in immunization booths had been set up. The booths were draped in flags with a large CCA emblem in prominent view.

It looks like some huge political convention that has overflowed into the streets, Resa thought.

Harland's name was conspicuous by its absence, but he was identified strongly, almost synonymously, with the CCA. It was a clever move. Even the most politically inactive person couldn't miss the flag symbolism. This was clearly government largesse.

Resa edged her car out of the stopped line of traffic and began maneuvering toward the freeway entrance. Ahead, a Highway Patrol car had pulled off the street and two officers stood beside it, casually inspecting the congested traffic.

They watched Resa's careful easing through the center of the packed street tolerantly, until she was close enough for them to spot the medical caduceus on her car. Then they went into action.

With a smile and a wave, the officers cleared the rest of the way for her. Today was a day that required no emergency to exist for medical personnel to receive preferential treatment.

Today, Resa thought wryly, we are VIPs.

WASHINGTON, D.C. (UPI) — *In a special news bulletin, the Russian News Agency has announced today that the Russian Federation will share its abundant supply of the new miracle vaccine for cancer with the People's Republic of China.*

Premier Nikolai Mikailovich Kolchak, speaking for Russia's President Aleksandr Ivanovich Vassilov, said that he is leaving immediately for Peking where he and the Chinese Prime Minister Ling En-huai will be on hand together for the first arrivals of the vaccine.

Supplies are now being loaded in the new Russian swing-wing, long-range bombers, bearing the NATO code name "Starfire III," which fly at three times the speed of sound and at altitudes over 20 miles.

Premier Kolchak said that the use of the new Russian bombers as vehicles for a peace mission was a good omen for a future of warm friendship and cooperation between the two nations.

The Premier said that this act is in the spirit of the 2001 Treaty of Good Neighborliness, Friendship, and Cooperation entered into by Russia and China to seek peaceable unanimity over border disputes between the two nations.

Chapter 6

Pacific Ocean Coastal Waters
Half Moon Bay, California

IN THE PACIFIC Ocean, some 50 miles west of the California coast, two men waited in cold, wet, discomfort on the flying bridge of a trim, 36-foot cruiser, the *Sea Nymph*. Around them the sea was churning; white foam from the breaking waves was blown in streaks by a southerly wind. It was a slate gray sea, cold and dark. There was no horizon, no moon, no stars, only a dark canopy blending into a dark turbulent ocean.

When they had left the marina at Sausalito that afternoon, the small-craft warning had been up: one red pennant, which indicated that winds up to 33 knots were forecast, dangerous sea conditions for small craft operation. And the warning had held true. But the bright flag must be ignored this night, for even if the wind had risen to gale force, the two men would still be where they were now: at this exact time, at this exact location.

The bad weather conditions had forced them to leave the marina far earlier than they had originally planned, but it would have been too great a risk to wait, to gamble that the weather would not worsen, for if it had they would have created too much curiosity by leaving for a pleasure cruise with a gale blowing. And curiosity could easily turn into suspicion, especially if the submarine they were waiting for was detected.

The skipper, Earl Chapman, had left nothing to chance. He was carrying an ample supply of extra diesel fuel, fully charged batteries, and an extra RDF—radio direction finder—in addition to his standard emergency equipment. He had taken care to avoid the vicinity of their present position during the ostensibly aimless cruising while they waited for nightfall.

On their last run, which brought them to the rendezvous point, he had used extreme care in plotting the radio bearings and had confirmed their position with frequent radar fixes. He was sure they were well within the 2° or 3° accuracy that is usually the best that can be expected using RDF without a visual fix.

The *Sea Nymph* was headed south into a high wind that was holding at about 33 knots, the upper limit of the near-gale category—a Force 7 on the Beaufort scale. The slow-moving California Current, which flowed generally southward along the coast until it took a sharp westward turn at Baja, had little effect against this wind. The wave height was close to fourteen feet now, but Chapman's practiced hand on the throttle kept the *Sea Nymph's* engine running at a precise speed—close enough to keep her bow rising to meet each wave rather than being pounded hard into it, yet fast enough to maintain enough headway for maneuvering.

Chapman checked his watch and then turned to his passenger, Ed Miller, who had been scanning the turbulent surface with a pair of binoculars.

"It's time to turn on our running lights," Chapman said as he pulled a switch on the dash. "Hold her steady on course and keep a sharp eye on the PPI scope. I want to take another fix on those coastal radio beacons to make sure we're holding our position."

Ed Miller nodded and moved into the helmsman's seat. He expected such caution from Chapman. This mission was vital: he had never before received such high priority instructions. It would require a coordinated effort from his best agents on the west coast, and, for seamanship, Chapman was the best.

Alternately, Miller checked the compass heading and the small PPI scope beside the helm. He knew the radar wasn't much good for a fix with the way they were rolling, but at least the scope would show the approach of any ships in the area.

Miller watched the bright radial line on the face of the scope, which represented the radar beam rotating in synchronism with the antenna. The distant shoreline showed up as points and patches of pulsing light that never completely faded out before the antenna made another rotation and restored their brilliance.

His main attention was directed at the area immediately around the center of the screen, for the center itself represented the position of their vessel. He was still watching it when a patch of light suddenly appeared close very near the center.

The submarine had surfaced.

The long, dark silhouette of the submarine, black against the foaming sea, lay about 100 yards astern of the cruiser and even as Miller turned from the scope to look, she was already maneuvering to come up parallel to the Sea Nymph's starboard side.

"Chapman, come up on deck," Miller shouted.

He relinquished the helm to the skipper and moved quickly to the aft deck. The submarine was alongside now, her speed matched to that of the cruiser, maintaining headway easily. He could see a group of men muffled in foul-weather gear moving on her deck.

"Stand by to receive lines." The sharp command came from somcone on the submarine.

Lines secured, Miller waited while the men on deck rigged the transfer chair. He was watching the wave action, and, so too were the men on the sub.

The transfer was swift and efficient: the new passenger reached the deck of the cruiser at the precise moment that she was steady in a trough of the waves. Miller hauled the man aboard, and both of them quickly cast off the lines.

As the men moved from the deck into the warmth of the cabin, the submarine was already starting to submerge, back to the safety of the deep water, moving swiftly from the enemy coast.

In the main cabin, Chapman went to the helm station; he would navigate from inside on the return trip since there was no longer any need to keep watch from the bridge. Both Chapman and Miller studied their new passenger with ill-concealed interest.

The man had removed the hood from his wet suit and was drying himself off with a towel. He was a powerfully built man in his late thirties: his hair was light brown and thick, with the hairline extending low on his forehead, his eyes were an unusual light shade of blue, and his face was big-boned with sharp planes and angles that were accentuated by the dim cabin lights.

So this is the famed Nikolai Gregorivich Rostov, thought Miller.

He had never seen the man before, not even a picture of him, but he knew his reputation well, for Rostov was the top agent in the Russian Foreign Intelligence Service, the SVR.

Rostov met his gaze. "You are Ed Miller?"

"Yes. And this is Earl Chapman." Miller nodded toward the skipper.

Rostov glanced at Chapman and then turned back to Miller.

"You have carried out your instructions?" It was more of a statement that a question, and spoken in flawless American English.

"Everything has been done," Miller replied. "I'll brief you on the way in."

He poured mugs of hot coffee from a thermos, passed them

around carefully, and then went to a small, built-in teak desk where he unlocked the drawer and drew out a thick folder.

Seating himself beside Rostov, he took a navigation chart from the folder and spread it out on the table, one arm bracing himself against the table to keep his balance as the boat surged in the heavy seas.

"This is our position now," Miller said, pointing at the chart. "We'll follow the coastline generally southeast to Half Moon Bay. Pillar Point Harbor, here, in the northern part of Half Moon Bay is where we'll drop you. There are no mooring floats in the harbor so fishing vessels and pleasure craft must anchor. If the harbormaster does come out in this weather to check on us, nothing will appear out of order; we are transients sheltering from the storm on our way down the coast. And you would be gone before he could reach us."

Rostov nodded his approval.

"We have scuba gear on board for you. The harbor is well protected by breakwaters so it will not be too difficult for you to reach shore safely."

Rostov studied the detailed chart. "Is this a military facility near the harbor?"

"Yes. It's an Air Force radar site less than a quarter mile north of Pillar Point. There's a building and two dish antennas that are quite conspicuous when one approaches the harbor in daylight. The personnel are used to vessels entering the harbor—even with the small-craft warning up. And who would expect an enemy agent to land in such a place?" Miller shook his head and shrugged.

"I agree," Rostov said. "It should be safe. Now, back to the harbor. Give me details of the layout."

"Right. Here's a sketch drawn to scale." Miller placed the drawing in front of Rostov. "On the northeast side of the harbor is an L-pier about 590 feet long. The office of the harbormaster is at the head of the pier; a restaurant is just north of the office, and at the end of the pier is a skiff hoist. Here"—Miller tapped the paper—"west of the L-pier, is another 600-foot-long pier, but we needn't be concerned with that area.

"There's a parking area, here, near the inshore end of the east breakwater where you'll find your car—a dark blue Corvette, license number RYY356."

Miller handed a set of car keys to Rostov. "The car is parked in the back of the lot, and you'll find a suitcase with extra clothing locked in the trunk. I've marked the most direct route to Palo Alto on this road map."

While Rostov studied the map, Miller checked his watch; he had timed his presentation carefully so that Rostov would be completely briefed when they reached the harbor entrance. He glanced at Chapman, who was watching the PPI scope.

"All clear and we're on course," Chapman announced.

Miller turned back to Rostov. "Now for your cover." He took the remaining papers from the folder. "You are Allan Sutherland, age 38, born in Chicago Illinois, but raised in different areas because your father traveled extensively—you can memorize the details later. Here are your papers: driver's license, social security card, credit cards, and a press card.

"You're a freelance writer selling mostly to *Trend* magazine, and for the past five years, have written a number of articles—mostly political, current events, economics type things—for them. There are back issues of the magazine at your apartment. The cover is solid. Jim Shaughnessy will telephone you in the morning to discuss your next article and to extend a social invitation: a dinner party at Paul and Catherine Linder's home, where you will meet Dr. Myles."

"Where is she now?

"She returned from Washington late today, had a staff conference which included listening to President Harland's broadcast, and left for her home shortly after that," Miller replied, and then continued with the briefing.

"You are renting an apartment at a place called Parkside Glen. It's about midway between Myles's home and the Stanford Research

Center. I have marked its location on this street map of Palo Alto.

"Your apartment number is 159, a ground-floor unit in the back of the complex, which borders on an orchard. Food, clothing, and all the supplies you requested are there. I had one of our people install special locks." He handed over a set of keys.

"And now that last item." Miller picked up a small sheet of paper. "This is a list of safe houses, drops, telephone numbers, and agents you may call on for any assistance. All have been carefully briefed." He held out the paper.

Rostov took the sheet and studied it carefully.

"We'll be approaching the harbor entrance soon," Chapman warned. "I'll take her in from the command bridge, so I'd better go up now and give my eyes a chance to adjust to the dark."

Miller moved over to the helm to relieve him.

"When I get up there, close all the curtains in the cabin." Quickly, Chapman put on a heavy slicker, took the binoculars, and left the cabin.

Through the binoculars, he could see the storm warning displayed along the coast: a lantern signal of a red light above a white light, the small craft warning for winds from 28 up to 33 knots. The storm hadn't gotten any worse; it still remained at near gale force. The anemometer mounted on the cruiser's masthead indicated that the wind was gusting at the upper limits of this category, around 32 to 33 knots. He took over the helm.

They were drawing closer now. He could make out the large black rocks that extended well south of the point. The entrance to the harbor itself was about 130 yards wide, between the east and west breakwaters. He could see the light marking the end of the west breakwater and could hear the fog signal sounding intermittently.

He was using extreme caution in his approach, for there was foul ground—rocks and reefs—off the harbor entrance. He could see the white water surging before the coastal inlet. Steep breakers and cross-seas were tearing about the inlet's mouth. He knew they wouldn't have a chance in those breakers if the cruiser broached—the impact pressure of even a smaller 10-foot inlet breaker was something over 4,000 pounds per square foot.

He put the thought aside and concentrated on guiding the *Sea Nymph* through the buoyed opening between the Pillar Point foul ground and the Southeast Reef, maneuvering to keep the sea crests breaking ahead and astern of her. It was the best time for running an inlet, just before the tide was reversing—the period between waves was at its greatest length and the wave height was not as steep.

Rolling heavily, *Sea Nymph* passed the breakwaters and entered the well-protected harbor, which seemed almost calm compared to the raging waters through which she had just passed. There were a few fishing vessels anchored toward the west side of the harbor, but Chapman could see no pleasure craft.

He steered toward the east side, and Miller came up on deck to drop the anchor. They could hear Rostov moving about in the cabin below, getting into the scuba gear.

Chapman cut the engine just as Rostov appeared on deck. He took the binoculars Chapman offered and made a quick scan of the harbor to get his bearings.

"You've both done well," Rostov said quietly, gripped the hand of each man in turn, and then slipped quietly over the side.

IT WAS A short swim for Rostov, but bitterly cold, even with the heavy wet suit to protect him. He was shivering when he reached shore and went quickly to the parking lot, automatically seeking out shadowed areas to hide him from curious eyes.

There were only a few cars in the lot, and he had no difficulty locating the dark blue Corvette, where hurriedly, with fingers stiff from the cold, he stripped off the wet suit and put on the warm clothing he had taken from the trunk of the car.

After a quick check of the road map, he swung the Corvette slowly out of the lot, enjoying the feel of the powerful engine throbbing smoothly under his hands, and soon he was on the freeway, merging into the anonymity of the traffic, sheltered by the mass of the enemy around him.

The pressure was easing off. Rostov began to feel more relaxed as he automatically went through the motions of driving, holding the car just under the speed limit so he would not attract the attention of any Highway Patrol cars. He never took any unnecessary risks.

He thought back to his final meeting with Vassilov in Moscow. "Dr. Myles must not be permitted to disrupt the immunization program," Vassilov had ordered. "If she speaks out against it—kill her. But remember, no suspicion must be aroused by her death, so you must make it look like an accident. The program must *not* be endangered."

Rostov's mission was critical to Russia's future.

Nothing must stop the Americans from destroying themselves.

RADIO STATION KGSH (Palo Alto, California) —

"Wil Welsh here with the latest News Roundup. Project Immunity is in full swing and it's happening worldwide.

"Millions of people are lining up for their immunizations. Cancer is no longer a deadly threat, and kudos go to our own CCA Research Center on the Stanford University campus here in Palo Alto for their key efforts in developing the cancer cure/preventive vaccine under the creative leadership of Dr. Resa Myles. You may remember that she was the scientist who isolated the first cancer virus."

Chapter 7

Los Gatos, California

FEELING RATHER PLEASED with herself because of the fast time she had made driving down from Palo Alto, Resa parked her car in front of Catherine's house and paused for a moment to admire the quiet countryside.

Everything always seemed more green and lush here in Los Gatos—even in the summer when most of the countryside was an ugly brownish green, these hills seemed to retain their freshness. There must be more springs or brooks in the area, she thought as she walked up to the front door of the sprawling, ranch-style house and knocked.

"Resa! I knew it was you, big sister. Since when do you have to knock on my door? You should have just come in," Catherine exclaimed before she could speak. She pulled her sister into the entrance hall and threw both arms around her neck in an intense hug. "It's so good to see you!"

"It's good to—"

"Do you realize it's been almost two months since I've seen you!" she scolded. "And every time we've talked on the phone you've had to cut me short and dash off somewhere. All I hear is, 'I'll get back to you, Cathy,' and bang—you're gone. Honestly, Resa, I don't know what—"

An insistent knock from the back of the house cut her off. Catherine dashed out of the room, muttering something about the caterers and the robots. And Paul, who had been quietly watching with a broad grin on his face, came forward and clasped Resa's hand.

"Welcome home."

Resa shook her head in exasperation and laughed. "Did she say robots? And did I manage to get two words in there edgewise, or was it my imagination?"

"I believe you managed three words this time," Paul replied in a mock serious tone. "And yes she did say robots. She's been dying to tell you all about them. The caterer will have them circulate through the crowd with trays of drinks and finger foods."

Resa smiled. "Only in Silicon Valley . . ."

"They're really quite simplistic machines from a computer science point of view, but don't tell Cathy that. She thinks they're the greatest thing since sliced bread."

"I'll be properly enthusiastic about them when Cathy springs her surprise."

"It's your own fault, anyway. You know what Cathy's like, big sister, and you're too far away for her to keep proper track of you, and *vice versa*."

"Thank heaven for small blessings. . . ." Resa sighed and made herself comfortable on the couch. "It has been one hell of a day," she said. "It's good to be here."

"I'll fix us a couple of drinks and then you can tell me about it."

Paul disappeared into the den, and Resa leaned back on the thick, comfortable cushions and surveyed the pleasant room.

It was long and spacious, with a large stone fireplace dominating the wall to her right. At Catherine's insistence Paul had had the architect include wide bay windows on each side of the fireplace: they were contemporary versions of the old-fashioned favorites, with roomy seat units built into each one. At the opposite end of the room, large panes of glass extended upward all the way to the cathedral, beamed ceiling, permitting a view of the hills that was magnificent.

Catherine had brought autumn indoors with her color scheme: deep orange, tan, gold, and yellows, warm wood-paneled walls, and accents of brown, vibrant red, and mossy green—she had done it without a discomfiting flamboyance, for one felt the warmth, the welcome, the comfort of the room immediately. The interior decorating appealed very much to Resa's artistic side.

Resa could hear music drifting into the room from Paul's stereo set, turned down low in the den. The wide double doors leading into the room were open, waiting for the milling guests that would scatter throughout the house.

Paul returned with a tall glass in each hand. "We have about fifteen minutes before the mob arrives. Let's have the news."

"Well—you heard Harland's broadcast?"

Paul nodded.

"Earlier that day I was in Washington for a brief meeting with him and found out that his reasons for starting Project Immunity are purely political. I tried to talk him out of it, but I couldn't convince him that it could be dangerous.

"Damn it, Paul, there's no good reason to immunize healthy people with a vaccine that has had relatively limited testing. The fact that they want it is not good enough. Harland's trading on the ingrained fear of cancer that has been pounded into people by the media. You know what I mean—check for lumps, danger signals, stop smoking, and so on. Admittedly, that kind of awareness is important, but it's also frightening.

"We're treating fatal cancer cases successfully with the benign virus, but we lose too many that I think we should be saving. I lost one today. . . ." Resa shook her head gloomily. "We don't know enough about the virus to suit me. It's benign—but any virus is benign until it invades a cell."

"When politicians provide the funding, they're almost impossible to stop," Paul said. "Caution and planning for the future have not been strong points in our political system. Look at the foul-ups just in our ecology. We still don't have clean air in the larger cities—even after years of clean-up programs. And then that big energy crisis in the mid-seventies that dragged out for so many years. . . . I don't know what to tell you, Resa. I sympathize—but from what I saw today, no one could stop that program now, especially with the Russians in the act. Apparently they've been stocking up on the vaccine too. The *Times* carried a small news item on it. But, at any rate, Harland beat them to the punch with his immunization program. And I think the average citizen would be up in arms if he were 'deprived' of his vaccine when so many people have already had theirs."

"Yes. I saw the crowds waiting for their shots. They were almost euphoric, but they could easily turn ugly," Resa reflected.

"Who's turning ugly?" Catherine asked.

"Not you, little sister." Resa laughed and patted the empty space on the couch next to her.

Catherine sat down and favored her with an especially sparkling smile. Obviously, all was forgiven. "Resa, dear— I've hired a caterer with the most darling robots you've ever seen. And I've had the portrait you painted of me framed and hung in the den. It's beautiful. The painting, I mean. And I've invited someone tonight who especially wanted to see you. You remember Paul's friend, Steve Sheldon, don't you. You two dated a bit some years ago."

"This is where I came in," Paul remarked.

"Cathy—" Resa started to protest and sighed as the doorbell rang and Catherine dashed off to greet her new guests. And Resa and Paul retreated to the den to escape the onslaught.

Paul studied the play of emotions on Resa's face with interest. "I never had any sisters," he said thoughtfully.

Resa grunted something unintelligible. She was not only sister, but also, for a few years, mother substitute for Cathy after they had lost their parents. Emotionally, it was devastating for both of them, but their parents left them with absolutely no financial worries.

Paul grinned. "Oh, well. Not to change the subject, but how is your *karate* coming along? Still improving?"

"What? A black belt isn't skilled enough?"

"Black, hey! I didn't realize you'd gone that far. I'm still at brown, but since I'm bigger than you, maybe we could have a match sometime."

"Paul, I'd just love to wipe up the floor with you. And I do mean, wipe it up with you, literally."

Paul laughed. "You're on."

The two rose to greet the first wave of arrivals who were being skillfully shepherded into the den by Catherine to make room for even more newcomers. Catherine made the introductions, her eyes sparkling as she kept up a constant stream of conversation, one ear listening for the next ring at the door, one eye watching the caterers put the final touches on the buffet table, and her grin a mile wide at the raves over her robot servers.

"I really enjoy Cathy at her parties," Paul said in an aside to Resa.

Privately, Resa had to agree. She had always been intrigued by Catherine's ability to carry on an intent conversation with one person, and, at the same time, be aware of what else was going on in the far corners of the room. But Paul enjoyed everything about Cathy. She had never seen two people more in love. Her little sister had been blessed in that department.

Resa was quickly engulfed in a flurry of introductions. A few faces were familiar, but for the most part the guests were new to her. Where did Catherine pick up all of these people? They were a wildly assorted crew. She gave up on her private game of trying to judge a person's occupation by appearance when a middle-aged, sedately dressed woman—whom Resa had mentally categorized as a teacher—became engaged with Paul in an avid discussion of the latest planes she had added to her charter flight service, while Paul boasted over additions to his own air freight company.

She drifted away from the flying enthusiasts, adroitly sidestepped around a robot that was announcing "Champagne" in a mechanical voice, and eased by a group of avid golfers absorbed in a detailed dissection of the current tournament that was going on at Pebble Beach. Slowly she made her way to the buffet table, intent on getting her plate fixed before the horde made a shambles of the carefully arranged delicacies.

As she fixed her plate, Resa caught a glimpse of Mac, deep in conversation at the far end of the room, partially obscured by a bare, shapely shoulder, a fatuous expression on his face.

Resa made a mental note to tease the devil out of him. He'll be tied up there for at least an hour, she thought, as she scanned the room for a halfway quiet spot in which to enjoy her dinner. If she had had more time, she would have eaten before she came, and then just snacked lightly throughout the evening to counteract the generous drinks Paul served.

She saw that the bay window on the far side of the fireplace was empty. It was still too early in the evening for the quiet corners to become occupied, for now there was movement and mingling, the momentum still building.

Resa sat sideways on the seat, half-turned toward the window, her full plate balanced precariously beside her. She didn't want to catch anyone's eye and end up with an impromptu dinner companion, so she concentrated her attention on the scenery outside, ignoring the ebb and surge of conversation around her. She dug into the delicious food, and it didn't take her long to polish off the whole plate. The next time one of the robots rolled by, she put the plate and cutlery on its tray.

The first few stars were out now, sharp pinpricks of light against a dusky sky. As her eyes became accustomed to the twilight shadows, she could pick out familiar landmarks on the hillside. And then her reverie was interrupted by the glare of headlights. The driver parked the car and approached the house. A late arrival, Resa thought, watching the tall masculine figure move slowly into the pool of light close to the house.

His stride was smooth, athletic, and Resa watched his approach with interest. There was something familiar about the way he moved, but the memory eluded her. He paused in the light, listening to the clamor from within the house, a half-smile of his lips, and Resa recognized him. Her heart gave a sudden lurch. He was the epitome of the tall, dark, and handsome *cliché*, if one could substitute ruggedly handsome into the equation, rather than movie star handsome. It was Steve . . . Steve Sheldon, her former lover. She had decided earlier that he probably wasn't going to show up, and chided herself at the spurt of eagerness she felt.

She stood up and glanced around the crowded room, trying to locate Catherine. When the doorbell rang, she saw her sister turn to answer it and she moved to intercept her. "Let me get it," she said.

Resa swung the door wide for Steve to enter. He looked up at her in surprise. "It's the right house," she said lightly.

At that, he smiled. "I know," he said quietly as he reached out and took her hand, holding it between both of his. "But I wasn't sure you were still going to be here this evening."

Resa reluctantly drew her hand back. "Well, I'm glad I came. It's been a long time." She had missed him far more than she thought she would. She couldn't help comparing other men she met with Steve, and no one quite measured up to him. Even now, after all this time, she felt an instant tug of attraction.

"It's been too long." His eyes met hers appraisingly.

Her heart started to race. It doesn't take much, she thought

74

wryly.

"I think you'll need a drink before you can face this mob, and I know just the quiet corner to have it in." She slipped her arm through his and guided him through the crowded room to the den. Paul was helping the caterer tend bar, and Resa signaled a request for two drinks to him, pointing back to the general area of the window seat she had just vacated.

"I saw you arrive from here," Resa said as Steve sat down next to her.

He glanced out the wide window. "I'm afraid I'm terribly late. It was all those lines of cars waiting for the immunizations that held me up. I promised to come early and give Paul and Cathy a hand getting things set up." He looked around the room. "I really should explain—Is that a robot?"

"Yes. Cathy's coup of the month. Don't worry. They know you're here. But I didn't even know you were in the area."

"I've only been here a week. The last time I talked to Paul he said he hadn't seen you in some time." Steve smiled. "That's why I was surprised you were here. I had the impression your life was now too much work and too little play. You're certainly in the news frequently."

Was there a hint of reproach in his tone? The gray-blue eyes meeting hers were cool and watchful, but she remembered the guilt and anger she had seen in them years ago when they had parted.

"I've been busy. Cathy informed me tonight that I've been out of touch for too long. In fact, she was quite verbal about it."

Steve laughed at the expression of Resa's face. "Cathy has always been quite verbal when she's objecting to something."

"You mean quite verbal, period."

"Yes," Steve agreed fondly. "But you wouldn't change her, and neither would I."

They were still laughing together when Paul arrived with the drinks. "Good to see you, buddy. It's been too long."

The two men shook hands, and then Paul turned to Resa.

"Your stronghold here won't last much longer. Cathy has two men in tow who want to meet you—literary types."

"Oh, no."

"Afraid so," Paul remarked lightly. "The price of fame, *et cetera.* But they're not all bad. Steve here is a sometimes literary type. It's his favorite cover, and you don't seem to be trying very hard to get away from him."

Resa turned to Steve. "Are you a literary type?"

He nodded. "Of sorts. As you know, I have several careers, but I never talk shop at parties so you don't have to worry about me talking you into an exclusive, inside story." His eyes glinted with amusement.

"Oh, that's too bad. I would make an exception for you." Resa raised one eyebrow in challenge. "But what about your former employer. Did you leave them?"

"No, not really."

"I see." So he was still with the CIA. That didn't seem to bother her as much as it did once. Over Paul's shoulder, she could see Catherine weaving through the clusters of people, two men following behind her. "Here they come," she murmured.

"Well, there you are," Catherine said brightly. "Resa, I have two gentlemen anxious to meet you. And I did warn them about not talking shop. This is Jim Shaughnessy, from Trend magazine, and this is Allan Sutherland." She completed the introductions with a practiced ease.

Resa shook hands with the two men and listened politely to Shaughnessy's explanation.

"We don't want to intrude on your evening with a business discussion, but I did want Sutherland here to meet you. He's a free-lance writer under contract to *Trend* and he'll be in this area for a few months."

"Resa glanced at the other man—cold blue eyes, heavily muscled build, a smile that didn't seem to soften craggy features and didn't reach his eyes.

"You may see me snooping around your Research Center, Dr. Myles. My articles are mostly politically oriented, but this new one for *Trend* will drift a little into your field. I'm researching the effects—good, bad, or indifferent—that political funding has on medical and scientific research programs," he explained. "Personally, I think too much control is being taken out of scientific hands . . . but I have a lot more research to do on it yet."

Resa nodded. "Well, I have to agree with you. Maybe when things quiet down a little at the Center we can discuss it more thoroughly."

"Thank you. I'd really appreciate that." Sutherland looked at Shaughnessy. "Now, I think we should raid that great-looking buffet.

"Good idea." Shaughnessy nodded to Resa. "A pleasure meeting you, doctor."

Resa watched the two men move away. "Well, that wasn't too bad. Maybe the magazine types are more courteous than the reporters I've been tangling with lately." She looked up at Steve, enjoying the fact that she could tease a smile out of him.

"Of course. I haven't been a magazine type for very long, but I'll try to live up to your expectations."

She glanced at the people clustered around them, wondering where and when Paul and Catherine had drifted off, and then turned back to Steve as he spoke.

"That's your work, isn't it." He was looking at the framed oil portrait hung in a place of honor on the opposite wall. "It's beautiful."

"Yes, it's mine. A gift for Cathy. She's a beautiful subject, but it was an experience getting her to sit still for more than half an hour at a time. I think I did most of it from memory. I wish I had more time for my painting, but I'm spread pretty thin right now."

"I'd like a chance to talk to you without shouting over the noise of the crowd, and without trying to pick up where we left off because of interruptions. What do you think? Want to head out for somewhere quiet?"

"Good—let's find Paul and Cathy and tell them we're leaving."

They gathered their coats and started shouldering their way through the crowd, heading toward the door when Catherine found them, and Resa explained that they were going to leave early. "It's a wonderful party. And I just love your robots." Resa hugged her sister. "Do you mind that we're leaving early?"

"Of course not, you can't talk here," Catherine said warmly. "Dash off, and try to come back tomorrow for lunch or dinner, or whatever suits your plans. . . . I'll see you soon."

She stood at the window watching the two leave. Paul come up beside her, slipped his arm around her waist, and brushed her cheek with a light kiss. "Score one for our side," he whispered in her ear.

She smiled, returning his caress with a light pressure of her fingers. "Paul, it's so good to see them back together again."

They were not the only ones interested in Resa's departure. From another window Sutherland watched the couple leave. Shaughnessy, beside him, spoke in a low voice. "Will the man be a complication?"

Sutherland smiled. "No. With her attention on him, she'll be off guard, distracted." His voice was cool with just a trace of contempt. "She's more vulnerable now."

THE COCKTAIL LOUNGE was dimly lit, the air acrid with the odor of stale food and alcohol fumes, but what one wasn't? Resa shrugged inwardly. At least it was warm and fairly quiet.

Steve glanced around the room and led her to a small table near a circular fireplace, away from the crowd around the piano bar and its diminutive dance floor. This was one of the few places where there was no live band or disc jockey to shatter one's hearing with music at an almost unbearable decibel level.

"What would you like, Resa?"

"Something sweet."

He ordered an old-fashioned for her and a scotch and soda for himself. He leaned back in the thickly padded chair, lit a cigarette, and smiled at Resa, studying her face.

"What do you see?" She ran her hand over the cap of soft, dark chestnut curls framing her face.

"I see a heart-shaped face and a pair of dark blue eyes a man could drown in. You are incredibly beautiful. You don't know how glad I am that no one snatched you up while I was gone."

She felt the color rise in her face. "I was too busy working. No time for anything serious."

He leaned toward her and took her hand, the look on his face serious. "I did a lot of soul searching after we broke up. I treated you badly. The timing was off for me. We met shortly after my divorce, at a time when I was still bitter about my marriage failing and I was pretty cynical in regard to the future."

"Steve," she protested, "you don't have to go into that."

"I know. But I want to. It took me some time to work out why I behaved as I did. I want you to know."

"All right," she said softly,

"At that time in my life no one woman would have been enough. I felt driven to make up for lost time, to snatch as much pleasure as quickly as I could, to sample a variety of women. But then I met you, and I cared for you more than the others so I lied to you. I wanted to keep you, but I didn't want to be tied down to one woman."

"I remember that well." She looked directly at him. It was probably best to let him get it all out, but it still hurt to remember. "I didn't want to be part of a harem. I broke it off, when I found out."

"Yes. And that really opened my eyes. I'm glad you were strong enough to dump me. At first, it was a relief not to have to lie, and I pursued my pleasures in a casual, no commitment way. But believe it or not, recreational sex became boring."

Resa raised an eyebrow. "Oh, really."

"Yes. It's just not the same without any emotional involvement or any significant companionship. I missed you. You can't imagine how much. I couldn't get you out of my mind. And you were gone out of my life completely. Until tonight."

"Was tonight an accidental meeting?"

"No, I practically begged Paul and Cathy to help me see you again. You wouldn't believe the threats they made if I did anything to hurt you."

"On the contrary, I would. They love me."

His nod acknowledged her words. He held her gaze for a long moment, his eyes roaming over her face. "I'm afraid I do, too."

Resa was stunned into silence. An admission of love was without a doubt the very last thing she expected from Steve. It made him so terribly vulnerable.

The waitress came to the table with their drinks and Steve released her hand. He raised his glass. "To a new beginning?"

She smiled. "Yes, to a new beginning."

They sipped their drinks and Resa turned the conversation to more casual things and they both indulged in some idle people watching.

She looked over the men and women seated at the piano bar passing a microphone around. Their attempts to sing snatches of a tune were amateurish, but each performance ended with vigorous applause.

"When I'm in a place like this, I often wonder if people like those are really having such a good time," Steve commented.

"I've often thought the same thing." She turned back to Steve. "To me they seem to be *desperately* having a good time," she added slowly. "Do you know what I mean?"

"Yes. It's almost a frantic pursuit of pleasure—no peace, no quiet, no relaxation." He shrugged. "Maybe that's one of the reasons I don't socialize the way I used to."

Her deep blue eyes met his level gaze for a long moment, and then she smiled. He *had* treated her badly, very badly. But it wasn't in her to keep him dangling, to make him wonder if she could forgive and forget. She was not going to belabor the mistakes of the past and ruin any future they could have.

Steve returned her smile with visible relief, relief and genuine pleasure.

"Will you be in the area for a while?"

"Yes. Two or three months, I imagine. I told the CIA Director, Jim Taggert, that I really needed a break."

"Good." She smiled broadly. "That's the best news I've heard all day."

"But you've had a bad day," he teased lightly.

"Cathy told you?"

"Yes. That's why I was afraid you wouldn't be at her party this evening."

"It *was* a bad day," she agreed. "In fact, it started way too early. I had a nightmare last night that was solely from this damned immunization program of Harland's."

"Tell me," he urged.

Resa described the giant spirals of her dream, the horror she felt at their crumbling, the people falling into an unknown darkness. "It was quite obviously the DNA molecule," she explained. "But I don't know why it fell apart like that. I couldn't do anything to stop it."

"Oh, but . . ." He hesitated and stopped, a look of dismay on his face.

"Go on, say it. It's all right." She grinned at his sudden confusion.

He smiled back. "Okay. I was just going to point out that it was *your* dream," he said gently.

Resa was startled for a moment. That fact had never entered her mind. "Of course," she said slowly. "It was my dream, and that means that I decided what happened, even if only subconsciously. I never thought of it that way. This will take some thinking about. It might be that I'm concerned about the wisdom of the program—and I am—or it could be wishful thinking that Harland would fall flat on his face because he just took over. . . . I hope it's not the latter, but you never know." She shrugged. "The mind's ability to rationalize is virtually unlimited."

Steve nodded in agreement. "It sure is."

Resa was pleased at his honesty. In the past he would never have attempted to examine the motives for what he did, for then he would have had to accept total responsibility for his actions. And then he would have had to modify his behavior to fit the image he had of himself, or accept as a part of himself the qualities he really didn't want to change. But it looks like after they parted, he did a lot of self-examination. Insight was such a wonderful thing to discover. Once you faced yourself honestly, your needs and desires and motives and goals, all that you were, then you could change what you really didn't like about yourself. There was a heady freedom in such knowledge.

He asked her to dance, and as she settled herself comfortably in his strong, familiar arms, the years they had been apart fell away. This is where I've wanted to be, she thought. She felt his arms tighten around her, and once his lips brushed her hair. She put one arm around his neck and molded her body to his. The heat rose from somewhere below her heart and radiated to the tips of her toes and the top of her head.

She wanted him. That hadn't changed.

He maneuvered her around the tiny dance floor skillfully, and they stayed there until it became too crowded to dance easily. They finished their drinks, and when Steve suggested they leave, Resa agreed readily.

"Let's go back to my place," she said. "You can build a fire and I'll round up some snacks."

THEY SAT ON an oversize, comfortable couch in front of the fireplace, the small logs crackling and the firelight gleaming on the champagne glasses Resa had just refilled. Isis lay sprawled between them, taking turns favoring one then the other with an intent look from her grass-green eyes. The cat had remembered Steve and had leapt into his lap the moment he sat down. And Steve, of course, had stroked her pale gray fur until she was rumbling like a small engine.

Resa had laughed and called Isis a traitor. On the other hand, she envied the cat a little. With a contented sigh, she leaned back and rested her head on one of the plump throw pillows scattered on the couch.

"Tired?" Steve asked gently.

She shook her head. "No," she said with a low laugh. "I'm happy."

They had talked for hours in the quiet, intimate room and now both were content to enjoy the fire and the soft music from Resa's stereo. Her hand rested lightly in Steve's and he pressed his lips to the smooth palm. Her fingers answered with a light caress, tracing a line down his cheek and along his firm jaw line.

Steve gathered Isis into his arms. "Sorry, Lady Cat." He placed her on the fluffy throw rug in front of the fireplace and sat back down on the couch closer to Resa.

Resa's relaxed contentment faded when Steve drew her up across his lap, her head pillowed beneath his arm at the end of the couch and began to kiss her face. His lips followed the soft curve of her cheek down into the smooth hollows of her throat and then back to the silken corners of her mouth.

She felt a hot surge of desire course through her body. She wound her arms around his neck and pulled him closer to her. She lifted her lips to his and he took her mouth in a long deep kiss.

"I wanted you the moment I took you in my arms when we danced," he whispered as his lips caressed the fold of her ear.

"I wanted you too," came her soft, breathless reply. She slipped her cool hands beneath his shirt and up over the taut muscles of his back. He kissed her once deeply with a restrained passion that sent her blood pounding, and then lifted her into his arms and carried her into the bedroom.

Leisurely, he undressed her, stroking and kissing each new expanse of the velvet smooth skin he exposed to his touch. She tore at his clothing but he quickly stripped it off and lay beside her, drawing her onto her side close to him so that the full length of their bodies touched.

"Oh, Steve," she whispered huskily, "It's been so long."

"I know, . . . I know." He turned her gently onto her back and buried his face in the valley between her breasts. She cried out softly when he cupped one breast in his hand and ran his tongue teasingly over the nipple. It hardened and rose beneath his questing mouth and he turned his attention to her other breast. Her arms closed around his head, drawing him closer. With his hands and his lips, he caressed every inch of her body until her skin was flushed with the heat of her excitement and she trembled uncontrollably.

She strained against him, and whispered, "Steve, I want you now."

He covered her mouth with his. "Not yet," he said softly. He murmured endearments and continued covering her with gentle strokes and kisses. His assured control released her last shred of restraint and she returned his caresses with a passionate abandon.

When he entered her, she moaned with pleasure and tightened her muscles around him, trying to draw him even closer inside her. He held her close to him, unmoving, while she savored the intense pleasure of their intimate contact. And when the need grew too great to remain still, she rolled their locked bodies over so that she was on top of him and began to move, slowly at first, prolonging the pleasure they found in each other, until both of them were caught up in a frenzied passion that swept away all such considerations.

Lost in her own driving need, she cried out, acutely conscious of the rhythmic spasms pulling her to a peak of pleasure that left her weak and shaken. She couldn't move.

Steve rolled over onto his side and drew her into his arms and kissed her, holding her tenderly until her trembling ceased and her breathing grew even. She rubbed her cheek gently against his, and then nestled close to him. Exhausted, she fell asleep in his arms and he stroked the tousled head resting on his shoulder until his hand grew heavy and he, too, drifted into a deep, dreamless sleep.

THE NEXT AFTERNOON Resa and Steve drove down to Santa Clara to meet Paul and Cathy at the *dōjō* favored by both Paul and Resa. The results of last night must be showing on both their faces, Resa decided, judging from the smirk on Cathy's face when she greeted them.

"Hello, Steve. So good to see you again," Cathy said sweetly. "You both look wonderful. So calm. So rested."

"Mmm, thanks to a little, matchmaking witch," Resa replied.

"Leave them alone, Cathy. I don't want Resa to hurt me." Paul slipped an arm around his wife's waist and pulled her back against him.

"She wouldn't do that." Cathy frowned and thought for a minute. "Or would she?"

'You'll have to just wait and see," Resa said airily. She turned to Steve. "Are you going to work out, too?"

"No, I don't want to hurt either one of you." Steve kissed her on the nose.

Resa laughed and pushed him aside. "Let's go change," she said to Paul.

They each went to their respective locker rooms and came out dressed for a match. Resa's pure white *gi* was secured around her waist with a black belt, and Paul's with a brown belt. They moved barefoot onto the polished boards of the *dōjō* and separated to begin warming up with karate *katas*.

Resa moved smoothly into the first of the basic *katas*, the *heian shodan*, and then segued into the second movement, the *heian nidan*, making the forms appear like an artistic dance. She soon lost herself in the predetermined moves and moved gracefully, but with speed, unleashing the concentrated power of her body in a quick burst of energy, when called for by the various techniques of defense and counterattacks.

When she stepped back, her *katas* completed, Steve and Cathy both applauded from the sidelines.

Resa shook her head at them. Fortunately, the *dōjō* was fairly empty, or she would have been very embarrassed.

"Are you ready?" Paul moved toward her.

"Let's do it."

Both assumed the closed fist ready stance and bowed from the waist. Paul immediately launched a grabbing attack, but Resa broke it easily by counterattacking with a front kick and a double back fist to his body.

"Don't hurt him!"

Cathy's shout threatened to break her concentration, but she managed to step back to block a kicking attack from Paul and struck his face with a back fist punch.

Paul countered with a reverse punch to Resa's face and followed through with a roundhouse kick to her neck as she retreated.

"Paul, don't you dare hurt her!"

Resa pivoted and moved in toward Paul while deflecting his fist blow and counterattacked with a palm heel strike to the groin followed up quickly with a throwing technique.

"Resa, stop!" Cathy's horrified voice shattered both her and Paul's concentration and they broke apart laughing as they bowed to each other to signify the end of the match. Cathy didn't seem to know that they were both pulling their blows so they wouldn't really hurt each other.

Resa shot Steve a stern look. He, of course, knew what was going on, but instead of calming Cathy down, he was doubled over laughing.

"Dinner's on you, Sheldon," Resa ordered.

Steve stopped laughing long enough to reply, "It would be my pleasure."

Paul motioned to Resa. "Let's get cleaned up. We'll do this

again without an audience."

"Sounds good to me."

They walked to the end of the *dōjō* and bowed to the *sensei,* who had stoically watched their match, and then they went to their respective locker rooms for a quick shower and change of clothing.

RADIO STATION KGSH (Palo Alto, California) —

"Darlyne Martinez here with updates on the president's Project Immunity. Officials of the World Health Organization (WHO) praised President Harland today for his actions in providing the anti-cancer Stanford vaccine to peoples on a worldwide, simultaneous basis.

"Because of the airlifts of vaccine supplies, immunizations are progressing as rapidly in the remote parts of the world as they are here in the United States.

"Locally, only minor traffic snarls marred the orderly procession of cars lining up at drive-in immunization booths, which are strategically located all over the city.

"A CCA spokesman estimated that at least 50,000, and probably more, immunizations have already been given here in the Palo Alto area alone.

"Immunization booths have been set up in a variety of places: health centers, fire stations, malls, drugstores, clinics, hospitals, etc. For more information on where to go here in the Palo Alto area, just go to our web site at kgsh.com for a complete local listing."

Chapter 8

Palo Alto, California

THE NURSE BENT OVER the bed and spoke soothingly to the frightened young woman lying there. "You're doing just fine," she said cheerfully. "It takes a little longer with the first one, you know."

The woman nodded and lay quietly watching while the nurse drew back the sheet, folded up the short hospital gown, and pressed a stethoscope on her distended abdomen. She felt her abdominal muscles tighten instinctively when the cold instrument touched her.

"Is the baby all right?" she asked, her voice rising tremulously despite the constant assurances from the staff since her admittance to the hospital some twelve hours ago.

"Fine, everything's fine," the nurse said smoothly. "You try to rest between the contractions, the doctor will be in to examine you shortly." She straightened the sheets on the bed and locked the side rail in place.

The door closed quietly behind the nurse and the young woman was once more alone in the room. She wished again that her husband would come back. It was easier somehow when Howard was there, easier to bear the pains, easier not to keep remembering that it was far too early for the baby to come.

Only a little over seven months, she thought, he'll be so small. But they have a special incubator for the premature babies, she reminded herself. Everything would be all right. It had to be all right. Her husband, Howard, said it would be, and he always knew best; he always took care of her. Didn't he get her a dose of the new vaccine before anyone else got theirs?

She felt again the warm satisfaction over the special consideration he showed her. Howard said that only the best would do for his wife. And he was so cautious. She remembered how he had carefully checked on the tests that had been done in that laboratory.

Howard said that their son would have no fear of the leukemia that ran in her family. He said the vaccine would pass to the baby through her blood stream. He said they wouldn't have to worry now about supplies of the vaccine running short on the program. None for himself . . . he said he would wait. But only the best and the safest would do for his wife, for his son.

She was so groggy from the injections the nurse had given her, but they helped so much. Oh God, how they helped. . . . She was terrified of pain; she didn't know labor would be so painful. How could she stand it if it really got worse? What if she made a fool of herself in front of everyone?

She put the thought out of her mind and tried to think about something else. The sun, warm and golden, slanted through the window blinds, and she watched motes of dust dancing in its rays. She closed her eyes, but could not relax.

The pain was building again. Her body was out of her control.

She gripped the side rails on the bed waiting for the peak to come, the rock hardness in her belly—and this time she felt an uncontrollable urge to bear down with all her strength, to force the child out of her womb. The powerful contractions made her body seem alien to her, an animal thing over which she had no control.

Frightened, she shouted for the nurse, forgetting the call button beside her.

And then the doctor was there. She felt his hands on her, heard his calm voice issuing instructions to the nurse. Then he spoke to her.

"You're fully dilated now, Mrs. Prescott. It won't be long. We're taking you to the delivery room, and I'll start a caudal on you. It will take all of the pain away. You remember, don't you, when we talked about it? You're doing fine. Just try to relax and don't fight the contractions."

They put her on a stretcher and wheeled her out of the room. There was Howard, waiting. Oh, thank heaven, it would be all right now!

He smiled and bent over the stretcher to kiss her cheek. "I'm here, darling," he said softly. "I got away from the Research Center as quickly as I could. I won't leave you, Angela."

The pains were so close together, so powerful. But the nurses didn't seem at all concerned. I wish they would hurry, she thought. I'm getting tired, so tired. . . . How many hours had it been? She couldn't remember. . . .

They lifted her onto the delivery table. Howard stayed at the head of the table—she could look up and see him bending over her. But he had a mask on now and his hair was covered with a cap, only his eyes smiled at her.

How silly he looks, she thought, her smile turning into a grimace as another contraction seized her.

Dr. Robbins was standing beside the table with his hand on her abdomen, easing the pressure of the contractions. "Just a few minutes," he said, "and the pain will be gone, when the anesthesiologist starts the block ."

The anesthesia took effect quickly, numbing her pelvic area; she could feel pressure, but no pain. She felt her taut muscles relax and smiled at Howard who was bending over her. When the doctor told her to bear down with the contractions, she could do so without that awful agony.

The nurses covered her legs with sterile drapes, and then lifted them into the stirrups. The support made her more comfortable; it gave her something to brace herself against. She gripped the handles on each side of the table as the next contraction began to build.

DR. ROBINS WORE a head stethoscope so he could check the fetal heart sounds and still keep his hands free. He was concerned about the irregularity he saw on the fetal monitor after the last few contractions. The fetal heart rate was too slow, at around 80 instead of the usual 120 or so, a definite sign of fetal distress. Although the heart rate normally slowed during a contraction, it usually recovered rapidly

He motioned to the nurse to remove the stethoscope from his head, and sat down on a small stool at the end of the table, between his patient's legs. The nurse handed him a folded sterile towel.

The woman's perineal area was bulging now from the pressure of the baby's head. There was a gush of amniotic fluid and a fetid odor filled the room as the membranes ruptured and the baby's head crowned the perineum. Robbins used his full hand to retard the progress of the baby's head and prevent its sudden expulsion through the vulva with consequent lacerations to the mother.

He took a pair of blunt-pointed scissors and made a small cut in the perineum that was now stretched thin from the pressure of the baby's head. An episiotomy, like any clean-cut surgical incision, was easier to repair and healed better than a ragged laceration. He employed the procedure routinely, especially in a primipara, although sometimes after a woman had borne a few babies, it was not necessary.

Maintaining pressure on the baby's head with his hand, Robbins delivered the head slowly, during the short intervals between the mother's pains. Then he passed his finger up above the occiput of the baby's head and felt for the umbilical cord around the infant's neck. He drew it carefully down and over the head to prevent pressure on the cord from the baby's shoulder interfering with its oxygen supply. The woman's uterus contracted again and the baby's body rotated, its anterior shoulder arrested beneath the pubic arch and acting as a pivotal point for the other shoulder, which was then delivered by a lateral flexion of the baby's head.

The newborn child lay on a sterile sheet on Robbins' lap; as expected, it was a boy. He stared at the reddened areas covering the small body: some had actually broken into open sores. There was a strange pale, almost anemic appearance to the rest of the skin. This infant would definitely score low on the Apgar scale.

"Is he all right? It is a boy, isn't it?" the mother asked anxiously. She lifted her head to try to see below the end of the table, because Robbins' back and shoulders were blocking her view through the mirrors that had been set up for her to watch the progress of her delivery.

The baby gave a weak cry. "It's a boy," Robbins said.

He motioned to the nurse. She handed him the clamps and scissors. His mind raced while he automatically clamped the umbilical cord, and then tied the ligature securely before cutting the cord. In all his years of obstetrical practice he had never before seen a newborn in this condition. He nodded to the nurse, and she wrapped the infant in a sterile sheet.

"Just one quick look at your new son. We want to get him right into the incubator, because he *is* on the small side." He kept his voice even, calm and unhurried, as he spoke to the new parents. They were exclaiming to each other, tears of relief on the woman's check, her husband pressing his face to hers.

"Notify Dr. Hallam that we have a premature baby for him to

examine," he instructed the circulating nurse.

"Yes, doctor," she replied.

Robbins knew that the nurse realized it was not the usual practice to have the Chief of Pediatrics examine any newborn, but she was too well trained to comment on the fact in front of the infant's parents.

Mechanically, Robbins checked the woman's uterus, massaging the fundus gently, feeling it contract and harden under his hand. The placenta was expelled with that mild contraction, and he examined it carefully before passing it to the nurse. "Save this specimen," he told her quietly.

With a practiced efficiency, he repaired the episiotomy, anxious to finish the suturing so that he could check with Hallam about the condition of the baby.

After Robbins finished, the delivery room attendants wheeled a stretcher alongside the delivery table and carefully transferred Mrs. Prescott onto it. Robbins stopped beside the stretcher on his way out of the room. He took the woman's hand. "You get a good rest now. I'll stop by to see you later on in the day," he said, patting her hand. "You did just fine."

When Robbins reached the small nursery reserved for premature babies, Hallam was already there, carefully examining the infant through the armholes in the incubator, a frown furrowing his brow.

"Well, what do you think?" Robbins asked in a tense voice.

"I'll be damned if I know," Hallam said laconically. "Is the mother all right?"

"So far, yes. She was a primipara so she had a long labor, but she held up well under the strain. She's in excellent general health. I think it was just uterine irritability that caused the premature labor."

"Parents' blood types okay? No Rhesus factor problems?"

"All okay. No incompatibilities in the prenatal checks."

"The only thing I can think of is some kind of an allergic reaction, and yet, the infant is too debilitated for just that alone," Hallam mused. "I'm going to get some stat lab tests done: a complete blood series and also some cultures from those sores. Then we'll know where we stand. In the meantime, see if you can find out if the mother was taking any kind of medication you didn't know about."

"Dr. Robbins, you're wanted in OB . . . Dr. Robbins, you're wanted in OB . . . ," a melodious voice called on the intercom.

Robbins went to the desk just outside the room and called the floor nurse on Obstetrics. "This is Dr. Robbins."

"Doctor, Mrs. Prescott is spiking a temperature—it's 103°."

"I'll be right up." He put the phone down and went back to the doorway of the nursery to tell Hallam, who was entering orders for the lab tests at a video terminal of the hospital's computer system.

"I'll go with you," Hallam said. He signed off the computer and joined Robbins.

The waited impatiently while the elevator rose slowly to the floor above. They stepped out and Robbins led the way to Mrs. Prescott's room.

A nurse was waiting, chart in hand. Robbins took it and checked the notes on the patient's vital signs. The temperature graph showed a sharp spike, pulse was rapid, blood pressure a little low.

"Well, now, I hear you don't feel too well," he said. "I've brought Dr. Hallam up to see you. He'll be taking care of your son, and I thought you'd like to meet him.

The woman smiled weakly. Her face was flushed and damp; she was breathing rapidly.

The nurse drew back the sheet, and Robbins examined the woman's abdomen—the fundus was firm and the perineal pads showed no heavy bleeding had taken place. He motioned to the nurse to untie the patient's gown so he could examine her heart and chest.

The skin over her chest was covered with red blotches. "This may be the trouble," he said mildly. "It looks like you have a rash starting."

She looked down at her chest in surprise. "I didn't notice it before. It must have just started. What is it?"

"Well, it's a little too early to say," Robbins hedged. "Have you ever had any allergy problems?"

"Never." She shook her head firmly.

"What about medications? Have you had any new kind of medication in the last few weeks? Some people can't take certain kinds of ordinary medications because they get a bad reaction from them.

"No, I don't—oh, that must be it," she said, relief in her voice. "I had the Stanford vaccine a few weeks ago."

Robbins looked at her in surprise. "A few *weeks* ago? Are you sure?" he asked.

"Yes. But it's all right," she said. "My husband knew about the program and got some for me before the public immunizations started."

"I see." Robbins stepped back so that Hallam could examine the woman. He waited until Hallam finished, and then said, "Let's check your back to see if the rash is anywhere else."

"My legs feel a little irritated," she offered.

There were only a few small red patches on her back, but her feet and the calves of her legs were a fiery red. A few areas were moist where the skin was starting to break down.

"I'll order something for that irritation, Mrs. Prescott. Now I want you to think hard for a minute. Is the Stanford vaccine the only medication you've had recently? It's important that you remember."

"Why, I'm positive," she said slowly, her eyes showing confusion. "It's the only thing I've had. Why? What's wrong? Won't it go away?"

"We don't know exactly why you're getting such a reaction. But—we'll check with the CCA people and see what they say."

Robbins deliberately held back telling her of the baby's more serious condition. After the strain of labor and delivery, she wasn't ready for that kind of shock. But, without a doubt, he would have to tell her husband—the infant's condition was serious.

In Robbins's office, the two physicians discussed what action should be taken. "We'll have to be careful how we handle this," Hallam commented. "It may not be from the vaccine at all. But, if it is . . ."

"Yes, if it is . . . ," Robbins echoed. He frowned as he mentally reviewed the courses of action open to him. "I know Resa Myles. Let me give her a call and ask her to take a look at Mrs. Prescott and the baby before we risk causing a panic with an official inquiry through CCA channels."

He picked up the phone and dialed a number. "This is Dr. Robbins at Connor Hospital. Could I speak to Dr. Myles, please?" He frowned at the reply. "Do you know where?"

Hallam's fingers drummed impatiently on the desk while he waited for Robbins to finish the terse question-and-answer conversation. "Well?"

Robbins shook his head and put the receiver back on the hook. "She left for Tahoe about three hours ago."

The tension in the silent room was an almost palpable thing as each man weighed his own thoughts. Hallam looked at this colleague and spoke in a tight, quiet voice. "I just don't like the coincidence. The whole thing doesn't feel right."

Robbins nodded. He, too, had learned to rely on his medical instinct, that intangible feeling that overrode diagnostic tests and textbook criteria.

He picked up the phone. "Get me the Highway Patrol."

THE TRAFFIC WAS still fairly light on Highway 80. Steve glanced at Resa and smiled at the intent look on her face. She was looking out the window, her eyes searching the rock-strewn, wooded hillsides gliding past them. He came up fast behind a Volkswagen laboring in second gear on the gentle hill, swung out to pass it, and then turned to her.

"What are you looking for?" he asked.

She turned to him, a surprised look on her face. "Why, snow, of course," she said in mock indignation.

"Oh, of course," he agreed seriously. "In a few hours we'll be knee deep in it."

Hampered somewhat by the seat belt and shoulder harness, she leaned toward him and took his hand. There was a current of excitement in her voice, and her eyes were bright with anticipation.

"I want to see the first patches," she explained. "It's been years since I've seen any." She squeezed his hand. "If we're lucky it may even snow while we're up there. It's so much better to see it falling, it's clean and fresh and new."

"I can see it now," he said. "You and I skiing down a difficult run at Squaw Valley in a blinding snowstorm."

Resa chuckled. "Silly goose."

"Make that silly gander," he protested.

"We're well out of Sacramento," he said. "Watch for an elevation marker. I think we're high enough that you should start to see some patches any time now."

He drove with one hand, his other still warmly clasped in Resa's. The miles slipped by in a companionable silence, and Resa reflected on how her outlook had changed in the short time since Steve had come back into her life. She felt a new peace and at the same time a sense of purpose, of direction to her life. The aimless socializing, the single-minded pursuit of career, the lonely emptiness in quiet moments had vanished. Her world had become a different place.

It was as if her perception, her very senses had been dulled and now suddenly pulsed with new life. There was pleasure in feeling the sun, the wind, the rain on her skin, pleasure in seeing the different textures of very ordinary things, from the blades of grass crowding the lawn and the rough pebbled cement in a walkway to the silken gleam of polished metal.

When they were apart Steve was there in her mind, not a distraction, but a comforting awareness that made the petty annoyances and politics and problems at the Research Center fall into a lesser perspective, and become easier to cope with.

Bless Catherine and her conniving, meddling ways, she thought. If it had been left to mere chance, she might never have seen Steve again. The thought was a cold one, and she clasped his hand more tightly.

She felt his eyes on her, but even as she turned to him and saw the soft smile, she knew there would be no need for explanations. Between them, there was that special kind of empathy that never demanded the sharing of private thoughts

Daylight was fading fast. They were in snow country now, well beyond the first tiny pockets of snow that hid from the sun in the shadows of small gullies and under spreading fir trees. Steve had reduced speed to maneuver more carefully on the slippery highway with its thick blanket of hard-packed snow. On each side of the road rose tunnel-like walls of snow, heaped high by the snowplows that worked continually to keep the highways open.

"Look," Resa said, "up ahead of us."

There were flashing lights and a large sign that said chains were required over the summit. A line of cars had formed haphazardly in the right lane where Highway Patrol cars, strategically parked with red lights flashing, blocked the passage of all but a few vehicles that were permitted to pass, their tires already encased in snow chains.

Steve pulled off to the right and joined the line of cars. It was a cheerful gathering. For the most part, cars were loaded with brightly clad skiers who laughingly called out instructions to their companions who had been elected to leave the warmth of the car to put on the chains. It was also a money-making opportunity for the young men from nearby towns; they routinely gathered at the road blocks to help motorists, and for a few dollars could have chains on a car and the motorist on his way in minutes.

As soon as Steve stopped the car, a pair of eager young men were at his window. "Need any help, sir?"

"We can manage, thanks." Steve turned to Resa. "I need to get out and stretch my legs. Want to watch me put on the chains?"

She nodded, tied a fur cap over her chestnut curls, and climbed out of the car to join Steve, who had opened the trunk and was untangling the set of chains. "Next time," he said, "you can do this and I'll move the car onto the chains when you have them all lined up properly under the tires."

Before she could reply to his teasing remark, a Highway Patrol car drew up alongside them, and one of the officers, eyeing their license plate, rolled down the window and called out to them. "Are you Dr. Resa Myles?" he asked.

"Yes, I am," Resa replied.

"We have an emergency call for you from Dr. Robbins at Connor Hospital. We can put you through from here."

Steve waited at the car for Resa. She talked for a long time. When she returned and got into the car, her face was set in an anxious frown. "I'm sorry, but we'll have to go back," she said.

He said that it was all right, but she scarcely heard his words as he wheeled the car around and headed back toward Palo Alto.

"What's wrong, Resa?" he asked.

"I don't know, exactly," she said absentmindedly. . . . She reached over and squeezed his hand briefly. "Robbins wants me to look at a mother and newborn infant who have some unusual symptoms. Apparently the mother had a dose of the Stanford vaccine before it was released, and Robbins thinks there may be some connection between that the symptoms she and the baby are exhibiting."

"You mean they're sick from it?" Steve asked.

"Oh, they're sick all right, but whether it's from the vaccine I can't tell yet. . . ."

"Oh, Resa, it can't be . . ."

"I don't know. But Robbins doesn't panic . . . and he sounded unusually concerned."

Resa wondered who had given the woman the vaccine. And how did he get his hands on it? The damn fool needs his head examined, Resa thought. He might have taken the wrong vaccine, maybe one of the test strains. But then again he could have gotten the right vaccine. Then Resa remembered Harland's secret stockpiles of the Stanford vaccine and the number of Bay Area laboratories that had been in on that program.

No, she decided, it wouldn't have been that difficult for anyone to get some of the genuine vaccine; in fact, it would have been far easier than the chance of getting a test strain. But why give it to a pregnant woman about to deliver?

Beneath the superficial conjecture of her thoughts was a cold core of fear that she avoided examining too closely. But it was there waiting, the crystallization of her doubts and concern over Harland's usurpation of the program, the acceleration of research, the limited testing

They left the cold clean air of the snow country behind and descended into the smog of the valley. Traffic was light and Resa was glad that Steve drove quickly, efficiently. She was anxious to reach the hospital and find answers to the questions that raced through her mind.

"Hey, I'm sorry about this. It's ruined our weekend, for sure. I don't know how long I'll be tied up at Connor.

Steve smiled. "There'll be other weekends. I'm disappointed, too, but . . ." He shrugged. "That's the way it to goes sometimes. Will you call and let me know what happens?"

"Of course," she said. "As soon as I can break free. We'll have a midnight breakfast if you're awake."

But midnight would come and go . . . and even the early hours of morning would find Resa back at the Stanford Research Center with key members of her staff, deeply involved in analyzing tissue and blood samples.

AT CONNOR HOSPITAL Howard Prescott sat alone in a modernly antiseptic waiting room that gleamed with chrome and glass, staring at the wall opposite him. A large abstract painting dominated the wall, its garish streaks of violent color making it the focal point of attention in the room, but Prescott saw neither the artistic monstrosity nor the brightly colored furnishings. He was oblivious to the people who entered and left the room, their pains, their hopes, their fears mirrored on their faces.

His son was dead.

He waited to see if his wife would survive.

The syndrome had begun.

CNN NEWS UPDATE—

There is a worldwide euphoria sweeping the planet. Joyous crowds are lining up for their cancer inoculations. Prominent at the centers is the United States flag, which is printed on the boxes containing the vaccine sent out worldwide under President Harland's Project Immunity program.

It's a proud day for Americans.

Chapter 9

Palo Alto, California

"MR. PRESIDENT, I want Project Immunity canceled immediately!"

Resa's voice was harsh and angry. She spoke from the Research Center over a secure line to the president that had been installed for urgent communications concerning the synthetic virus.

"Impossible," Harland replied coldly, "the program is almost completed. I'm not going to authorize canceling it just because you've found someone with a bad reaction to the vaccine. I consulted with my medical advisors after I got your message this morning, and they have assured me that this is not unusual—an allergy of some kind.

"Of course, I sympathize with the young couple. In fact, I'll send my personal condolences to them. But millions of other lives will be saved by the program." His voice lost its persuasive timbre and became impatient, annoyed. Harland was determined—and who could gainsay him?—to continue the program.

"Stop grasping at straws, Resa. You were against the immunizations from the outset."

"My personal views are beside the point, Mr. President. Since I sent you that first message, we've received reports of other cases where healthy individuals took advance doses of the vaccine and are exhibiting severe reactions. We have to stop the program and—"

Harland cut her off. "Look, my word is final. The program continues and that's an order. You listen to me, doctor. If you stir up any trouble for the CCA, you're out! Is that clear?" Harland was almost shouting in anger.

Resa's reply was sharp and brief. "Perfectly clear, Mr. President." She hung up the phone and drew a deep breath to relax her own throbbing anger.

She thought of the infant body lying in the Center morgue, and the young mother in a coma kept alive by the equipment in the Critical Care Unit. She thought of the new patients she had not yet seen, who were reported early this morning, after the urgent call had gone out describing the new syndrome and requesting any cases be reported at once.

Resa pressed a button on the office intercom. "Marge, have the chiefs of staff assemble in my conference room stat."

"Yes, doctor," her secretary said.

"Then set up a press conference—major news—to follow the staff meeting. . . . And, Marge, try to keep it quiet. No leaks until I make an official announcement."

"I'll take care of it, doctor. Would you like coffee served at the staff meeting?"

"Yes. That's a good idea. Thanks, Marge."

Resa went to the private dressing room adjoining her office, splashed cold water on her face, and then put on a fresh blouse. She had been up all night and working at a hectic pace since her decision to transfer Mrs. Prescott from Connor Hospital to the Research Center's Critical Care Unit late yesterday evening. Her face was haggard and drawn, and she knew that soon she would have to stop and get some sleep or she wouldn't be able to function with any claim to efficiency.

Resa joined the men and women who had assembled in the conference room, took her chair at the head of the table, and glanced through the latest report Marge Bryson had placed there. Then she put the papers down and spoke to her chiefs of staff.

"I've just finished talking to the president, and he refuses to authorize cancellation of the immunization program," Resa said quietly. "So let's have a quick recap and see where we stand on the problem. You lead off, Mark. How many cases of the new syndrome have been reported?"

Mark Ashton referred to the papers in his hand. "As of ten minutes ago, we have reports on 476 cases. All had a preliminary dose of the synthetic virus, and we advised that each be transferred to the nearest CCA center for treatment. Three of those have expired. We have some initial computer printouts on the results of lab tests from about 200 cases, but we're still waiting for complete cell studies."

"How many of these cases are local?" Resa asked.

"We'll be getting about twelve of them here," Ashton replied.

Resa turned to Dr. Maria Schiller, who was handling Mrs. Prescott's treatment.

"Mrs. Prescott is still comatose. I left orders to prep her for surgery. The only chance she has is a complete blood replacement, and I'm not sure she'll survive the procedure. Her blood is loaded with the virus and it's attacking normal cells. I hope the blood replacement will buy us time to find a way to stop it. . . . I think Whitman can tell us more about the latest photomicrographs than I can."

"I can add very little, I'm afraid," Whitman said. "The synthetic virus is very definitely penetrating normal cells and multiplying. The syndrome seems to result from the action of the virus in inhibiting normal cell regeneration. Why this doesn't happen when the patient has cancer cells in his body, I don't know."

"Anyone else have anything?" Resa asked. The others murmured negative responses. "Then let me summarize very briefly what facts we have. First, it is definite that the Stanford vaccine is producing this syndrome. Second, the syndrome varies widely in severity from an allergy type of reaction to a complete breakdown of the body's normal defense mechanisms. Third, we don't know how to treat it, other than symptomatically. The antivirals we're using don't seem to be effective against this virus. And, lastly, we don't know how many people took advance doses of the vaccine, so we have no way of knowing what percent of the people that had advance immunizations are having a bad reaction. It could be anywhere from 1% to 100%."

Resa paused. "In my opinion," she said carefully, "we must issue a public announcement of these facts so that the people will stop taking the vaccine."

There was silence in the room while the group considered her statements.

"They'll panic," observed Ashton.

"Aye, that they will," MacBride asserted.

Resa nodded. "Yes. There will be panic."

Ashton looked surprised at Resa's agreement. "Then we can't make a public announcement."

"On the contrary. The panic will come. It's simply a matter of when. The syndrome exists. We can't change that. Right now we're seeing the reaction from only those people who had the vaccine in advance of the regular immunization program. Can you imagine the panic when the syndrome starts to appear on a mass scale?"

Resa had given some careful thought to what would happen in the cities then. The controls of civilization would be shattered, and she had determined to find some place of comparative safety for her family before that happened. From the sober, reflective looks on the faces of the men and women in the room, Resa knew that they, too, were contemplating the personal dangers their loved ones would be facing.

"Mark, would you get us a reading on the current percentage of the adult population that has *not yet* received the vaccine? A percentage of the clean population, if you will," Resa asked.

Ashton went to the conference room computer terminal and keyed in the query. The researchers watched the instant response appear on an oversize video screen on the wall.

PROJECT IMMUNITY
STANFORD VACCINE
PERCENT NOT GIVEN
BASED ON ADULTS
CURRENT CENSUS
UNITED STATES: 41%

Resa sighed. She had hoped for a much higher number. "Let's see a listing by state."

Ashton keyed in the request, and the words faded from the glowing display to be replaced by another, longer message that began to scroll across the screen:

PROJECT IMMUNITY
STANFORD VACCINE
PERCENT NOT GIVEN
BASED ON
CURRENT CENSUS
ADULTS BY STATE:
ALABAMA: 31%
ALASKA: 40%
ARIZONA: 33%
ARKANSAS: 26%

CALIFORNIA: 48%
CONNECTICUT: 42%
DELAWARE: 24%

"That's enough, Mark, thank you."

Resa jotted down some figures on the writing pad in front of her. "Please look at the percent of California's population that has not yet received the vaccine. I think the state population is somewhere around 25 million, so with 48 percent of the population still—I'll use the word clean again—we're talking about roughly 12 million people. And this is only one state. Remember, Project Immunity is a worldwide program.

"We have no choice. The program must be stopped, in spite of the president's attitude. I, for one, am certain that this syndrome we are seeing will snowball, that it's not a few isolated cases caused by individual idiosyncrasies, but a flaw in the vaccine itself. Do you agree?"

Resa looked first at Ashton, who said heavily, "Yes, I agree. In time it will be apparent to everyone, even the president. We'll need all the healthy people we can get. . . . A nation of sick to care for. . . . God help us."

"And God help the millions of children who won't have parents to care for them," MacBride added.

The two men spoke for all of them in the room. The others nodded agreement as Resa scanned their faces.

"Thank you, all of you," Resa said. "I will personally make the announcement at the press conference. I don't want any of you to be there. The president has made it clear that anyone who disrupts the program is in for trouble. I can't begin to understand his attitude; political expediency can only go so far. There's just no way to hide from the facts. We have to move now or there will be more than panic, there will be chaos—and on a worldwide scale. From this point on, our top priority is to develop a counteragent to the synthetic virus."

She turned to her secretary. "Marge, the press conference?"

"In conference room 6, doctor." She glanced at her watch. "In fifteen minutes."

"Thank you." Resa excused herself and left the room hurriedly. There was just enough time for her to stop by the operating room and see how Mrs. Prescott was progressing.

The O.R. supervisor directed her to the room where the surgery was taking place. In the glass-enclosed gallery that encircles the amphitheater, Resa looked down on the operation in progress. The patient was hidden beneath a mass of equipment.

The members of the surgical team worked together as if directed by one mind, their movements swift, precise, with an economy of motion Resa had always admired, and she felt a surge of pride in these people; they were among the best in the world. If any one group could stop this syndrome, it would be these people here at Stanford. Here, where the synthetic virus was born. And she felt again the heat of anger. If Harland had let them expand the testing slowly, with the first small group of healthy volunteers, they would have known something was wrong.

She left the gallery, her step sure and purposeful. She had yielded once to the politicians, and they had used her research as a political weapon. Now it was backfiring on them and they would try to hide their culpability. But Resa was determined to salvage all she could from the insanity they had bred, and not even the president himself could stop her now.

Conference room 6 was routinely used for small lectures and for press conferences. It was a spacious room filled now with reporters, radio and television crews, and their media equipment. Resa was glad to see that a CNN crew was there. Worldwide exposure was needed desperately.

The camera and microphones were in place and directed toward a raised platform that occupied one wall at the head of the room. The rows of chairs along the back of the platform were empty and the lights and cameras were focused on a small lectern, which stood in front of the chairs and held the speaker's microphones. Resa went directly to the platform. She held no notes and stood relaxed at the lectern, waiting for the room to quiet.

Robert Neilson, the Center's public relations director, joined her on the platform to make the brief introduction. "Ladies and gentlemen of the press, . . . Dr. Resa Myles, director of the Stanford Cancer Research Center, will make a major announcement for immediate release to the public."

Resa spoke clearly and distinctly, and in the hushed room the attention of everyone present was directed at her. "I know you are all familiar with the worldwide ramifications of Project Immunity, which is being sponsored by the Control of Cancer Agency, so I won't go into any background details on the program. I'm here to give you some facts of which you are not yet aware. It has come to my attention—"

She stopped speaking as the door to the conference room opened and a group of people filed quietly into the room and took seats behind her on the raised platform. James MacBride led the group, followed by Mark Ashton, Michael Fournier who was a Nobel laureate in chemistry, and Michael and Susan Leonardo from immunology. They were followed by others until every name scientist in the Research Center was there, every chief of staff. A low murmur rippled through the room, and the reporters, taking notes furiously, did not miss the unspoken show of solidarity. The scientific community had closed its ranks firmly behind Dr. Resa Myles.

Resa felt her throat tighten, but only someone who knew her very well would have been able to see how this gesture from her colleagues had touched her.

"It has come to our attention," she went on, "that some people—desperately anxious, frightened people—obtained doses of the Stanford cancer vaccine before the public program began. Among these people a very serious syndrome has appeared as a direct result of the vaccine they took. The syndrome manifests itself along a broad range of symptoms, from a severe allergic reaction to a complete breakdown of the body's vital processes. There have been 476 new cases reported in the last twenty-four hours.

"I want to emphasize that the syndrome is only beginning. We are seeing the reaction in only those people who received the vaccine *before* Project Immunity started. There will be more people affected by the vaccine, many more people.

"We advise everyone who has not yet received the vaccine *not to take it*. It could be lethal to them.

"You will be given handouts with a complete description of the syndrome. Any person who begins to exhibit these symptoms should seek medical attention immediately. We ask that all who received immunizations before the program started go immediately to the nearest CCA Research Center. This is an urgent request. We will *not* bring any charges against you. We simply want to examine you and take a blood sample to determine if you're going to have any negative reaction to the vaccine.

"It will also help us to know exactly how many people received the vaccine before the formal program started. When we determine just how many had early immunizations, we'll be able to calculate what the percentage is of those having dangerous reactions. Right now we don't know if 1 percent or 100 percent of the people who have been immunized are going to be adversely affected by the vaccine. Please notify your nearest CCA Center. I repeat, no charges will be filed against you. We're concerned only with the state of your health.

"Thank you for your attention. Are there any questions?"

Resa held up both hands to stem the barrage of questions from the audience. "One at a time, please." She pointed to a reporter in the first row.

"Dr. Myles, are you saying that everyone who has taken the vaccine will be affected?"

"I'm saying many of them will. I cannot estimate how many, because I don't know how many people took the vaccine in advance. Therefore, I have no total against which to compare the number of people having adverse effects. I know only that we have received reports that over 400 of this unknown number of people are seriously affected. In a matter of weeks we'll know more."

She pointed to another reporter. "Next question, please."

"Doctor, has it been definitely established that the Stanford vaccine has caused this syndrome?"

"Yes." Resa's reply was emphatic. "There is absolutely no doubt. We have photomicrographs that show the action of the synthetic virus clearly."

"Then it is very probable that everyone who has had the vaccine will have some reaction from it?" the reporter continued.

"I would say yes. It's almost a certainty. . . . I have time for just a few more questions." She pointed to Hauser from the wire services.

"Dr. Myles, why hasn't this announcement come from the president?"

Resa eyed him coldly. "I do not speak for the president, Mr. Hauser. You'll have to ask him. But just remember that he is a politician, not a scientist or physician," Resa added quietly but firmly.

But Hauser pressed the issue. "But he is the Director of the CCA, doctor. What is his reaction to the announcement?"

"You'll have to get that from the president himself. . . ." Resa pointed to a hand raised at the back of the room.

A woman stood. "What is being done about treating all the people who will need medical aid?"

"We are sending directives to every hospital, every Red Cross chapter in the country. We are also in close contact with the other CCA Research Centers worldwide. Needless to say, we have already started work on trying to find out how to stop the syndrome."

She glanced at her watch. "That's all I have time for. Thank you all for your attention. Neilson will distribute printed releases to you."

As Resa turned from the crowd of reporters and joined her colleagues, the reporters hurried from the room to telephones from which they could file their releases: within minutes the news would be announced by special bulletins over radio and television.

IN ANOTHER PART of the city, at his Parkside Glen apartment, Rostov waited with controlled impatience for a report from the agent he had ordered to cover Resa's press conference. As soon as he had heard from the agent planted at the Research Center itself that she had called for a press conference, he had contacted his agent in the television media.

He moved restlessly around the room, glancing frequently at his watch. Inactivity irritated him, and he disliked the caution and the surveillance activities required in this assignment. When the telephone rang, he answered sharply. "Yes?"

He listened carefully, and let the agent complete his report without interruption.

Then Rostov said, "I'll contact you later," and hung up the phone.

He crossed the room, turned on the television set to CNN, and sat down to wait. The screen came to life, and he looked with disdain at the program in progress. But his wait was a short one. A television announcer appeared and an unseen voice spoke.

"We interrupt this program for a special news bulletin."

And then the announcer came to life. "Dr. Resa Myles, director of the Cancer Research Center at Stanford, has issued a warning that the Stanford vaccine administered under the CCA-sponsored Project Immunity is producing dangerous effects. We will now show you a videotape recording of her announcement."

Rostov watched the recording of the press conference intently, and when it was over he switched off the set. He was not concerned with the broadcaster's summary and speculation.

His mind was occupied by the information he had gathered from the broadcast. The agent's report had been good, but he had missed a major point. Dr. Myles and her group were already seeking an antidote—and the full-scale syndrome with the chaos it would bring had not yet erupted. She would have to be stopped immediately.

Rostov had not planned on any preliminary news of the syndrome reaching the public—he had underestimated the doctor. He thought she would be afraid to go up against the president. The woman's immediate action could disrupt the whole plan severely.

But the president would be an unwitting ally. Rostov was sure that Harland would try to disassociate himself from the program, and Myles, acting without presidential approval—as was obvious from the press conference tapes—would be the logical scapegoat. Censure directed toward the scientific community, and Myles in particular, would help Rostov immeasurably.

Now he must set other forces into action quickly, forces that would point the way for Harland to act. Public opinion must be turned against the scientists. Demonstrations must be arranged.

It would not be difficult.

Rostov had at his call agents who had been under deep cover for up to twenty years, among them agents who controlled a major part of the illegal drug traffic in the country. These agents had a great influence on the people who bought their drugs. Minds dulled and crazed by drugs were easy to direct, and a killing rampage by crazed addicts was not uncommon in this country, not at all uncommon.

He unlocked a briefcase and from it took a file containing detailed information on Myles: her habits, her possessions, her career, her friends, her loved ones. He studied a photograph of Myles's car and another with an enlarged view of the car's license plate.

Rostov picked up the phone and dialed a number. He identified himself by code only, and then began to issue concise, explicit instructions.

WIRE COPY — *THE WHITE HOUSE PRESS SECRETARY HAS JUST*

ANNOUNCED THAT THE PRESIDENT IS QUOTE APPALLED AT BEING MISINFORMED BY TRUSTED SCIENTISTS OF THE CONTROL OF CANCER AGENCY (CCA) END QUOTE. STOP. THE PRESIDENT IS NOW MEETING WITH ADVISORS. STOP. (MORE) IN HIS CAPACITY AS DIRECTOR OF THE CCA, PRESIDENT HARLAND HAS REQUESTED THE RESIGNATION OF DR. RESA MYLES AS DIRECTOR OF THE STANFORD CANCER RESEARCH CENTER IN PALO ALTO, CALIFORNIA. STOP.

Chapter 10

Palo Alto, California

FROM AN OFFICE window high on the top story of the gleaming Cancer Research Center, Resa looked down with distaste on the milling, ant-like figures clustered around the building. The noise did not carry this far, but she had shouldered her way through that mob a few hours earlier and knew first-hand of the venomous shouts and obscenities that filled the air.

Uniformed security guards stood shoulder to shoulder in front of the entrance to the building, watching the demonstrators who shouted and cavorted around the fringes of the mob. A half-dozen police cars were parked nearby and the officers were circulating around the outer edges of the mob. It was not the type of mob she had been expecting. These were not your serious, sedate, middle-class protestors. There was no family, no professional type of presence.

Filthy, ragged, and demented, the gutters of America had spilled over into the street; encouraged by the numerous television cameras, the mob shrieked their venomous insults with abandon. Eyes glittering with insane delight, they performed gleefully for the newsmen who dutifully, even avidly in some cases, televised and reported every facet of their spontaneous protest.

But beneath the façade of spontaneity, Resa was sure that the demonstration was shrewdly organized. But who, she wondered, and why? Harland, of course, would want to steer public attention away from himself. She fully expected him to blame her for the syndrome that was appearing, but she didn't think he would use the kind of mob that had appeared.

Resa looked away from the posturing figures below and turned to speak to her sister, Catherine, who had been trying to persuade Resa to leave the Center for a few hours and join her in the house-hunting expedition she had asked Catherine to undertake several months ago.

"But Resa, it's your house we're going to look for. I have a whole list of good prospects ready. And, besides, I hate to go alone. And you're working too hard anyway. You really need a little time away from this place. Anyway, you're fired."

Mac came into the office just in time to catch part of Catherine's plea. "How's my little Cat," he said to Catherine.

"Oh, Uncle Mac, hello!" She threw her arms around his neck. "I haven't seen you since my party."

"And that was so long ago, don't you know!" Mac teased. He turned to Resa. "It'll do you good to get away for a while. It'll give us time to decide how best to 'share' you among the staff."

He slipped an arm around Catherine. "Little Cat, we don't agree with the president firing Resa. We've hired her back as a special consultant."

"Oh, good for you! Resa, you didn't tell me."

"I would've when it was my turn to talk!" Resa quipped and they both laughed.

"Who knows how long that will last. If Harland gets wind of it, I'll be out again." Resa knew that the time left to stop the syndrome was short, that the staff as a whole had ignored the advisory from the president relieving Resa of her post as director.

And now they looked to her for direction, but Catherine was right. She'd have to vacate her office. And it might be that eventually she'd have to keep in touch with the staff by computer from home.

Also she had needed and wanted a larger place for quite a while—her two-bedroom townhouse just wasn't big enough, and if she did have to work from home, her small house definitely wouldn't cut it.

"All right." Resa yielded gracefully. "The two of you are too much to argue with. Besides, I can get more work done this evening. And by then maybe that disgusting mob outside will have thinned out at least a little."

Mac escorted them down to the lobby. "Go out the back door," he said. "I don't want you fighting your way through that mess."

Resa nodded in agreement. "We'll take my car. It's parked in the back lot, and I just filled the tank up this morning." The women left the Center by the back door and managed to avoid the mob at the front of the building. Resa drove off the campus and sighed with relief. "That mob is unbelievable," she said to Catherine. "I'd like to know who planted the idea of protesting in their little minds."

"They're gross," was Catherine's succinct reply. "I didn't think Harland would stoop so low."

"No. It's not Harland. The CCA is his baby. He wouldn't want it tarnished in any way."

"Well, I'm glad we'll be house hunting out in the country. The city's a mess right now. . . . You know, Resa, you surprised me at first with this decision to buy a house out of the city, because it will be a much longer drive into Stanford for you. But now I think it's a really good idea."

"Yes, and I think things will get much worse in the cities when more people get sick. . . . Riots, break-ins—you can imagine how chaotic it will be."

"You're right. I hadn't really thought it all out. When I told Paul about it, he said it was a wise decision. I guess we're lucky that we already live out in the country."

Resa turned the car toward the freeway. "Where is the first stop?"

"Oh, wait." Catherine rummaged through her purse for the list she had secured earlier that morning from the real estate agent she'd been using.

"Head for Skyline Drive and I'll give you directions."

"Skyline it is." Resa headed toward the mountains. It was a sunny day and unusually clear for the valley, with the sky a cool bright blue. A good day to be outside, she thought.

Catherine unfolded a road map and studied it intently for a few minutes, her face puckered in a frown. "Fine, we're all set now," she commented.

"I'm glad to hear it."

"Paul has a good day for flying," Catherine remarked. "It just doesn't feel like a Saturday to me for some reason."

"Maybe because I was working, and you're house hunting instead of grocery shopping, and Paul is off on his emergency trip to Pasadena."

"Yes." Catherine laughed. "Paul's not here—that's what's wrong. If that computer on the satellite had to go haywire, I wish it had done so during the week."

"Well, you picked out a genius at computer science. Look at it this way. Paul's computer skills brought in the money he needed to start his air freight company."

"That's true," Catherine conceded. "And he loves those planes. He's like a kid with his favorite toy. But the thing I like best about the weekends is that Paul is home instead of at work."

118

"I know," Resa said fondly. "It shows all over the two of you."

"After five years!" Catherine said in mock indignation.

"Yes," Resa said dryly, "after five years. Now, where do I turn? Skyline Drive is just ahead."

"Go about two miles and turn right on Oak Road. . . . I *am* paying attention, you know."

"Of course you are."

The first house on Catherine's list was rejected after only a cursory inspection. Back in the car she lined through the listing vigorously. "I can't believe they want that much money for a rattle-trap house! It's practically falling apart. And the kitchen! . . . Well—on to the next place. This one will be better—I saw a picture of it at the agent's office and it looked like it might be just perfect."

"Well why didn't we go there first?"

"Logistics, my dear," Catherine said lightly. "We scientists' wives understand these things. In plain English, it wasn't the first stop if we're to follow a circular route that will take us right back to Palo Alto."

"I beg your pardon. Where to?"

"Back to Skyline, turn right, and then proceed about five miles." Catherine folded up the map and settled herself back in the seat.

"Oh, Cathy," Resa said with ill-concealed laughter, "if I didn't know you better, I'd say you look downright smug."

"Not at all," Catherine said equably, but the complacent smile didn't leave her face. "Here's Skyline. That's a right we take."

"I know." Resa shot a sidelong glance at her sister and smiled when Catherine winked back at her mischievously.

Resa turned from the side road onto the wider highway and increased her speed slightly. She enjoyed driving on an open road with no traffic to fight, no pedestrians darting across in front of her. Automatically, as she usually did when edging over the speed limit, she glanced at the rear-view mirror.

"Oh, Cathy. Look what's coming up behind us," she said in

annoyance.

Catherine turned around and looked out the back window. A group of motorcycle riders was coming up fast behind them, weaving in a crisscross fashion across both lines of the highway.

"Oh great," Catherine said, "a bunch of clowns. Let's take the next turn and let them go by us. They act like they're high on something."

"That's a good idea," Resa said, watching the riders rapidly closing the gap between them. "I don't want to wreck my car dodging those idiots."

She made a sharp right turn onto a side road and slowed down, watching in the rear-view mirror for the cavalcade to pass.

But they did not pass. The roar of the motorcycles grew louder as the riders turned and came up behind the car.

"Oh, Resa," Catherine said slowly. There was fear in her voice. "Don't stop. Keep going."

Resa felt her heart lurch. She pressed her foot down harder on the accelerator and the car shot ahead of the riders who had clustered behind them. They kept coming.

She clenched the wheel tightly, braking at the last second for the frequent sharp curves on the narrow road and accelerating strongly to pull the car out of them. But she couldn't stay ahead of the cyclists.

Two of them swung out and came up on the left side of the car. They shouted at her but the words were unintelligible over the roar of the bikes' motors.

Resa glanced briefly at them, her main attention on the road, and caught only a glimpse of helmeted figures in battered leather jackets with long, stringy hair flying out from under their helmets.

The speedometer was vacillating around eighty and she was having trouble easing the car off the shoulder on the sharper curves. Suddenly, in a short open stretch, one of the huge bikes roared ahead, cutting her off. She eased back on the accelerator instinctively.

"Keep going! We can't let them stop us!" Catherine shouted. She yanked open the glove compartment and, frantic with terror, pulled everything out in her search.

"What are you doing?" Resa cried. She couldn't turn to look, but had seen Catherine's frantic movements out of the corner of her eye.

"I'm looking for something we can use to defend ourselves, " Catherine sobbed.

"There is nothing. I don't have any guns in the car. And that's what we need. Cathy, take my cell phone out of my purse and call 911."

Terrified now, Resa watched the riders move in even tighter around the car. There were six of them. They were grinning arrogantly. She half listened to Catherine's call and the directions she gave to the police.

Resa felt the sick trembling within her, the feeling of weakness, fade and turn to cold anger. "Tighten your seat belt as much as you can," she said sharply to Catherine, "and do mine—I need both hands on the wheel. Hang on, Cathy, we'll get out of this. You watch for a house or some people in a field."

Catherine obeyed her with trembling hands.

"Good," Resa said firmly. "Now, on the next open stretch, wedge something—a pen or nail file—down around the horn so it stays on. Tie it down. Use my scarf, anything. Take care you don't tangle my arms."

Resa alerted her sister, "Hurry—now!"

The sudden strident blare of the horn startled the cyclist in front of the car and his machine wavered. Gaining confidence in her ability to control the car, Resa increased her speed, concentrating intently on the movements of the cyclist weaving in front of her and the layout of the road directly ahead. The loud noise of the horn did not disturb her, it was reassuring, a danger signal broadcasting their need for help.

They were approaching a narrow curve to the right. She waited until the rider in front of her started to swing left to take the turn on the outside, then she floored the accelerator and, ignoring the other riders close to the car, moved up fast to the left of the rider, forcing him into too tight a turn. The bike skidded on the gravel shoulder and disappeared over the bank.

"That's one down," she muttered grimly, "five to go."

The other cyclists fell back behind the car. She watched them through the mirror. Her action must have angered them. Their sly grins were gone and they were shouting and gesturing to each other. Two of them reached into their saddlebags, but she couldn't see what they were doing.

"Cathy, watch them," she ordered tensely.

Catherine twisted around in the seat to look out the rear window. "Oh, my God," she groaned. "They have chains! Resa, there are big metal balls on the end of the chains . . . like bolas."

There was a sharp crack and the rear window of the car shattered into frosted white. Resa began to weave the car across the road in a dangerous fashion. She knew if the riders got around to the front and shattered the windshield, they were finished.

"God help us," she whispered.

The cyclists were raining blows all over the car, but she dared not take her eyes off the road to see exactly where they were. And then there was another sharp crack, and the front windshield went white. She saw Catherine smash at the windshield with her fist to try to remove the shattered glass, but only a small hole appeared.

For a few more seconds, Resa held to the road by watching the shoulder out her side window, but then she missed a sharp turn. The car lurched and went over a bank. Everything around her was spinning as the car tumbled end over end down the hillside. She heard Catherine scream, and then there was a sharp pain in her head and a wave of darkness engulfed her.

Resa felt as if she were struggling in a red haze. She heard something—it was Cathy screaming loudly over the noise of the horn. She had to help her. Her eyes opened and they felt sticky.

There was something wet all over her face. She looked around her. The car was on its side and she was wedged in the wreckage with her head leaning on a heavy branch that had come through the windshield. She was vaguely aware of shadowy forms in a small clearing near the car.

Then her vision cleared and the shadowy forms came into focus. The five cyclists stood in a circle around Catherine. She was almost naked. They were passing her around the circle, each man tearing at her clothing in turn. She screamed and fought, and they jeered gleefully at her.

Resa tried to move and a violent pain shot through her head. She had to help Cathy. Frantic, she eased her arm from the wreckage and groped for the release on the seat belt that held her tightly in place.

Two of the riders had grabbed Catherine now and each held one of her arms so that she was stretched out between them. She was trying to kick at them, but they held her at arm's length and she couldn't reach them. Two of the others had removed their pants and their white, naked buttocks below the heavy jackets looked obscene in the sunlight. They moved toward Catherine.

"Hey, man, get the other one."

"I think she's dead."

In the car, Resa strained to reach the release button on the seat belt . . . and finally the tip of one finger touched it. She pushed hard. The belt released.

Her body started falling.

There was one moment of excruciating pain and then all sensation ceased.

A PERSISTENT SOUND brought Resa slowly out of her unconscious state. She struggled to identify the noise, her mind clouded with pain and confusion, and then she realized it was Cathy's voice screaming for help. The shock brought her awake. Memory flooded back and she turned her head to see the small clearing near the car where the men had taken Cathy.

She was on the ground now, struggling against the four men holding her arms and legs spread apart. They were laughing at her and seemed to enjoy her screams and lunges. They made no effort to stop her cries and only restrained her arms and legs enough to keep her from flailing out and clawing at the man who was kneeling between her legs, thrusting himself viciously into her.

Resa cried out in horror when she saw them, but her weak cry was lost in the clamor of Cathy's hysterical screams and her rapists' laughter.

The man raping Catherine finally rolled away from her. "Take her arm, it's my turn," said one of the others. He stood over her, his penis swollen erect. "She's a bloody mess," he muttered, nudging her pelvis with his bare foot. "Turn her over."

"Hey, wait. I got a better idea," said one of the others. "Let's use that boulder." He motioned with his head toward the far side of the clearing.

They yanked Catherine to her feet and Resa saw clearly the cuts and bruises on her sister's ravaged body. A trickle of fresh blood ran down her thighs, which were already stained red from the brutal raping she had suffered.

"Let me go!" Catherine sobbed. "Please!" She tried to pull away from the two men holding her arms.

"Baby, the fun's just started." They dragged her to the boulder and threw her face down over it. Then they gathered around her, yanking on her arms to draw her up over the rounded top of the boulder so that her feet dangled freely, a few inches off the ground. Two of them grabbed her legs at the knees and forced them apart, spreading her for the man who came up behind her and blocked her from Resa's view.

Catherine's animal-like scream of pain made Resa retch with spasms of nausea. Sobbing incoherently she tried again to move, to free herself from the twisted metal imprisoning her within the

124

wrecked car. She wanted to tear those animals apart, but she was trapped. Her attempts to move caused jagged pains to shoot through her head. A piece of sharp metal pierced her shoulder and she could feel the warm blood trickle down the inside of her blouse.

She lay there helplessly, tears streaming from her eyes as she listened to Catherine's screams. It seemed like a long time before she felt a merciful numbness begin to creep over her, blurring her vision and softening the tormented cries of her sister ringing in her ears.

Resa welcomed the closing darkness and, unresisting, let herself fall into it.

SAN JOSE MERCURY NEWS
OBITUARY NOTICE —

Angela Prescott, age 32, passed from this life on February 6 at the Stanford CCA Research Center in Palo Alto, California from complications following the birth of her first child.

Mrs. Prescott was preceded in death by her newborn son, David Prescott, who passed away one week earlier.

She is survived by her husband, Howard Prescott of Palo Alto, California. Prescott is a laboratory technician at Edmonton Laboratories in San Jose.

Services for Angela Prescott will be held on February 12 at the Laurel Grove Funeral Home chapel. Interment will follow at the Laurel Grove Memorial Park.

Chapter 11

Palo Alto, California

THE MORNING SUN sent tiny shafts of light through the partially closed blinds at the windows, brightening the hospital room perceptibly.

Why is it that sunlight always makes the brightest of artificial lights seem weak in comparison? Steve thought. A part of him chided himself for the foolish way his mind snatched at the most minute observation, cherished any distraction to avoid facing the memories of the night, agonizing memories.

The call from the police department when they found the wreck . . . the long, endless-seeming drive . . . the horrified look on Paul's face when he lifted the blanket and saw Cathy . . . the flame from the acetylene torches the police used to get Resa out of the wreckage. . . . Resa.

He looked again at her still figure in the hospital bed; she had not stirred for hours.

Once during the night her eyes had opened blankly, but it was only a random movement in the coma. He had moved quickly to her side, but her gaze had only wandered aimlessly around the room, unfocused, unseeing, and then her eyes had closed again.

The door to the room opened quietly, and a nurse leaned in. "Mr. Sheldon, there's a Detective Brennan from the police department asking to see you."

Steve nodded and rose, then hesitated, glancing at Resa.

"I'll stay with her, if you like," the nurse offered. "The detective's at the nurses' station."

"Thank you, I'd appreciate it." Steve went quickly down the hall and joined the man waiting at the nurses' station.

"Detective Brennan?" he asked. The detective looked to be in his late forties. He had salt and pepper hair, which he wore trimmed short, and heavy, craggy features that seemed at odds with the keen intelligence reflected in his eyes.

"Yes. I take it that you're Steve Sheldon," he said extending his hand.

"Yes." Steve returned his firm handshake.

"How is Dr. Myles?" Brennan asked.

"Still unconscious, but her vital signs have improved since they gave her the blood transfusions. There were no skull fractures, just the lacerations and a severe concussion, and shock, of course. She lost a lot of blood, but she'll be all right," Steve replied.

Brennan nodded. "That's good to hear." He looked around him. "Is there somewhere we can talk privately? I'd like to discuss the police report with you."

"Yes, of course," Steve replied. "Here, let's use the consultation room."

He led the way to a small office. Brennan placed his briefcase on the desk and sat down. Steve pulled up a chair beside the desk and watched Brennan open his briefcase and rummage through some papers.

Steve, highly trained in observation, was more acutely aware of the subtle signals that said Brennan was trying to reach a decision about something than the average person would have been.

"Spit it out," he said casually.

Brennan, startled by the crudity that seemed out of context, looked at Steve sharply.

Steve's face was pale, drawn, almost haggard from exhaustion and worry, but he returned Brennan's look with a cool steady gaze. He was still very much in command of himself.

Brennan grinned and relaxed. "I think someone's trying to kill Dr. Myles," he said flatly. "She has no next of kin. Her brother-in-law Paul Linder recommended that I deal with you regarding details of the investigation. He didn't seem to be in any condition to cope with this right now, so here I am."

Steve was startled. "Kill Resa? Why do you think that?" Steve knew that the police were investigating Catherine's murder, but that surely could have no connection with the statement the detective had just made.

"The attack on the women was deliberate. And they were in Dr. Myles's car, not her sister's, so it's logical to assume that Dr. Myles was the target."

Steve frowned, the skepticism clear on his face.

"Hear me out," Brennan went on. "The police report says that both license plates were removed from her car after it was wrecked. So, I think it's safe to assume that the motorcycle pack was after that car specifically."

"But they may just have wanted a trophy," Steve said bitterly.

"That doesn't wash. One plate missing and I'd buy that, but not two. Also, the usual trophies taken by the psychopaths you're thinking of are mostly something belonging to the victim of the attack, something personal and usually intimate . . . like a piece of jewelry or clothing or a lock of hair."

Steve nodded, and held the sudden spurt of pain aside. "Go on."

"They chased the women for a long time. There were signs of skid marks on the paved road and motorcycle tracks on the shoulders only a few miles off Skyline Drive. From there to the location of the wreck was about 23 miles. A long chase, and a dangerous one for the attackers. They were in an upscale area. We had about six 911 calls from people in the area who heard the car horn blaring or saw the chase.

"Dr. Myles ran one of them off the road. He's dead. And, contrary to popular opinion, these gangs usually respond to strong resistance by retreating. Also, the women were within three miles of a Ranger Station when they were finally forced off the road. Help was close by. There were two signs about the Ranger Station along the road, so chances are some of the bikers noticed them.

"And last, but not least by a long shot, is the coincidence that the mob protesting at the Stanford Research Center seemed to be made up of rather sleazy gangs, just like the bikers that attacked the women. I think it likely that they followed Dr. Myles's car from a safe distance right from the Center, and then launched their attack when they were well out in the countryside."

Steve's thoughts were racing. He shook his head hopelessly. "Why? She has no enemies, at least none that I know of."

"I had hoped you could tell me why. I think the bikers took those plates as proof that they had attacked her car, and ostensibly her as well, to get some kind of payment for the job."

"But that means that someone planned the attack very carefully and very deliberately. Someone who didn't want to risk being connected with killing her himself."

"That's right, exactly," Brennan said emphatically. "And whoever set it up wanted it to look like some bizarre accident. Maybe he couldn't get close enough to her to stage a more usual accident. I don't know. In fact, it almost worked. If the officer hadn't noticed that both of the plates had been taken, my suspicions probably wouldn't have been aroused."

"Maybe that's a flaw in your case, though," Steve observed. "Why would this cautious, imaginary killer do something as foolish as requiring both of the plates as proof of the attack?"

"But perhaps he didn't. He might have asked for only one. The bikers may have taken both plates on their own initiative."

Steve sighed. "We're just guessing."

"Of course we are," said Brennan, "but that's half my job—outguessing criminals."

"What do you want me to do?"

"Right now, nothing, except to be on guard for a so-called accident when you're around Dr. Myles. I'm putting a uniform on her door around the clock while she's here in the hospital. If you notice anything that seems out of the ordinary, get in touch with me right away."

Steve nodded in agreement.

"In the meantime, I'll try to get some leads on that gang. We have some fingerprints from the wrecked car. Apparently, they cut the seat belt holding Mrs. Linder and dragged her out of the car. Dr. Myles couldn't have been removed without equipment. With all the blood she lost, they may have assumed she was already dead. Probably did, in fact, or they'd have finished her off somehow. Possibly Dr. Myles will be able to give us some descriptions when she regains consciousness."

"Damn it. Don't you think she's been through enough. It won't bring Cathy back."

There was both understanding and pity in Brennan's eyes. He spoke gently. "It exists . . . it happened. . . . She can't bury it in her mind; she has to face it and then let it heal. Don't sell her short, Sheldon. She put up a fight—they both did—and it wouldn't surprise me if she wanted very much to do all she could to help us catch the killers."

He paused. "We have five different sets of DNA from Mrs.

Linder's body—blood, skin, and semen samples. She put up one hell of a fight. The very least we owe her is justice. I want her killers. I want them bad."

Steve stared at him somberly and just nodded.

"Let's see what shape Dr. Myles is in when she wakes up," Brennan said quietly. "I won't put any pressure on her that I don't think she can handle."

"Thanks." The relief Steve felt evident in his voice.

"Well, that's it for now." Brennan reached for his briefcase and then paused. "How is Paul Linder taking it?"

Steve frowned and shook his head. "He needs heavy sedation to get any sleep. He's here at the hospital a lot to sit with Resa. I think he'll come out of it all right. He's basically very stable, but he and Cathy had a special kind of marriage. They were deeply in love."

"I have the autopsy report," Brennan said heavily, "and it's bad."

Steve winced. "He'll ask. When he snaps out of this shock, I know he'll ask what happened to her. Would it be all right if you let me read the report, and I'll tell him only what he has to know."

Brennan took the report from his briefcase and handed it to Steve.

He started to read, and the medical detachment of the first words sent a shock through him.

"The victim is a white female in her late twenties, well developed with . . ." This was Resa's sister, and his friend. This was Catherine, not some nameless victim on a stainless steel autopsy table.

He continued to read. ". . . widespread ecchymosis over the face and torso from extravasations of blood into tissue . . ." Brennan said she had put up one hell of a fight. ". . . analysis of skin, hair, and blood obtained from fingernail scrapings shows multiple blood types and . . ."

Steve fought a wave of nausea when he read the detached description of the clinical evidence of repeated rape and sexual perversions committed on her, the wounds from mutilation, and, finally, the cause of death—they had cut her throat. He knew that he could not tell Paul all of it.

He handed the papers to Brennan, and got his emotions under control. When he spoke there was a cold, quiet hate in his voice. "I want those bastards dead."

"So do I." Brennan snapped the locks of the briefcase and stood.

Steve joined him and they left the room. "I don't know how Resa escaped."

Brennan shrugged. "They couldn't have gotten her out of the car, but I don't think they even tried—she looked like she was dead according to the first officer at the scene."

"Thank God for that. She's needed so much now. If anyone can stop this killer syndrome, it's Resa and her team."

Brennan looked thoughtful at Steve's words. "She's that good?"

"You bet she is. There's not another molecular biologist that comes anywhere near her."

He stopped at the elevator. "I'll keep in touch. And if anything new turns up, I'll let you know right away."

"Good," Steve said. "Hey, wait." He reached out and held the door of the elevator. "Did you take the Stanford vaccine?"

Brennan smiled. "No. I read the news article on that interview Dr. Myles gave two weeks before the program started." He grinned. "She was cautious in what she said, but her negative reaction to the program was obvious. That was good enough for me. I decided to wait and see what happened."

The elevator doors closed. Steve hoped there were more cautious ones like Brennan, many more. He went back down the hall to Resa's room.

When he opened the door, the nurse was standing beside the bed, bending over Resa. "She's restless. She started moaning a few minutes ago. I think she's coming out of the coma. Her vital signs are good. I'll notify her doctor."

"Thank you, nurse. I'll stay with her now." He sat on the edge of the bed and took Resa's hand in his. She was moving her head back and forth on the pillow and murmuring unintelligible words.

He spoke softly to her. "It's Steve, Resa. You're safe, darling. I'm here . . . everything's all right now."

Her eyes opened and looked blankly straight ahead of her, then focused on him. "Steve," she moaned. "Oh, Steve."

He took her in his arms and held her tightly. She cried softly, and he could feel her wet tears on his cheek.

"Cathy?" Resa whispered in a choking voice.

"She didn't make it," he said softly.

"Oh, no." She sobbed uncontrollably. Steve could feel the deep shudders shaking her body.

"Oh, my God, what will Paul do without her . . . I saw them, Steve. I saw them. I tried so hard to get to her. I couldn't get out. I couldn't help her. I'm supposed to take care of her. She's my little sister."

"Later, darling, later. You must rest now."

"I'll make them pay," she cried, tears running down her face. "I'll make them pay."

"It's all over. Get well first. Lie back and rest—I'll stay right here beside you."

He eased her bandaged head back down on the pillow, and wiped the tears off her face. "Close your eyes . . . sleep."

Obediently, she closed her eyes, but held tightly onto his hand. Tears still flowed from her closed eyes. Her eyes fluttered open as she started to relax, and then, reassured by the sight of him, closed again until finally she fell into a restful, natural healing sleep.

RADIO STATION KGSH (Palo Alto, California) —

"Wil Welsh reporting and the news is not good, folks. I'm interrupting this program to bring you a special news bulletin. Unconfirmed but reliable sources indicate that riots and uncontrolled violent demonstrations are sweeping the major cities of every nation in the

world. Civil authority is breaking down everywhere as more and more people succumb to the deadly Project Immunity syndrome."

Chapter 12

Palo Alto, California

RESA PUT ASIDE the photomicrograph she had been studying and rubbed her tired eyes. The last few weeks had passed like something out of a nightmare for her, even though she had made a rapid recovery from her injuries. The staff at the Research Center, herself included, had worked continuously, and all of them rapidly neared a state of collapse until Resa issued a directive that no one could work more than fourteen hours out of every twenty-four. It had been a necessity; exhausted people just didn't function at the peak of sharpness the research required.

Many had objected, but they obeyed the directive. It wasn't easy to leave the anodyne of work for the panic in the streets. Outside the

Center it was a different world. In the last few days the toll of sick had risen sharply, with a corresponding rise in panic and confusion and riot.

For Resa, the only bright note had been Steve's supporting presence. She wasn't sure how long he'd be able to stay here on the coast with the way disruption had been breaking out worldwide, but she was grateful that he was here now, when she needed him most.

Detective Brennan had put several police officers on around-the-clock watches outside her townhouse, and Steve and Paul, both spoiling for a fight, were on the inside staying with her. Resa had had to give up her idea of finding a larger and safer house outside the city—time had run out.

Paul . . . Resa felt a helpless pang whenever he thought of her brother-in-law. Resa was having a hard time dealing with the ugly pictures she couldn't get out of her mind. She was glad Paul hadn't seen what she had seen. But he had withdrawn into some private world of his own since Catherine's death. At her funeral, he had stood stone-faced, not a trace of emotion touching his features, his eyes cold and somber.

She had been present when Steve had given him a brief description of the coroner's report; Paul had listened stoically. Only the explanation of the reason behind the attack—Brennan's theory of the cause—had touched him. Resa remembered how Paul's eyes had suddenly come to life.

"It was planned?" he had asked slowly.

"Detective Brennan is pretty certain it was planned and that it was aimed at me," she said.

"Who planned it?"

"I don't know, Paul. I couldn't give Brennan any leads. I can't think of anyone who'd want to kill me."

"When they find out who it was, I want to know, Resa. I have to know." His intense words had demanded a promise.

"You will," Resa promised. "You have my word on it."

From then on, Paul had dogged Resa's footsteps like a second shadow. He had moved into the guest bedroom in Resa's townhouse and whenever she left the place, Paul was there waiting to accompany her.

Finally, in exasperation, Resa had said, as calmly as she could, that she didn't need Paul's protection.

"I'm not protecting you, Resa," Paul had replied with a slow smile. "You fight better than I do. Remember, I'm not a black belt."

"Then what *are* you doing?"

"When he tries again, I want to be there," had been Paul's reply. "His hirelings blew it. Next time, I think he'll come himself—whatever the risk. And I'll be there, waiting for him. He's mine, Resa."

"I don't think he's going to challenge me to hand-to-hand combat."

"No. I was teasing you about the black belt. I'm armed, Resa."

The implacable determination in his words had forestalled any objections Resa might have had. And, as the days passed, she became used to Paul as well as Brennan's men watching her. They became a part of the background, blending unobtrusively into her daily activities until she scarcely noticed them.

"It's time to call it a day, Resa." Mac's voice broke into her thoughts. "Go home and get some rest."

"What about you?"

"You had a head start on me today," Mac replied. "I'll be going along soon—when my fourteen hours are up." He grinned at Resa, who was too tired and distracted to notice the gibe.

"All right, Mac."

Resa rose wearily, took her coat, which she had tossed over a chair many hours earlier, and started toward the door. She had no office, of course, since she had been relieved of her position by the president, and spent her time helping wherever she was needed most.

"See you in the morning," she called back to Mac, who had already busied himself with the photomicrographs Resa had been analyzing.

"Aye, . . . get some rest."

She left the Center and drove as quickly as she could through the streets that were partially obstructed by abandoned cars and piles of rubbish. It reminded her of the way the streets had looked after the last big earthquake. Except now there was still electricity on in most areas, not dark like it had been when all the power went down.

WHEN SHE REACHED her townhouse, some of her weariness had vanished and she looked forward to spending a quiet evening with Steve. She let herself into the house by the side door near the garage, and Steve greeted her with a warm kiss. She savored being held in his arms and then, reluctantly, stepped back. "Are you hungry?" she asked him with a smile.

"Starved."

"Good. I have a casserole in the freezer that I can put in the microwave. I thought we could all have a quiet dinner in front of the fire."

"Sounds good, but Paul said he won't be eating with us. He's going out again tonight."

"Is he still here?"

Steve nodded.

Her face clouded momentarily, but before Steve could ask her what was wrong, she was ushering him out of the kitchen. "Dinner will be ready shortly. Go, relax for a while in the living room. Keep Paul company."

"All right," he said laughingly.

Paul was in the living room, poking at the burning logs heaped in the fireplace. "What happened to the housekeeper?" Steve asked.

Paul turned around. "Resa sent her home this morning. She said she was perfectly well and could look after things herself. It's quite an improvement, Steve. Wait until you taste Resa's cooking.

138

Cathy and Resa could both cook up a storm."

"Well, I guess it's her call." Steve sat down on the couch.

Resa came in and joined them. She slipped her shoes off. "Oh, does that feel good."

"Rough day?" Paul asked.

"Frustrating," Resa commented. "The analysis is not going well at all. We're flooded with tissue samples, blood samples, all kinds of samples, but no one has come up with any ideas for stopping the syndrome."

'You will," Paul said.

"Thanks for that vote of confidence. I hope you're right."

Paul smiled.

Resa studied her brother-in-law; Paul's face still had a withdrawn look. No, that's not quite it, Resa thought. It's more like a mask, hiding the thoughts in his mind.

"Steve said you're going out again."

"Yes." Paul's terse reply discouraged any further discussion of his nightly excursions.

"I had a call from Brennan today," Steve said.

Paul looked at him sharply. "And?"

"Nothing substantial, really. His informers say there is talk that a newcomer, a man with powerful connections, is giving the orders now. This fellow apparently has some high-up syndicate influence. That's all. No name, no description. The word is that no one ever sees him."

Paul nodded. "Thanks, Steve," he said quietly.

Resa went back to the kitchen and returned with a tray.

Steve rose and took the tray from her.

"Well, goodnight you two," Paul said. "I'll see you in the morning."

Resa watched Paul's retreating back with a strange, worried expression on her face.

"What is it, Resa?"

She shook her head. "Later, Steve. Let's relax for a while and enjoy dinner."

"All right," he said equably. "It looks great."

She lay the dinner out on the large oak coffee table in front of the fireplace. They sat down on plump cushions beside the table, and Isis curled up beside Resa and leaned her head on Resa's leg. Isis seemed to know that something was wrong, and shadowed Resa every moment she was home.

While they ate, Resa explained how she had prepared the casserole. "It doesn't have a name," she insisted. "I just memorized the recipe from a friend who used to concoct all sorts of gourmet dishes. It was a hobby with her. Cathy used to call it our 'exotic dish.'"

They both made an effort to shut out the world, at least for this brief hour. Steve described his first attempts at bachelor cooking for Resa, and set her laughing. "I don't believe it," she said.

"It's true," he said seriously. "The recipe said 'thicken with flour,' so I shook some into the pot and it just ended up a thick, goopy mess—all lumps." He leaned over and kissed her cheek.

"Did you eat it?"

"Sure, it wasn't half -bad."

"Now I know you're kidding."

"I kid you not," he said. "But that did end my cooking career. There's a lot to be said for a good restaurant."

After they finished eating, they carried their dishes into the kitchen and returned to the living room with steaming cups of coffee laced with brandy.

Resa put a CD of her favorite music on the stereo, turned the music low, and settled comfortably on the couch. She leaned her head against Steve's shoulder; they watched the fire and sipped their hot drinks.

Steve stroked Resa's hair. "Tell me."

She stiffened and didn't speak for a few minutes and then the words came, low and strained. "It's about Paul. He's hunting those men. That's what he's been doing all these nights when he goes out alone."

"How do you know?"

"This morning, when I put his jacket in his room, I saw photographs of the drawings I did for Brennan on Paul's desk. He must have left them out. There was a map of Palo Alto, too, drawn off in sections—about ten of them were crossed out."

Steve remembered the drawings. Brennan had shown them to him the day after he had questioned Resa about the attackers. Resa's artistic skill had paid off for Brennan. It had been a shock to see those lifelike faces in the drawings; Resa had captured a malevolent glee in their expressions. He had never spoken to her about them. Intuitively, he knew what it had cost her to draw them.

"You're probably right, darling," he said gently, "but there's nothing we can do about it." He took her in his arms, and she buried her face in his shoulder. He understood her reaction; she had had enough of horror, of death, of killing. But deep inside him he felt a fierce glow of satisfaction, and, in silence, he wished Paul good hunting.

"Don't mistake me, Steve. I'd go with him if he'd let me. I'm worried that he's out there alone. It's dangerous."

"Well, maybe we should insist on helping him. But Resa, with the hours you're putting in at the Research Center, I don't think you could do it. And that's critical right now."

"I know. That's why I'm here and not out there with Paul. But I don't have to like it," she added angrily.

ON THE EAST side of Palo Alto, Paul parked his car near the service entrance of the third bar on his list. The garish marquee in front of the bar, which Paul glanced at briefly, advertised live sex acts and featured a group of photos of nude girls in coy poses.

He went in and stood for a moment just inside the door to let his eyes adjust to the darkened room, and then took a seat at the far end of the bar.

The large room was crowded and noisy. From his vantage point at the bar, he could study the occupants of the room covertly, through the mirror lining the wall opposite him. It was a run-down place, the air filled with the odor of stale sweat and alcohol and filth. But Paul hardly noticed, for all of the bars in which he searched were third-rate, and he concentrated only on the occupants, searching for the five faces etched in his memory.

"I said what'll you have, mister?" the bartender repeated impatiently.

"Scotch." Paul tossed a bill on the counter.

He sipped at the drink while his eyes searched the room, studying each face carefully. And then he saw one of them, a long-haired, unkempt youth ogling the bare breasts of the girl serving him. Paul felt a mixture of relief and excitement surge through him, for he had begun to think he was wasting his time, but his persistence had paid off at last.

He signaled the bartender.

"Yeah?"

Paul placed a hundred-dollar bill on the counter and smoothed it carefully.

The bartender stared at it, . . . and then came quickly around the bar to Paul's side.

"What do you want, mister?" he asked in a low voice.

"I want one of your customers thrown out of here—the kid in the leather jacket eyeing the blond. The side door . . . right after I leave."

"That's all?"

"Yes," Paul said quietly, "that's all." He held out the bill.

The bartender stuffed it in his pocket and grinned broadly. "You're on, buddy."

Paul left through the side exit. He leaned back against the wall next to the door, took the gun from his shoulder holster, and waited.

I'm getting closer, Cathy. Soon, my love, they will pay.

A few long minutes passed. Finally he heard loud noises . . . the door opened, and the straggly haired youth was sprawling in the dirt.

The door slammed shut. Paul moved toward the young man, who was shouting obscenities at the closed door as he struggled clumsily to his feet.

Paul hit him in the head with the butt of the revolver and carried him to the car parked at the end of the alley and rolled the unconscious body into the trunk.

He drove slowly out of the city and headed for Skyline Drive. When he reached it, he turned off on the same side road that Resa and Catherine had taken, and followed it to the spot where they had been forced off the road.

Paul got out of the car and looked down the bank: the wrecked car had been removed, but the surroundings still bore marks of the wreck; broken branches, torn bark, long cuts in the earth. He opened the trunk and carried the man down the bank to the small clearing where Catherine's body had lain.

He sat down on a boulder at the edge of the clearing and waited.

It was a cloudless night. The small glade was lit by a bright moon, and Paul saw that time, although it had only been a short time, had already erased the crushed grass and the pool of blood from the ground where Cathy had lain.

An hour passed before the crumpled figure lying on the damp grass stirred.

Dispassionately, Paul watched him shake his head and moan, and then crawl to a sitting position.

"Who the hell are you?" the sullen figure muttered as he caught sight of Paul. "Who hit me?"

"Look around you," Paul said in a deceptively mild voice.

The youth looked slowly around the clearing, and then his eyes darted to the bank where crumpled brush and bits of metal and broken glass still spoke of the tragedy. His face paled; his voice trembled. "Hey, man," he said cajolingly, "you got the wrong guy."

"Her name was Catherine."

"Hey, man . . ."

"She was my wife."

"I didn't touch your chick!" the youth shouted, and scrambled to his feet.

Paul shot him in the knee.

The youth screamed in pain and grabbed his leg with both hands.

Paul's voice was cold and implacable. "Where are the other four?"

"I don't know! They're all sick. . . . They had those shots." He moaned in terror and pain.

"Who hired you?"

"We never saw him," the youth sobbed. "Please man, we didn't mean it!" He began to scream hysterically.

Paul motioned with the .38 caliber revolver. "Where are the other four?" The cold finality in his voice shocked the youth out of his hysteria.

"I'll tell you, mister. I'll tell you. But I didn't fuck your chick! They did it all! I just watched!"

"Where are they?"

"We got a pad in the hills." He babbled the directions and then, at Paul's command, repeated them more carefully. Paul stood slowly and the youth started trying to crawl away, screaming incoherently. "I didn't fuck that bitch! . . . Damn you! You bastard!"

Paul raised the revolver and fired—the screaming stopped abruptly. He stared at the bloodstained body in silence, his eyes veiled with other thoughts,

"That's one of them, Cathy," he said softly.

He took a handkerchief out of his pocket and wiped his fingerprints off the gun and tossed it far into the brush. He climbed back up the bank and got into his car, but before he started it, he unlocked the glove compartment, took out another .38, and slipped it into his shoulder holster.

Driving back toward the main highway, he glanced at his watch and nodded in satisfaction.

There was still time.

CHANNEL 7— BREAKING NEWS

"This is Dee Miller, reporting from the Channel 7 chopper over San Francisco. We're bringing you live coverage right now on what is one of the worst disasters in the city's history. I'm high above the downtown area and can see rioters and protestors fighting with the police who are trying to keep some kind of order in the besieged city.

"Fires can be seen in several buildings in the Market Street area and seem to be spreading. Fire crews and first responders are having difficulty reaching the fires. Roads are blocked by abandoned vehicles and the lights are out in most areas of the city.

"This just in: I've been told the Governor has called out the National Guard to help keep order in California cities that have been hardest hit by the deadly syndrome that is claiming lives daily. San Francisco is certainly high on that list. I'll continue to circle the city to keep you informed.

"Law enforcement personnel have been decimated by illness, and emergency services are swamped. Medical personnel are calling for volunteers to help with the sick. Call this station for further details on how to volunteer."

Chapter 13

Washington, D.C. and Palo Alto, California

AT THE WHITE HOUSE, President Harland paced the floor impatiently. "I can't reverse my position now, Dave. The people are on my side."

His voice was petulant, and David Blair, listening carefully, steeled himself to respond calmly. The president had changed markedly in this emergency. He was always on the defensive now and reacted in an almost paranoid way to the slightest hint of criticism. Blair chose his words with great care.

"The nation is in a state of chaos, Mr. President."

"That's not *my* fault," Harland said angrily. "I'll be damned if I'll take the blame for it! It's those God damned scientific bastards—"

"I meant no suggestion of blame to you, sir," Blair apologized. "I didn't make myself clear. The people need the security of a strong hand in charge during this emergency . . . civil authority has broken down."

"So, I'll declare martial law."

"Yes, sir. That's an important first step," Blair agreed. "But then there is still the problem of all the scientific and medical establishments—even hospitals—that people are attacking indiscriminately."

"We'll get that under control in due course."

Blair sighed inwardly. "There may not be time. The country will collapse if the bulk of the population is incapacitated, and the people are attacking the one group that has a chance to stop this syndrome."

"You can't expect me to send Federal troops to stop these riots! You know damn well the people will associate that with me, personally," he said harshly.

"That's true, sir," Blair said slowly. "If only there was someplace you could have the scientists taken, someplace where they would have all the equipment with which to work, to help you stop this . . . new syndrome. The people surely wouldn't object to the scientists being removed somewhere by Federal troops."

Harland thought for a minute, and then smiled triumphantly. "There is a place," he said. "The underground laboratories set up when we had that biological warfare scare right after the terrorists took out the World Trade Center. The best equipment available was put into place, and it's been updated on an on-going basis."

"That would be perfect, sir."

"Yes," Harland said firmly. "Have them moved there, Blair. Tell them it's protective custody."

"Yes, sir"

"And take care of that martial law announcement."

"Yes, sir."

Blair closed the door of the Oval Office quietly. He felt sick inside. Harland was in a major state of denial. He would tolerate no indication of blame for his part in activating Project Immunity over the objections of Resa Myles. Blair was cautiously feeling his way in his daily dealings with Harland. He was very uneasy about the way the president was reacting. He seemed to think the problem would just go away by itself.

"It's Armageddon," Blair murmured to himself.

MOONLIGHT FLOODED THE broad, abandoned quarry, giving Paul a clear view of the weather-beaten shack that stood alone in its center, like some forgotten sentinel. He was about three hundred yards from the shack, in the shelter of a small stand of fir trees on a hill overlooking the quarry. For an hour now, he had watched patiently and there had been no sign of movement around the windowless structure, but from the faint glow of light escaping through some broken boards, he was sure someone was inside.

Slowly, gun in hand, he moved down the hillside and into the quarry, walking carefully through the loose stones to keep them from rolling. He reached the door and noted that it was surprisingly sturdy as his hand silently pressed the latch and pulled the door outward. Quickly, he stepped inside and backed against the wall, his gun leveled at the occupants. The room was lit by a kerosene lantern that stood on an upended crate.

Three of the bikers were sprawled on a dirty mattress in a corner of the cluttered room—they stirred feebly but made no move toward him. On a second mattress a young girl huddled next to the fourth man, the leader of the gang. He seemed more alert than the other three but obviously ill, Paul decided, judging from the sores on his face and the fevered look in the narrowed eyes meeting Paul's.

He had found them at last. Paul felt a blend of elation and hate rise in him as he scanned their faces, disfigured now by disease, but clearly recognizable as the images in Resa's drawings.

"What d'ya want?" muttered the leader, raising himself slightly

148

on the soiled mattress.

"Don't move." The menace in Paul's voice and a motion of the gun he held stopped the other. Reaching inside his jacket, Paul drew Catherine's picture out and approached the gang leader slowly. He held the picture in front of the man and watched the play of emotions on the disfigured face—recognition and then fear, which was quickly replaced by a look of furious hate.

The man lunged for Paul, snarling, "You son of a bitch!"

But Paul kicked him backward, and he fell against the girl who whimpered in fear. When she moved, Paul saw her swollen abdomen straining against her skirt. She carried an evil spawn inside her. He hesitated, torn for a moment between the desire for vengeance that drove him and the old values he had once cherished. She belonged to this vicious gang, but a part of him was repelled by the thought of destroying her.

"Get out," he muttered to her. "And make it fast!" Her gaze darted to the others in the room and then back to Paul. Warily, she crawled across the mattress in front of him, and then fled from the room, moving swiftly despite the girth of her abdomen. The sounds of her rapid steps faded away and the room was silent.

Paul glanced at the picture in his hand, and then back at the hate-filled eyes glaring at him. "Now it's your turn to pay," he said in a hard, quiet voice. "All of you."

The leader glared at Paul. "She was good ass, buddy," he sneered.

Paul flinched at the vicious words and his finger tightened on the trigger of the gun, but then he saw the expectant look on the man's face.

He's trying to goad me, Paul thought. He shook his head. "That's too quick for you bastards," he said coldly. Tucking Cathy's picture back safely into his pocket, he moved toward the kerosene lantern.

With a short curse, the leader leaped at Paul and grabbed him around the legs. It was a short struggle. Terror had given the sick man a spurt of strength, but he was no match for Paul. Almost casually, Paul moved into an offensive stance, and delivered a sharp blow to the biker's head, followed by a high kick to the chest. Groaning, the man reeled back, stunned, and crumpled to the floor. He shook his head, trying to clear it.

The bikers on the other mattress stirred, but were too weak to stop Paul, who lifted the lantern off the crate and smashed it in the middle of the room. The flames raced through the spreading pool of kerosene and licked hungrily at the edges of the mattresses.

Paul grabbed the crate that had held the lantern, backed toward the door, and stepped quickly outside. He smashed the crate and jammed the latch on the door shut with a few slats of wood from the crate. Then he moved a short distance from the shack.

Smoke was pouring through the broken boards. He heard clearly the shouts of the bikers. Something crashed against the door—it shuddered and held. Paul was almost disappointed. One short, almost inhuman scream invaded the quiet clearing and then there was silence. His face impassive, Paul watched the small building until it was completely burned, and then he put his gun away and left the quarry.

There's one more, he thought, the bastard pulling the strings, the one who ordered the attack. He'd be more difficult to find, but Paul was determined to find him.

IT WAS LATE in the day at the Stanford Research Center. Resa was still at work analyzing the molecular structure of cell nuclei in the photomicrographs prepared from the latest biopsy specimens. She studied the glowing structure on the screen. "Mac, look at this."

MacBride went to the console and looked at the screen.

"Now watch," Resa said. "I'm going to put up a split image."

She keyed in the new instruction and the screen changed.

"They're both the same."

"Yes. That's the problem," Resa said. "The one on the left is from the last biopsy on Thurston; the one of the right shows the new syndrome."

"But Thurston was a prognosis-fatal cancer case," Mac said slowly. "The synthetic virus is acting as expected on the cancer cases—it's only the healthy people that are getting the untoward reaction."

"I know. That's why this may be significant. Let's take a look at Thurston's earlier photomicrographs." Resa's fingers moved over the keys.

The image changed; they studied the screen intently.

"It looks like the standard pattern of the synthetic virus reacting with the cancer virus to me," Mac observed.

"It is. Now I'll call back the last one we did on him."

"Oh, my God," Mac murmured. "The new mutation pattern."

"Yes. But this is the only cancer case that I've found with a double virus pattern. Why?" Resa spoke aloud, but her question was directed at herself.

Mac leaned over Resa's shoulder and typed in a new instruction on the console: a summary of Thurston's treatment appeared on the screen.

Resa scanned the glowing letters quickly. "Massive doses, Mac. That's what did it. When the patient had cancer the Stanford vaccine acted as it should, the benign virus attacked the cancer cells, stopping the wild cell growth and proliferation. But with massive doses the attack was also launched at the body's immune system."

"Aye," Mac said heavily. "I think that's it. I'll have someone write us a quick program to pull out all the cancer cases with massive dose regimens. Then we'll be able to check the photomicrographs we have on them."

Resa nodded. "Well, it's a start, Mac. We can use the standard antiviral drugs to slow down the syndrome until we find a way to stop it cold." She quickly typed instructions into the computer for the rest of the team, attached the pertinent photomicrographs to the message, and hit the send key. "The pharmaceutical companies must have a lot of antivirals on hand. At least we—"

A woman's piercing scream from the corridor outside the door cut off her words. Both of them ran to the door. Resa jerked it open and caught one quick glimpse of a howling mob flooding into the corridor from the stairwell, smashing everything and everyone in sight. She had to stop them.

She bolted into the hallway and attacked the man in front with a low, flying front kick followed by a vicious lunge punch to his face. He fell hard. She leaped over him to block the next man's attack, delivered a powerful reverse punch to his mid-section and a spear hand to his face.

"I'm behind you, Resa!"

She heard Paul's shout and shot a quick look backward even as she moved forward with a roundhouse kick. Paul had taken a baseball bat from one of the rioters and was using it to stop the mob from circling behind her. What a good idea! She had time to think before turning her concentration to the fight she herself was waging.

She was choosing vulnerable points for her free- fighting moves, trying to incapacitate as many of the rioters as possible until security or the police arrived. Then a bat-wielding man came out of the crowd and moved toward her.

"Just what I need," she muttered.

She grabbed his free arm to distract him, then moved in close and suddenly thrust her palm heel into his face. When he attempted to block her, she executed a brutal reverse punch to his body. Although stunned, he managed to raise the bat.

Resa grinned and delivered a powerful front snap kick to his exposed armpit. The man grunted and dropped the bat, which Resa quickly snatched up, and in one smooth motion, jabbed him strongly enough with the heavy end of the bat in his solar plexus to put him out of action.

"Back!" Paul shouted.

Resa half-turned and saw another mob running toward them from the opposite end of the hallway.

She caught a glimpse of a familiar face . . . the big fellow who was at Catherine's party. Sutherland. He had a camera around his neck and it was aimed at her. Paul pulled her back and took up her place, holding off the rioters with vicious swings of his bat.

At the same time, Mac leaned out of the room and yanked her from the hallway, shoving her back into the room. "Keep back!" he shouted.

A shot rang out, overloud in the confined space. Mac grabbed his chest and crumpled slowly to the floor.

"No!" Resa ran to him. She saw the blood bubbling out of his chest, staining the white lab coat a bright red. She tried to staunch the wound with direct pressure, but the blood pulsed out around her fingers. She glanced at the mob. The gunshot had halted them and now armed police, who must have been close on their heels, were holding them back. She saw that Sutherland was being forced back down the hall with the rest of the unruly mob.

And then suddenly Paul was there, helping her lift Mac onto a stretcher.

"You'll be all right, Mac. Your right lung has collapsed," she said. "Get a thoracic surgeon up here," she shouted to the trauma team that surrounded Mac.

"We'll take it from here," one of the doctors said as he placed an oxygen mask over Mac's face to help him breathe.

Mac pulled it aside. "Paul get her out of here!" he managed to shout before the doctor pushed his hands away and put the mask back in place.

Resa watched the team wheel Mac away, and her face was grim as she turned to her brother-in-law.

Paul was staring intently at the retreating mob. "He was close tonight, Resa," Paul said softly. "I could feel him. He used that crowd for cover to get closer to you."

"That shot was meant for me?"

"I think so."

"Damn him," Resa said in a choked voice. "Why doesn't he

come out in the open?" First Catherine, she thought, and now Mac. Resa could feel her control slipping; she was filled with rage and frustration.

Paul took her arm. "Come on. Let's get you out of here."

"I can't, Paul." Resa pulled her arm away. "I have to see how much damage this damned mob has done to the equipment."

"It doesn't matter."

She looked at him incredulously. "What do you mean, it doesn't matter?"

"You're being moved out. All of you here at the Center." Paul spoke in a low voice.

"How do you know?"

"Blair called the house from a phone booth. He said all calls leaving the White House were being monitored, and also all calls from the Center, here, as well. But he wanted you to know in advance, so he called the house. That line's clear," he added. "Steve checked it out himself."

"Well, I'm not going anywhere."

"You'll be taken into protective custody along with all the others here, . . . and their families. Tonight. Blair wants you to go along with it, Resa. All the equipment you'll need will be available. And he said he'd keep in touch. It's on Harland's orders."

Resa shook her head in exasperation. "Paul, Harland can't do that. It's still a free country, you know, and I'll tell the damned fool as much."

"Resa, hold on a minute. Harland *can* do it. He's going to declare martial law. The military will be running the country and he's the Commander-in-Chief. That freedom you speak of is now an illusion."

"Martial law? . . ."

"It had to come. Civilization, as we've known it, is falling apart."

"I hoped . . ." She shook her head. "All right, Paul. Let's go home and pack up some things. Does Steve know?"

"You bet. He was in the room when Blair called so I told him about it briefly, before I left. He's pulling some strings at the CIA so he'll be coming with us."

"Are you going, too?"

"Yes. Where you go, I go, big sister."

His copying of Cathy's favorite endearment, sent a spurt of pain through her heart.

Paul led the way to his car, which he had parked at the back door to the Center.

Resa hesitated as they approached it. She had left her new car in the front lot.

"Get in. You won't need your car."

Paul drove quickly back to Resa's house; the two were silent, each occupied with private thoughts.

As Paul turned the car into the driveway, he broke the silence with a dry comment. "He'll have to come out in the open now, Resa. Where we're going, it won't be easy to hide."

"Well, it can't be too soon for me. I want him," she said bitterly.

"So do I. Remember, he's mine."

RADIO STATION KGSH (Palo Alto, California) —

"This is Wil Welsh with the News in Brief on the International Scene. It was announced today that Russian President Aleksandr Ivanovich Vassilov has imposed martial law in Russia. Russian officials have clamped a tight censorship on all news leaving the country. Travel to or from the Russian Federation has been curtailed. For all practical purposes, the Iron Curtain has once again risen."

Chapter 14

Palo Alto and Moffett Field, California

IT WAS CLOSE to midnight before the military escort arrived at Resa's house to take her into protective custody.

She heard the cars stop in front of the house, and then there was a short knock on the door. She opened it. A tall figure in an Air Force uniform stood on the step, and at the curb were parked three military vehicles.

"Dr. Myles, I'm Jim Carlson," the man said pleasantly.

"Come in." Resa's voice was cool as she stood aside for him to enter. When he moved into the light, Resa saw the silver eagles on his uniform and was surprised that a full colonel would have been sent on this kind of mission.

Standing easily in the center of the room, Carlson was an impressive figure. He was a tall man, broad shouldered but trim. His hair was cropped short and slightly grayed, his eyes a dark hazel, his jaw firm and blunt, but softened now by a pleasant smile.

"I must apologize for the late hour, but I had to fly up here from Vandenberg and had a little trouble getting a plane," he said easily. "You must be Paul Linder." Carlson held out his hand to Paul.

"Yes." Paul shook his hand.

Steve came into the room and before Resa could speak, Carlson said, "And you must be Steve Sheldon."

"Yes." Steve looked at Resa questioningly, but she looked just as confused as he felt. He turned back to Carlson. "How do you do, Colonel?" he said gravely, exchanging handshakes with Carlson.

"I'm here to make your trip as . . . comfortable . . . as possible, Dr. Myles. I hope you'll overlook the late hour."

Resa nodded. "I understand."

"If you're all ready," Carlson said, "I'll have the men take your luggage out."

"We're almost ready," Resa said shortly, and wondered to herself what was going on with this red carpet treatment. "I just have to put Isis in her carrier." Her pet hated the carrier and Resa had to bribe her from her hiding place behind the couch with a handful of kitty snacks. "It won't be for long, sweetheart," she said in an attempt to console her.

Isis favored her with a look a supreme disdain.

Carlson went to the door and beckoned to the waiting men. While they carried out the bags, Steve held Resa's coat for her and picked up Isis waiting in her pet carrier. The three of them followed Carlson outside to the cars.

"I think we can all fit in my car," he said smoothly, differentiating his vehicle with its Air Force driver from the armed Naval escort in the other two cars. "Mr. Linder, would you sit with my driver in front?"

"Sure. Let me take Isis for you Steve."

"Dr. Myles, Sheldon . . ." He held the back door open. Resa stepped into the car, followed by Steve and then Carlson.

The first armed escort car pulled away from the curb slowly, and Carlson's driver followed. Resa glanced out the back window and saw the remainder of the armed guards in the last car close in behind them. Neatly sandwiched, she thought. This was the treatment usually reserved for either the most important personages or the most dangerous criminals. Wryly, she wondered in which category she belonged

Resa felt Carlson's eyes on her. She met the Colonel's gaze and was surprised to see understanding and amusement in his eyes.

Carlson lifted his shoulders eloquently. "I'm sorry," he said with a hint of laughter in his voice, "but there's a limit to the influence I have on a Navy base. I hadn't planned to meet you with this mob. In fact, I told the base commander at Moffett that it was ridiculous." He paused and smiled. "Maybe that was my mistake."

Despite his annoyance, Resa could not help but like the man. She smiled and the atmosphere in the car thawed noticeably.

"We have a mutual friend, Dr. Myles," Carlson explained. "Dave Blair called me earlier in the evening and asked me to hop a flight up here and stand in for him. You know, . . . give you a hand with the local militia."

"So that's it," Resa said slowly. She should have guessed that Blair's fine hand was behind the special treatment . . . and that explained how Carlson had known about Steve and Paul.

Carlson laughed. "Could you see Blair with this crew?" He motioned toward the escort cars with their serious-faced, armed men.

"Not in a million years." Resa said, picturing Blair, with his quick intelligence, his impatience with petty details, leading an armed escort. "But I approve of his choice of an emissary," she added with her usual frankness.

"Thank you," Carlson said graciously. "However, I must plead guilty to monopolizing the conversation, and I've neglected to introduce all of you to my driver. This is Lieutenant Bob Schaeffer. Actually, we were playing cards when Blair called, so I drafted Bob to fly me up here. We had a hell of a time getting a plane, and then when we got here—no driver. So—"

"So I was drafted again," the Lieutenant said with good humor.

"Truthfully," Carlson put in, "it was a favor. We've been friends for a long time."

Resa admired the smooth way Carlson had let them know that Schaeffer was to be trusted. Even though she had assumed that was the case when Carlson first brought up Blair's name, it was reassuring to have definite confirmation.

Paul engaged the Lieutenant in a conversation about flying; and Resa, her eyes growing heavy in the warm car, leaned her head on Steve's shoulder and closed her eyes. The half-hour trip was going to take at least twice that long. They were moving along very slowly and taking frequent detours because of the number of roads that were blocked with abandoned cars and debris.

"What did Blair have to say when you talked to him?" Steve asked Carlson quietly. "For a minute there, I thought you were from Langley."

"No. But Blair told me that the CIA is cooperating," Carlson replied.

Steve grinned at that news. "I'll bet they are. Did Blair say anything else?"

"Well, I know you're with the CIA. He told me that, otherwise nothing specific," Carlson said, "but one hell of a lot of innuendoes—and that's not like Blair. Something is very wrong, and I mean something other than the obvious problems that we're all aware of."

Resa stirred. "I wish he could have talked to me," she said. "Paul told me that Blair wanted me to go along with this protective custody, but I don't mind telling you I don't like it one bit. It's Harland's order, I know. But why is Blair going along with it like this?"

Carlson shook his head. "I don't know, Dr. Myles. But I am sure of one thing—Blair always has a reason, a good reason, for everything he does. And he never acts on impulse. . . . But he said a few things by way of explanation that . . . seemed a little cryptic."

"Like what?"

"Well, he said that civil authority was breaking down and shortly there would be no protection at all for scientific groups," Carlson explained. "At the time I didn't think too much of it—we know civil authority is being swamped, but under martial law federal troops would be responsible for keeping order, so, on the surface, it would appear that the protective custody order is . . . redundant?" He shrugged. "There is one thing he was specific about. In fact, that's why he ordered me out here. But I'm sure you know about it."

"I don't think so," Resa remarked.

"Dr. Myles, at all costs you are to be protected."

"My sentiments, exactly," Steve put in.

"Oh." Resa was thinking hard. The points Carlson made were quite valid, but it was still a fact that Blair was strongly pushing the protective custody. Why? There had to be some danger under the martial law set-up that was not apparent. "What if the federal troops didn't want to waste time protecting the research groups?"

"No," Carlson replied promptly. "Every sane-thinking person knows this mob reaction is just the result of panic. Our only chance to save a vast portion of the population lies with a medical breakthrough in finding a treatment. Harland would *have* to order that the research groups be protected. . . ."

"Maybe," Resa commented. But the pieces of the puzzle don't fit together, she thought. She hoped Blair would indeed "keep in touch" as he had said, because Resa felt a growing conviction that there was something more than a deadly syndrome threatening the country—and for some unknown reason, she was in the middle of it.

Detective Brennan was probably right about the attack on Catherine being aimed at her; Max's injury while trying to protect her reinforced that premise. And now Blair was reaching out from Washington to forestall some new unknown danger. That much, at least, was clear. But what was the danger? She felt again the frustration of fighting shadows, of guessing the nature of an unseen enemy, of guarding every move against an unknown danger, of waiting for the next disaster to strike.

"Well, here we are," Carlson said.

The cars slowed at the gate to Moffett Field while guards inspected passes presented by the drivers, and then waved them on through with snappy salutes.

The streets on the base were clear, and Lieutenant Schaeffer drove directly to a large house that was finished in white clapboards and set back on a broad, well-cared-for lawn.

"I requisitioned one of the Navy's VIP guest houses for the night," Carlson explained, "or what's left of the night. Your plane is scheduled to leave at ten in the morning, so you'll be able to get a little rest anyway."

He led the way up the paved walk to the house, pointedly ignoring the Naval escorts who had also left their cars and stood on the sidewalk looking somewhat discomfited, and presumably waiting for further orders.

Carlson turned to the commander of the naval escort. "Establish a perimeter around the house. No one gets in. And I mean no one. I'll be inside with the lieutenant."

"Yes, sir," the commander replied.

They were greeted at the door by a pleasant, elderly woman who explained that she was their housekeeper and asked if they would like any refreshments before retiring.

Resa declined, saying she wanted only someplace to sleep, and the others followed suit. Morning was not far off. And who could tell what a new day would bring was Resa's wry thought. She let Isis out of her carrier and gathered her pet into her arms.

The cat favored the people around her with a very cool, haughty look, before she licked Resa's chin affectionately and tucked her head under Resa's chin, snuggling close as she was carried up the stairs.

"Lady Cat, you're spoiled," Steve whispered, following them up the stairs.

Resa grinned. "That's no way to talk to a goddess," she admonished.

A GENTLE KNOCK on the door awakened her. Disconcerted, Resa looked around the sunny, pleasant room and then memory flooded back.

"Breakfast will be served in half an hour, ma'am," said a feminine voice beyond the door.

"Thank you," Resa called out. She looked at Steve's empty place beside her in the bed. The pillow still held the indentation from his head. I must have really been beat, she thought, not to have heard him get up. Another look around the room showed that Steve had taken Isis with him.

Quickly she showered and dressed, and then went downstairs where the sound of voices from the dining room told her that she was the late riser in the group.

"Good morning," she said, taking a place at the table next to Steve, who smiled at her warmly. The morning sun, streaming through the windows, felt welcome on her skin, and she could feel the warmth on her head as the sun gleamed on her dark chestnut curls.

"You're beautiful," Steve whispered to her.

She smiled and touched his hand lightly. "So are you." She laughed when Steve rolled his eyes at her.

"The goddess had a nice run out back and now she's eating like a pig in the kitchen," he said with a grin.

"Thank you." Resa couldn't hold back a laugh at Steve's words.

She served herself from the platter held by a maid standing at her side. "Coffee, ma'am?"

"Please."

"Well, how was your brief sleep?" Carlson asked.

"Great," Resa replied, and she had slept well, but whether it was because of sheer exhaustion or the comfortable bed, she wasn't sure.

Breakfast was finished in a pleasant, leisurely fashion, and then Carlson suggested that they leave for the airfield. "I'll see you off," he said, "and then I'll be on my way to Washington for a meeting with our friend."

"Tell him I look forward to hearing from him," Resa said in a dry voice.

"I'll do that." Carlson smiled at Resa's impatient tone.

Their luggage was once more packed in the trunk of the car, and Isis was persuaded to get into her pet carrier once again. They left for the short drive to the airfield, which was located on the other side of the base. Lieutenant Schaeffer drove directly onto the flight line where a sleek, gleaming Lear jet stood waiting.

"There's a little beauty," said Paul as they alighted from the car and he spotted the plane. A smaller version of the large commercial jets, this one was designed to accommodate about a dozen passengers in luxurious comfort.

They exchanged farewells with Carlson and Schaeffer and boarded the plane, where a Navy flight attendant escorted them to their seats with the usual pleasantries more typical on commercial flights. They were the only passengers. Resa looked out the window and saw Schaeffer directing the ground crew, who were removing the luggage from the car. Carlson stood on the fringe of the airstrip and raised his hand in a brief salute when he caught sight of her.

The jet engines roared into life; the plane taxied to the end of the runway and took off in a smooth graceful climb, then banked and turned east. They were still fairly low when they flew over the city, and Resa had an overall view of the damage caused by the riots. She ached inside for the chaos below. Somehow, she thought, it's almost worse than seeing isolated examples of the destruction from the ground.

The city dwindled from sight and was replaced by open country. They unfastened their seat belts and went to a small lounge where the attendant served coffee. Resa let Isis out of her carrier and the cat proceeded to explore the plane.

"Well, we're on our way," Resa remarked.

They drank hot coffee and conversed quietly, watching the changing countryside beneath the plane and speculating on their destination. They were flying over desert when the flight attendant came back to the lounge.

"Please return to your seats and fasten your seatbelts," she said. "We'll be landing in a few minutes."

Resa held Isis for the landing and looked out the window, but saw only empty desert, and, in the distance, hazy, blue mountains shimmering in the heat waves from the desert floor. But then the plane banked, and she caught a glimpse of a small group of buildings, a large radar dish, and a long paved runway. The plane landed smoothly and as they taxied past the buildings, she noticed a large, weathered sign on one of them that read:

U.S. AIR FORCE
WEATHER OBSERVATION STATION

I'll bet, she thought.

They turned off on a short strip of runway that led directly to a hangar where two men were rolling the tall doors open. The plane stopped inside the hangar and the flight attendant said, "Please keep your seats. We will be descending to a lower level." The doors to the hangar were shut and then they heard the whine of hydraulic machinery. The area of floor on which the plane stood began to sink.

"Look!" Resa exclaimed.

They were descending into a vast, underground hangar gleaming with florescent lights and polished tile. The hydraulic lift stopped.

"You may unfasten your seatbelts now," the attendant said.

A ramp was wheeled into place and they went down the steps to where a man in a blue jumpsuit stood waiting beside an open, electric-powered car.

"Welcome to Survival Six Access," the man said pleasantly. "I'm Sergeant Wilcox and I'll be your guide through the Access Area. . . . If you'll step into the car we'll be on our way."

Resa got into the back seat with Steve, who was holding Isis in her carrier, and Paul sat in the front next to Sergeant Wilcox. Their luggage was put on racks on the back of the car by other men in blue jumpsuits, and then Wilcox drove them down a long, well-lit corridor. "We've been expecting you and your companions, Dr. Myles. The rest of the Stanford staff arrived last night," he said.

"Was Dr. MacBride with them?"

"Yes, ma'am, he was. He's in the infirmary despite his many objections, and he's doing well."

"What is this place?" Paul asked.

"It's one of a series of underground shelters built by the government some time ago. Top secret, of course. Usually, we only have a skeleton staff here, but with this emergency we're bringing people in daily. This particular shelter can accommodate about 200,000 people; it's rather small in capacity because its main purpose is the preservation of scientific equipment in the event of nuclear war. And all of the shelters have self-sustaining life support systems. . . . Here we are."

He pressed a button on the dashboard and a portion of the wall slid open to reveal a large elevator. He drove into the elevator, and they descended rapidly. The elevator stopped. The doors opened automatically and Wilcox drove onto a wide platform—at the end of it stood a large, bullet-shaped train.

"This is where I leave you," Wilcox said. "The train will take you to the first level of Survival Six."

"I thought we were already in the shelter," Resa said.

"Only the Access Area, ma'am."

They took the luggage off the racks and stepped into the train where Wilcox showed them how to fasten their seat belts. "You're going about fifty miles across the desert through an underground access tunnel," he said. "It's perfectly safe, so don't be concerned . . . enjoy the ride."

"How does this thing work?" Paul asked.

"I'll operate the controls from out here to send you through." Wilcox pointed to a control station on the platform. "A security measure . . . ," he explained. "All set?"

Steve nodded. "We're ready."

He pressed a button on the panel. The doors of the train slid shut, and it moved swiftly into the tunnel. Through the transparent dome, they could see the tunnel lights flash by in rapid succession, blurred into streaks of light from the speed of the train.

"Fifty miles should put us under those mountains we saw off in the distance," Steve observed.

"I think you're right," Paul said.

"Did Wilcox means there are other bases like this one scattered around the country?" Resa asked.

"I've never heard of them, but it sounded like that to me. He said this was one in a series," Steve said.

"Did you catch the small capacity of 200,000?" Paul remarked.

"Yeah, I sure did," Steve said. "Say, it feels like we're slowing down some."

"We are," Paul said. "Look at the lights on the tunnel walls—they're becoming more distinct."

The train continued to decelerate and eventually it came to a smooth, quiet stop. The doors snapped open. Another guide, in an identical blue jumpsuit, stood waiting on the platform.

"Welcome to Level 1," he said. "Please follow me. Leave your luggage—it will be taken care of later. . . . We have an urgent message for Steve Sheldon. You're to call Taggert immediately. This way, sir," he said as Steve stepped forward.

The guide led him to a communications center at one side of the room and handed him a phone. "It's encrypted, sir." Resa and Paul moved to his side.

"Thanks." Steve called Taggert, and they conversed in low tones for a few minutes. He hung up the phone and turned to Resa and Paul.

"I have to leave for Washington immediately," he said. "Sorry, darling, but I've been half expecting it. The FBI ranks have been seriously thinned, so the CIA is supporting them. We're under orders to pull all suspected Russian agents in the country out of circulation immediately." He drew her off to one side. "I'll miss you. But I'll try to stay in touch. At least I know you'll be safe in here."

"Thanks a lot. I'd rather not be here. You *will* call?"

"You bet I will. You'll be sick of hearing from me."

She smiled. "That won't happen."

Steve turned to the guide.

"I'll send you right back, sir. A plane is waiting to take you to Washington."

"Thanks." Steve shook Paul's hand and asked him to keep an eye on Resa. He gathered her in his arms and gave her a brief, hard kiss."

She watched him until the train doors snapped shut. They hadn't had that much time together. All she could do was hope that would change in the near future. Make that the very near future.

The guide led them to a room that was partitioned off into small cubicles. "You will have to leave your clothing and all jewelry, wallets . . . everything, here. They will be returned to you. Storage containers have been provided in each cubicle for these items. Please put on the jumpsuits and footgear that you will find in the cubicles and return here."

He directed them to specific cubicles. "The red button on the left both closes and opens the door. Remember to remove everything you are wearing."

"What about Isis?"

"A vet will come to check her out, and you'll be reunited with her shortly."

Paul gave Resa an encouraging nod and entered his cubicle. Resa entered hers and pressed the button. The door slid shut. With quick movements, she undressed and placed everything in the container, which, she noticed in surprise, already had her name on it. She put on the blue jumpsuit and plastic-soled slippers, pressed the red button again, and left the cubicle.

When Paul came out of his cubicle and joined her, the guide said, "Follow me, please." He led them through another set of sliding doors (they're all over the place, thought Resa) to a room that was empty except for a series of sliding doors.

"This is the ID Section," the guide explained, "where your handprints and other information will be recorded in the computer files. Entry to the lower levels is entirely under computer control. You will receive booster immunizations and prophylactic wide-spectrum antibiotics as a precaution against carrying any infection into the lower levels. This was set up when the government was seriously concerned about biological warfare attacks. We have facilities for extensive decontamination procedures before entry, which are quite time consuming, but you will go through only minimum aseptic procedures. . . . Are there any questions?"

"Too many to waste time with," Resa said bluntly. "Let's get on with it."

The guide directed them to two sets of sliding doors. "You'll go through the process in parallel. "Press the button and enter."

Resa passed through her sliding doors and stepped on a platform. Her weight activated a system response: a panel directly opposite her opened to reveal a large CRT screen and a mechanical voice said, "State your name. Last name first."

Resa hesitated, startled by the verbal request, and then replied, "Myles, Resa."

"Place your right hand, palm down, on the glass rectangle to your right. Place your left hand, palm down, on the glass rectangle to your left," the voice continued.

Resa placed her hands as ordered, and the glass posts glowed with light. On the screen opposite her, appeared the words:

MYLES, RESA

HANDPRINTS RECORDED

A pedestal with two apertures rose out of the platform floor right in front of her. "Please look through the two, lighted openings for a retinal scan."

Resa complied and then stepped back when the lights went off and the equipment sank back into the floor. On the screen she noted the new information added under her name:

RETINAL SCAN COMPLETE

A laser beam from an aperture below the screen traversed her body slowly, from head to toe; and she saw additional words appear on the screen:

Height: 5 feet, 8 inches

Weight: 122 pounds

PHOTOGRAPH CODED

The system will recite a series of words, the mechanical voice intoned. "Repeat each word in the sequence until you receive a stop request. Alpha . . ."

"Alpha," Resa responded

"Beta," the computer said.

"Beta," she echoed.

"Gamma," the voice went on.

"Gamma." Resa continued responding in sequence until the system was satisfied and the voice told her to stop. On the screen, another phrase was added:

VOICEPRINT CODED

To the right of the screen, a door in the wall opened. "You may now exit through the door to your right," the mechanical voice said.

As soon as Resa stepped through the door, she was bathed in a wide beam of light from an aperture in the wall. After a moment, the mechanical voice said, "Identity confirmed . . . Myles, Resa," and, simultaneously, the doors behind her snapped shut. Resa looked around the seemingly empty room and wondered idly what would have happened if she had not been "Myles, Resa."

"Remove all clothing and footwear," the flat voice said. "Place them in the receptacle on your right." A scoop-shaped container appeared out of the wall. Resa removed her clothing and placed it in the receptacle, which disappeared with a sucking sound. Then in front of her another door opened, revealing a long corridor covered with nozzles spraying a sudsy solution. "Close your eyes and enter the shower tunnel," the voice said. "Do not walk. The beltway will move you through the tunnel."

With a sigh of resignation, Resa stepped onto the belt and closed her eyes. She felt the tingling jets hit her from all sides.

"Raise your arms. Keep your eyes closed," the voice instructed.

She raised her arms and was moved forward a few paces and then felt the slickness of the sudsy spray change to a warm liquid. "You may open your eyes and leave the shower."

Resa found herself standing on a platform in front of steps that led down into a pool filled with a pink solution, which she guessed was some kind of disinfectant. Opposite her, a transparent shield descended about a foot below the surface of the pool, dividing it in half, and through the clear wall she could see steps on the other side leading out of the pool and into another shower corridor.

"This is a total immersion bath," the voice said. "Keep your eyes open when under the solution. Proceed to the opposite side of the bath."

Resa walked into the pool and swam under the dividing wall; the solution irritated her eyes slightly, but it was not painful. After she went up the steps on the other side, the mechanical voice continued: "Pass through the next series of showers. Avoid getting excessive amounts of the spray in your eyes."

After the last shower, Resa was hit with blasts of warm air from blowers that dried her completely. She walked toward a sign market EXIT, and entered a small room bathed in ultraviolet light. Sensors must be tracking her, she thought, because when she had been in the room for some indeterminate time, a door slid open and the mechanical voice said, "Aseptic procedures have been completed. Go to the next room."

"Please sit down," said the voice after Resa entered.

Resa saw that the only place to do so was in a large, padded chair that stood in the center of the room facing a CRT screen on the wall. She sat down on it and wished they would give her some clothing. She wasn't cold, but she was somewhat uncomfortable parading around naked.

"Please remain still. Mandatory laboratory tests will be performed."

A dome device was lowered over her head and she felt leads being attached for an electroencephalogram. On the CRT screen, words appeared:

EEG RECORDING
AVERAGE RESPONSE ANALYSIS

The words were followed by tracings of her brain waves, flashed in quick succession on the screen. They showed a rapid, spiky pattern that Resa knew was typical of those seen with an alert subject. The recording session was a short one—about five minutes. During that period, she had been asked to close her eyes and relax for part of the time. She knew this was necessary to get a good recording of her brain alpha rhythm, best obtained when a person was resting quietly, with eyes closed, but not asleep.

The leads were withdrawn and the dome rose. "Please lie back," the mechanical voice said. Simultaneously, the chair in which she was sitting tilted back and extended itself into a padded table. Mechanical arms, directed by electric eyes, arose from the sides of the table and attached electrodes to her chest and four extremities. Obviously for an electrocardiogram, Resa thought, and looked at the screen.

Tracings showing the electrical activity produced by her heart flashed on the screen, and Resa studied them with interest. The recording took only a few minutes, and then the mechanical arms withdrew the electrodes.

"Are you allergic to eggs, chicken, feathers, or any antibiotics?' the mechanical voice asked. "Answer only yes or no."

"No," Resa replied. She felt a sharp sting in her left arm accompanied by a hissing sound. "Hey!" Resa objected.

You have just received a pneumatic injection of booster immunizations and broad-spectrum antibiotics."

The table folded itself and raised her to a sitting position. A clear box-like object with finger holes appeared on the left side of the chair.

"Please place your left hand in the glove box. A sample for blood type analysis will be taken."

"My blood type is A, RH positive," Resa protested. On the screen appeared the words:

RESPONSE CANNOT BE CODED

The mechanical voice began to repeat the request, and Resa muttered, "Oh, hell!" and placed her left hand in the box, which closed gently, holding her hand snugly. She felt a cold spray on her fingers, and then the box released her hand. The screen glowed with the message:

BLOOD SAMPLE TAKEN

Curiously, she examined her hand and saw a small puncture wound on one finger. She had felt no pain, so she assumed that the cold spray must have been a topical anesthetic.

"Please lie back."

With a sigh, Resa relaxed as the chair tilted back, extended itself and became, once more, a padded table. A panel in the wall in front of her opened and she was surprised to see the familiar cylindrical shape of an MRI whole-body scanner. It was the most sophisticated of medical diagnostic tools, and this one was larger than any she had seen. The device slid out of its recess to the end of the table and then Resa felt the table lift and begin to move into the hollow scanner.

"Please place your arms above your head. This is a magnetic resonance imaging scanner. Please do not move."

The tube began to rotate around her. During one of its 360-degree revolutions the scanner would take hundreds of thousands of measurements from which cross-sectional images of her body would be formed and stored in the computer. With this detailed information on the size, location, and configuration of her organs, a physician could pinpoint just about any abnormality.

When the procedure was finished, the motorized table withdrew from the MRI chamber. The voice said, "Entry procedures are completed. You may dress and exit to your right."

A white jumpsuit and plastic-soled slippers appeared on a shelf that opened out of the wall. Resa dressed quickly and went toward the exit. As she passed the screen she glanced at it, and shook her head at the words that appeared:

BLOOD TYPE: A, RH POS

"I knew that," she muttered. She approached the closed door marked EXIT and it slid open. Her arm began to ache a little from the injection.

She entered a lounge area where a man clothed in a green jumpsuit rose and greeted her, "Welcome to Survival Six, Dr. Myles. I'm Jack Swenson, the shelter security officer." He looked at Resa rubbing her arm. "I hope you didn't find our entry procedures too annoying."

"On the contrary, they were most entertaining." She looked around the lounge. "As soon as my brother-in-law arrives, I'd like to get to work. I believe the emergency still exists?"

"Yes, ma'am, it certainly does," Swenson replied, undaunted by Resa's irritation.

"Would you like some coffee while we're waiting?"

"Resa nodded curtly. Swenson led her to a self-service counter at the end of the lounge and showed her how to select items from the menu on a CRT screen. "We have central kitchens here," Swenson explained, "and all ordering is under computer control."

"That figures," Resa commented.

"It's really the most efficient method to use," Swenson said in mild defense, "especially when a large number of people must be fed. The shelter is self-contained; everything needed for survival can be made right here, within the shelter itself."

They took their coffee to one of the tables. "How many people are here?" Resa asked.

Swenson shook his head. "That's classified," he said with a

smile.

"That's ridiculous."

"Well—" Swenson's remark was cut off by the hiss of sliding doors. Resa looked up.

Paul appeared, fully dressed in civilian clothes. "How did you get through so fast?" Resa asked.

"I think I was moving a little ahead of the voice recording," Paul admitted. "An interesting process . . . the input from the sensors overrides the time triggers on the recording. I guess I had the system in a constant update mode. These programmed processes are so simple you really don't have to wait for all of the instructions, as long as the computer itself is keeping up with you."

Resa shook her head in resignation. "I guess you didn't even stop to argue with it?"

"With a machine?" Paul laughed. "That's a good one, Resa."

Resa smiled. "You don't know how good," she said cryptically. She decided she'd die before admitting her mild disagreement with the computer.

Swenson left the table and approached them, but before he could launch into another welcoming speech for Paul's benefit, Resa said, "This is Jack Swenson, the security officer. . . . We are ready, Mr. Swenson."

Swenson gave up, "Follow me," he said. "After you dress, I'll show you to your quarters first and then the research areas."

They followed him down the corridor.

"By the way," Paul asked, "what happens in that first room if someone else tries to go through in your place—where the system says 'identity confirmed'?"

"Lasers happen, Mr. Linder," Swenson replied blandly.

CHINA BLASTS RUSSIA'S "RUTHLESS SUPPRESSION"

Wire Copy — China's official news agency said today the Russian gov-

ernment is "sitting on a volcano," with its "ruthless suppression" of the people, arousing strong resistance from Russian citizens.

The official Hsinhua News Agency said that the action of the Russian Federation's government in the present world crisis is a prime example of this "ruthless suppression" of the people. The government has imposed a rigid censorship on all travel and all news media. Russian citizens are "sealed in behind an impregnable iron curtain."

"Society in Russia has never been 'stable' and 'harmonious' as Vassilov and his like have described it," Hsinhua said, referring to Russian President Aleksandr Ivanovich Vassilov.

Hsinhua said that since 2001, the government has expanded its "machinery of Fascist dictatorship," reinforcing the police and special agents. In addition to new prisons, it said, the Russian government has set up many labor camps "for the suppression of revolutionary people."

Chapter 15

Survival Six Underground Shelter, Nevada

THE LIVING QUARTERS at Survival Six are surprisingly spacious, Resa thought, as she looked through the suite of rooms to which she had been assigned: living room, dining area, bedroom, and bathroom. All, of course, in the same modern, streamlined styling as the rest of the shelter with a liberal use of tile and plastics. There were no rugs, no fabric upholstery, no draperies—nor windows to put them on, for that matter. Everything possible seemed to be disposable, the bed linen as well as her clothing. There was no kitchen; all food was ordered from a central kitchen through a computer terminal in the dining area, and all eating utensils were sent down a disposal chute with the leftover food. Isis had explored the suite of rooms several times and Resa had the impression that the cat didn't much care for their quarters.

She studied the map that Swenson had provided, showing the levels on which she would be working. There were apparently eight levels in the shelter. Their living quarters, the scientific data processing area, and various laboratories were on the fifth level. Other scientific laboratories and equipment occupied the entire sixth level. There were no details on the map concerning the other levels, only an outline which designated their existence.

A knock on the door interrupted her ruminations. Resa opened it and saw Paul. "Come on in. I'm checking out this map Swenson left. It looks like we're not supposed to wander off outside the areas described on it."

"Yes. I noticed that on my map, too. Swenson seems to be unusually security conscious—you'd think we were plotting to blow up the place."

Resa was inclined to agree with him. "Well, that's typical of the military mind though," she said. "We're outsiders . . . and apparently the existence of these shelters has been a well-kept secret up to now." She wondered how the military planned to keep the secret after the protective custody was no longer necessary, but then dismissed the idle thought. She had far more important work to do than conjecture about military problems.

Resa glanced at her watch, one of the items she found waiting for her in the bedroom that she had left in the Access Area earlier. "I've got to go to the research area and get started."

"Shouldn't we wait for Swenson?" Paul asked. "He said he'd be right back."

It's been over an hour since he left, Resa thought. He must be tied up with some security problem.

"I'd rather not wait any longer. Besides, with these maps we really don't need him. And we'll have to find something for you to do," Resa said.

"Well, I can help out in the computer area with the data processing."

"That's a good idea, Paul. And I'll be spending a lot of time in there myself." Neither of them had forgotten the hidden danger. It had cost both of them too much, Resa thought as they continued down the corridor, her heart aching with thoughts of Cathy. With an effort she pulled her mind away from those painful memories.

"When Steve calls, there is something I want him to do, though," she said. "It's been on my mind. I'm going to ask him to use his CIA contacts to check out Allan Sutherland."

"The magazine writer we met at the party?"

"Yes."

"Why?"

He was with that mob that broke into the Center. It was strange, Paul. He had a camera, but he wasn't photographing the people in the mob. He had his camera aimed at me! And what bothered me was the way he looked at me. I could tell from his look that he recognized me. But his face was cold, not quite angry, but there was something wrong there. He almost looked like he hated me."

Paul frowned and looked concerned. "Did he take a picture of you?"

"I'm not sure. Mac yanked me back in the room right when Sutherland was looking my way through his camera. I don't think he had time."

"Damn! That was right when Mac was shot. Did you see anyone in the mob with a gun?"

"No. That's why I was so stunned when the shot rang out. No one had a gun. Well, the police probably did, but they were still behind the mob at that point."

"Hmm . . . So you didn't see a weapon, just a camera. I've heard of cameras that have guns inside them. Sutherland could have had a gun in his camera."

"My God, Paul! Do you really think so?"

"It's certainly possible. If you don't connect with Steve first, I'll ask him to call his contacts at the CIA."

"Good. I won't worry about it anymore." She smiled. "My other priorities are more than enough."

They passed a number of people who were moving busily in and out of the rooms that opened on the corridor, but Resa recognized no one. She looked at her map. "Let's stop in data processing. It's right up ahead."

Resa was astonished at the size of the data processing area—it was at least ten times as large as the one at the Research Center and crammed with what looked like the most advanced equipment available. She looked around the area and saw many familiar faces. The guide had been correct—the entire senior staff was here.

Mark Ashton spotted her and came over quickly. "Thank heaven you're here, Resa! We really have to move. The reports are coming in like a flood—and the death toll is rising fast."

"Is this computer tied in with the CCA network?" Resa asked.

"Yes. All the data are there, but—"

"Good." Resa cut him off. "Mark, I want you to retrieve the photomicrographs on a patient named Thurston that we had at the Center. I'll show you something I noticed just before the riot that last night at the Center.

"Also," Resa went on, "I want someone started on writing a program that will locate all the records on patients who were treated with the synthetic virus on a massive-dose regimen."

"I can write that program for you, Resa," Paul offered. "I'll just need some medical record information for the sorting sequences."

"Good. Mark, get him some help there, will you?"

In just a few minutes, Resa was totally involved in moving the research program back into action. It was as if the brief interlude with its annoying relocation had not intruded. Once again, the world was shut out, concentration undivided, personal problems forced into the background.

IN WASHINGTON, D.C., President Harland had called a special meeting—a private conference with carefully chosen officials, and, as usual, David Blair was there, recording the entire session for Harland's private records.

Harland's proclamation of nationwide martial law had placed him in a unique position of control, thought Blair. In the most powerful country in the world, his authority was virtually unlimited.

Historically, military commanders of areas under martial law could be called upon to justify actions they had taken during the emergency, but this was only after martial law had been removed, and even then their actions were judged solely in the context of the emergency situation that existed at the time the martial law was in effect, rather than according to the way their actions appeared in the light of later developments.

Blair wondered how history would treat the actions Harland had taken so far, and he wondered too, with a growing concern, what future actions Harland was planning to reinforce the power he was drawing to himself. Blair had been letting his mind wander during one of Harland's long discourses to the small group of men assembled in his office. Now, all of them except Taggert of the CIA had been dismissed, and Blair paid close attention to what Harland was saying.

"The next item on the agenda is control of the missile bases, or rather," Harland amended, "assurance of the reliability of the commanders of those bases. We have too few bases left to risk anything going wrong at even one of them." He handed a list of names to Taggert. "I want a fast but complete loyalty check on these men. As you can see, some of them are already in command of a missile base, and others are not, but are qualified to be should any changes in command be required."

"Yes, Mr. President," Taggert replied, studying the list, which was actually a computer printout.

"Make no mistake in my meaning, Taggert," Harland said softly. "When I say 'loyalty check' I meant loyalty to me. Find out how they feel about me, how they feel about the martial law proclamation."

"I understand, sir," Taggert said quietly.

"Good. And hurry it up. I think you'll find that we have to get some new orders cut, some changes made," he said briskly. "See me or Blair here, if I'm tied up, as soon as it's done. . . . And you better check on their physical condition, too, while you're at it," he added. "I don't want anyone with this damned *syndrome* in charge of a missile base," he said in annoyance.

Harland shuffled the papers on his desk and made no comment. He seemed distracted, momentarily withdrawn, his mind focused on some inner problem, and then his eyes cleared and he continued talking as if the lapse had not occurred.

"The next matter," he said, "involves priority in treatment of the sick. I want orders sent out immediately that all military personnel and their dependents are to receive priority over all civilians. You attend to that, Blair."

Blair almost protested that such an action could not be justified, but he held back. He knew from the set tone of his voice that Harland wouldn't listen, knew that it could enrage him, set him off on one of his diatribes that were becoming all too frequent. And Blair was about to bring up a point he wanted very much to win.

"While we're on the subject of the sick, sir, I'd like to ask if you have any orders concerning the problem of the children?" Blair said.

"Children?" Harland frowned. "What children?"

"The vaccine was not given to children under six years of age, sir. The Red Cross has been trying to take care of them, but it needs all the available facilities for the sick, and the number of children whose parents are either ill or dead is mounting. I thought perhaps we could send them to the survival shelters." Even as he finished speaking, Blair could tell that Harland did not like the idea. "They may be the very Americans that will help you rebuild the country one day," he went on persuasively. "And as I said, they are not ill, merely homeless or without parental care. Also, they are in danger because of the riots that are still going on."

181

"Yes," Harland said slowly, distractedly. "They could be trained in the shelters." His eyes cleared. "They could be cared for in the shelters," he said, "far more easily than on the outside. You attend to it, Blair."

"Yes, Mr. President." Blair felt chilled by Harland's words, but the important thing now was to save the lives of these children. The training, the indoctrination Harland implied was a long way off in the future. And, in that moment, Blair promised himself he would not let it happen.

"And now," Harland said, "we come to the last, but most important, item on the agenda." He picked up a file marked PRIVATE, and spread it open on his desk. "I have made extensive additions to the Enemies of the White House list. In the present crisis," he said slowly, "it's vital that no one be permitted to undermine my authority . . . to endanger the survival of the nation . . . or to interfere with my direction of the government. Taggert, I want you to report to me on the current status and the whereabouts of every person on this list." He handed the list to Taggert.

"Yes, Mr. President," Taggert said quietly.

"That is all for the present, gentlemen."

Blair and Taggert left the room. Outside the door, Taggert asked if Blair had time to discuss an important matter with him, privately.

"Certainly," Blair replied. "Let's go to my office."

As the two men walked quickly down the hall, Blair's alert mind was sorting the facts he knew about Taggert. The man was excellent in his job: his direction of the CIA was outstanding, but he was close-mouthed and never voiced political opinions, which made it difficult to judge where his loyalties were. Blair had known him to be completely ruthless when he felt the situation called for it, but at times he would urge patience and diplomacy with equal vigor. In short, Blair decided, Taggert was an unknown quantity as far as his reaction to Harland's orders was concerned . . . and Blair would have to handle him accordingly.

The two men sat down in Blair's office and Taggert immediately came to the point. "I've received reports that indicate a Russian agent was landed on the coast of California and that he is interested in Resa Myles."

"Dr. Myles! What do you mean by interested?" Blair asked sharply.

"I'm not certain yet exactly what that means. There's a remote possibility that this agent was sent to kill her. I've talked to a police detective in Palo Alto named Brennan, a pretty sharp man, and he feels that someone has made attempts on Myles's life, but there is no concrete evidence. Also, even if it's true, it need not necessarily be the Russian agent behind the attacks. There are other possibilities to explain the agent's interest in Myles. . . ."

"Such as?"

Taggert shrugged. "Defection . . . sabotage . . ."

Blair shook his head. "No, . . . no chance."

"You're sure?"

"I am positive," Blair asserted. Did the man suspect everyone?

"You seem to have great faith in Myles's loyalty," Taggert observed.

Blair began to feel irritated. "I would not call it faith. The word implies a belief without reason, without facts. When you check on Dr. Myles's background, you'll see what I mean."

"Then why would the Russians want her killed?"

"You tell me," Blair countered. "She's the world's leading molecular biologist. Maybe that's a clue . . ."

"Hers is also one of the names on the president's Enemies list," Taggert said with equal coolness.

So that's it, Blair thought. He nodded calmly. "I'm not surprised. In fact, I'd be more surprised if her name was not on it. She argued with Harland rather strongly; she was very much against starting the mass immunization program. She said that it was too soon, that not enough testing had been done."

"I didn't know that," Taggert said slowly.

"Few people did." Blair's level gaze met Taggert's. It was time to push a little to find out what was going on in Taggert's mind. "Why did you come to me with this?"

"Because I have a feeling," he said slowly, "that there's more here than there appears to be on the surface. I knew when I checked her out that you had known Dr. Myles for a long time, and that you were friends. Neither of the facts fits with a subversive action on her part. And yet, why a threat to her life?" He shook his head. "And there are other things, apparently unrelated."

"Like what?"

"The Russians' top agent has disappeared. We lost track of him over a month ago. He should have surfaced by now, there should have been some hint of where he went. We keep a very close watch on him," Taggert said slowly. "When Rostov appears, there's trouble."

"What about this agent they landed in California? Could that be Rostov?" Blair asked.

Taggert shook his head. "It doesn't fit. Rostov gets in and then out fast—he doesn't fool around with any prolonged assignments. He's their best, and they send him in when a situation is critical. Usually, he has completed his assignment and is on his way somewhere else when we're just finding out what happened," Taggert said bitterly. "He's an elusive bastard. . . . God, how I'd like to get him," he added softly.

For a moment he seemed lost in private memories. "I have a top deep-cover agent in Russia that I managed to contact before things got locked up too tightly. He's good, very good, in fact. I've given him a free hand to nose around and try to find out what's going on over there.

"As far as the California Russian agent I'm trying to get a line on goes, there's another item that doesn't fit," Taggert went on.

"The man we got most of this information from said he was ordered to comply with any request from the agent landed on the coast, no matter what the cost, no matter how many other agents were lost or endangered. And this man, himself, had been under deep cover for about twelve years—a valuable agent to lose for something minor like trying to subvert a leading scientist."

"Then why did he talk?" Blair asked curiously.

"He's been cut off by all of his contacts. He took the vaccine, and he and his whole family are quite ill. He gave the information in return for treatment—it's next to impossible to get a bed in a hospital now.

"Unfortunately, he never saw this agent or spoke to him. We're still questioning the man, but I don't think we'll get much more information than we have now."

"I wish I could be of more help," Blair said, "but I'm stumped. The only thing I'm sure of is that Dr. Myles is not involved in any shady deal with the Russians. . . ."

Taggert nodded. "Well, thank you for listening. I didn't think it wise to dump this in the president's lap—he has enough on his mind right now and most of my concerns here are based too much on conjecture."

Blair studied the man, looking for some sign of a hidden meaning. "I think you made a wise decision," he said quietly. "Dr. Myles is safe at an underground shelter, from both the mobs and the Russians, if there is a real threat from that direction."

"I know." Taggert smiled.

What the hell didn't the man know? "Will you keep me posted?" Blair asked as Taggert rose to leave.

"Yes, I certainly will." He paused. "In fact, I think another meeting will be necessary in the very near future." Taggert folded the president's list carefully and placed it in his pocket.

He left . . . and Blair pondered the meaning in his last words.

LATE THAT NIGHT, in the quiet privacy of his office, Blair was no longer able to concentrate on the papers on his desk and he put them aside. Phrases that Harland had spoken, images of his erratic behavior kept intruding into Blair's thoughts. He went to the large Webster's dictionary on the file cabinet, leafed through the pages and found the word he was looking for:

par-a-noia . . . 1.: a rare chronic nondeteriorative psychosis characterized chiefly by systemized delusions of persecution or of grandeur that are commonly isolated from the mainstream of con- sciousness and that are usually not associated with hallucinations 2 .: a tendency on the part of individuals or groups toward suspiciousness and distrustfulness of others that is not based on objective reality but on a need to defend the ego against unconscious impulses, that uses projection as a mechanism of defense and that often takes the form of a compensatory megalomania.

"Megalomania," he murmured. Lost in thought, he closed the book and left the office.

CNN NEWS REPORT —

Martial law is now the law of the land in the United States of Ameri- ca. Because of the breakdown of civil authority, the president has de- clared a state of martial law to preserve public safety. When asked how long this temporary rule by military authorities would be im- posed on the civilian population, a spokesperson for the White House stated that it would depend entirely on how long it would take to stop the syndrome that is devastating countries the world over.

Chapter 16

Obninsk, The Russian Federation

BORIS IVANOVICH PEROVSKAYA approached the guardhouse at the gates of the Bolotnikov Laboratories in Obninsk and rummaged in the pocket of his heavy coat for his work pass.

Reluctantly, the guard stepped out into the bitter cold night and examined Perovskaya's pass. For the past five years, Perovskaya had passed through these gates, but orders must be followed, every pass must be checked. The guard always stopped him.

Perovskaya trudged slowly through the snow toward a side entrance of the building. The guard inside the door took his usual cursory look at the small bag of food Perovskaya carried for his break and waved him through. The building was quiet tonight for the first time in weeks. Technicians had been working on full shifts around the clock, preparing vaccine for the mass immunizations, but now the rush was over.

The old man went down the steps to the basement where all the cleaning supplies were kept, and opened the door to the small cluttered room in which he usually left his belongings; it was crowded with brooms, mops, pails, boxes. Dimitri Gregorivich Shuiski—who usually worked this late shift with him—was already there, sitting on an upturned box, his head resting on his hand.

"Ah, Dimitri, my friend, we have a lot of work to do tonight," Perovskaya said. "The laboratories will be empty, and what a mess they'll be after these past weeks."

Dimitri nodded his head dejectedly and did not speak.

Perovskaya took off his coat and hung it on a hook. "What's wrong, old friend?" he asked. "You haven't said one word to me."

Dimitri sighed heavily, "Forgive me, Boris. I can think of nothing but my daughter and her little one. They are so ill . . . and I'm so afraid for them."

Perovskaya sat down on another box beside Dimitri. "Have you taken them to a doctor? I can help you with the money."

"No, no. I don't dare. You don't know," Dimitri said painfully.

"Tell me. You know you can trust me. Maybe I can help you," Perovskaya urged.

Dimitri took a deep breath. "I must tell someone," he said. "I don't know what to do. . . . Her fool of a husband paid a technician from the Obninsk Research Center to give the whole family injections of the new cancer vaccine. The technician had stolen it from the supply sent to the Chinese—you remember how we all had to wait for the new supply," he said bitterly. "Something was wrong with the vaccine they sent to China, Boris. The technician is dying. I saw him myself—all covered with sores and burning with fever, just like my daughter and her family are now."

"Then you must take them to a doctor."

"No!" Dimitri said gruffly. "The technician went to a doctor at the Research Center, and the SVR took him away. Don't you see, Boris? They knew the vaccine that went to the Chinese was bad. They must have put something in it."

Perovskaya clasped Dimitri's shoulder; he was thinking hard. "I know what you must do," he said quietly. "Take them out of the city. I'll give you money to rent a car. Take them to a country village and find a doctor there. The SVR would not dare alert all of the doctors to watch for such an illness—then the secret would become known. They probably only watch the cities around the Research Centers."

Dimitri's eyes brightened. "Yes," he said slowly. "I could do that. You are a good friend, Boris, a good friend."

"Hush," said Perovskaya. "Take this money." He pressed some rubles into Dimitri's hand. "Go, now. Tell the guard you are not feeling well. I will clean the laboratories."

Still protesting his gratitude, Dimitri left. Quickly, Perovskaya gathered his cleaning supplies and went to the first large laboratory wing. He had waited anxiously to get in here ever since the news blackout had been imposed. He locked the laboratory doors behind him and moved briskly down the aisles. Gone was the stooped, trudging gait, the dulled peasant look in his eyes—he had shed twenty years. He examined the labels on the flasks lining the counters carefully. Then he went to an assembly area where the vials of the new vaccine that were being sent to all the Russian cities were filled. He broke open a vial and prepared a smear of the vaccine on a slide and examined it under a microscope. Then he placed a sample in an analyzer and waited impatiently for the results to be printed out.

That's it, he said to himself, looking at the report. There was no doubt now—his suspicions were confirmed. The Russians were passing off sterile distilled water for Russian citizens in place of the real vaccine, because the real vaccine was deadly.

Now he knew that the fragmented broadcasts he had tried to tune in were true. Now he knew why the FSB had prohibited travel into or out of the country.

189

The whole world, he thought bitterly, the whole fucking world. What had Dimitri said about his daughter? Covered with sores and burning with fever . . . and the Russian Federation, strong and healthy, waiting to move in and take over.

Thank God, Taggert had given him a free hand to try to find out what was going on with this sudden return to iron-clad secrecy.

Perovskaya, whose real name in the CIA files was Phillip Jordan, took what looked like a battered, old-fashioned cigarette lighter, but was in reality a miniature camera, out of his pocket and photographed the flasks and vials spread over the counters, as well as the printed analyses. He put a few of the filled vials in his pocket.

While he worked, his mind was racing—how to get the information out of Russia? The country was sealed shut, and the rest of the world probably thought the Russians were coping with disaster in their usual secretive fashion. He couldn't risk getting the message out through the American embassy, because if it had not been closed down, he was sure it would be under Russian control—the SVR would have seen to that.

Jordan had been operating in isolation from the other agents in Russia, under deep cover—there was no help from that source. It would be impossible for him to send a radio signal out of the country; the Russians were jamming all frequencies in the news blackout. He couldn't even get a message out; everything, including the internet was monitored and locked down. He had to take the news and the samples out himself.

That left only one way out for him—the emergency escape route that had been set up as part of his cover over five years ago, to be used only as a last resort. If it was still intact . . . He shrugged. There was no other choice. That was the fastest way, maybe the only way, out of the country.

Jordan put the lighter back in his pocket, gathered his cleaning supplies, and left the laboratory, becoming Perovskaya once more—and for the last time. He decided to chance leaving the building before his work shift was over. The guards were not as particular about who left the premises as they were about checking workers who came in . . . and time was critical.

It was snowing lightly when he left the laboratory, large moist flakes that clung to his coat and crowned the old fur cap he wore on his head. Head bent low and huddled in his coat, he trudged slowly toward the gate, staying directly in the path of the bright yard lights so the guards would see him approaching. They waved him on with scarcely a second glance when he paused at the gates.

Leaving the laboratory behind, he moved more quickly through the quiet, deserted streets to the room he rented in an apartment building about eight blocks away. Dawn was still many hours away but he had much to do in the dark hours of the night.

Quietly, so as not to disturb the neighboring tenants who might wonder why he had returned at this hour, Jordan let himself into his room. It was shabby and small and dark, but it was in the back of the building on the first floor, near an exit leading to a rear alley—an important consideration for an undercover agent. He drew down the shade on the one small window in the room and turned on a light.

Now he had to move quickly. From underneath the bed he dragged an old, battered footlocker, which had a strong lock in surprisingly good condition underneath the chips and scratches on its exterior finish. He unlocked the small trunk, tossed the contents on top aside, and released the inner lock that exposed the false bottom in the trunk.

Here lay his new identity: expensive clothing, papers, money, and a leather briefcase. When he left the shabby room he would be Yuri Iosifovich Kamenev, an affluent businessman, owner of a small electronics firm in the Leningradskaya Oblast.

Yuri Iosifovich Kamenev, he repeated the name to himself and refreshed in his mind the details of his new identity (which he had committed to memory years ago and reviewed periodically) while he shaved off his beard and washed in the tiny bathroom adjoining his room. He dressed quickly, studied his appearance critically in the mirror, and then took his briefcase and left the room without a backward glance. More than his appearance had changed: he moved with a poised, confident stride, with the air of assurance that success in one's chosen field invariably brought.

THE TAXI DRIVER pulled up at the curb reserved for departing passengers at the Moscow Airport, and turned to the man in the back seat with a smile.

The well-dressed Kamenev nodded his approval. "You made good time, my friend." He handed over the sum of money agreed upon for the trip from Obninsk, which was some thirty-five miles southwest of Moscow, and added five extra rubles to it.

Thanking him profusely, the driver pocketed the money, and then got out of the taxi quickly and opened the back door for his generous passenger.

Kamenev walked briskly through the terminal, which even at this predawn hour was thronged with people, to the ticket desk where he purchased a round-trip ticket to Leningrad. The SVR had not extended their restrictions to travel within the country; there was no difficulty in securing the ticket. He took care to make sure he requested a round-trip ticket, since he carried no luggage except the briefcase. An unexpected, but very important business trip—not at all suspicious, if the man looked every inch the successful businessman.

"Your plane leaves in thirty minutes, sir," the flight attendant said, "from gate 6."

"Thank you." Ticket in hand, Kamenev went to the passenger lounge at gate 6 and obtained a boarding pass. He was all ready when ten minutes later the loudspeaker announced that his flight was boarding passengers.

He settled himself in his seat with the boredom of a businessman who traveled frequently. Before the plane had taken off, he had opened his briefcase, removed some papers, and, using the case as a desk, began busily jotting notes in the margins of the papers. He hardly noticed the whine of the jet engines as the pilot built up power at the end of the runway, and then maneuvered the plane smoothly into the air in a steep, graceful climb and turned northwest.

It was a short trip. Leningrad was only 400 miles from Moscow and about an hour after the jet had left the ground it was circling for landing at the Leningrad airport. Dawn was breaking, brightening the sky, and Jordan, alias Kamenev, had a clear view of the sprawling industrial city. It stood on the Neva delta—which was still frozen solid and would stay that way until breakup began sometime in April—at the head of the Gulf of Finland.

Finland . . . Jordan thought, so near, its border so heavily guarded. His pulse raced as he thought ahead to when he would make his attempt to cross that distant border, but not here, not from Leningrad. It would have been impossible.

The thud of wheels on the snow-covered runway broke his reverie. Once more the efficient executive, he left the plane and made his way briskly through the busy terminal to a car rental desk.

"For two days, please," he told the attractive young woman at the counter. She gave him the keys to the car, his receipt, and a dazzling smile.

His destination was Vyborg, a smaller city of the Leningradskaya Oblast with a population of only about 60,000; it stood at the head of Vyborg Bay on the Gulf of Finland some seventy miles northwest of Leningrad, close to the Finland border. At one time it had been part of Finland and had then been called Viipuri, but some fifty-odd years ago it had been ceded back to Russia.

Jordan knew that the Russian internal security, the FSB, would be watching the border points in the city closely, which was the major reason he had chosen to rent a car and drive there, rather than take the direct railway connection from Leningrad into the smaller city. Vyborg was on the main Leningrad-Helsinki line, but he knew that the train was being stopped now at the border and passengers exiting at Vyborg would be closely scrutinized.

In the early morning hours, traffic was still light in Leningrad, and Jordan left the city quickly, driving carefully through the winding streets to the main highway. It would take him longer to drive to Vyborg than the flight from Moscow took. But caution was more important than time right now. He couldn't be sure that any other agents had realized what was going on before the powerful FSB and SVR had sealed the country. He had to go on the assumption that he was the only agent left to get the information out.

Two hours later, he had driven through Vyborg and was on a highway on the outskirts of the city. He left the highway, and took about twenty minutes more weaving his way among narrow side roads before he stopped at a small rustic-looking house. It was set in open country among the many small tributaries that fed nearby Lake Ladoga.

His nearest neighbor was over three miles away. The house was thought to be a vacation home of a wealthy industrialist from Leningrad who was only able to get away from the pressures of work on rare occasions to use the small lodge.

Jordan saw that the farmer he paid to keep the long, private road to the lodge clear of snow had been performing his job conscientiously. The straight stretch of road had recently been plowed clear—his luck was holding.

Quickly, he unlocked the heavy door to the lodge and went inside. A fast look around assured him that nothing had been disturbed. Jordan smiled and felt a rising confidence in his ability to get out of the country.

He entered the garage, which was attached to the lodge, through a door in the kitchen, and removed the tarpaulin from the small, single-engine plane that almost filled the small garage. The plane was painted white, with fictitious numbers and a large Red Cross emblem on its side. Years ago it had been shipped here in separate parts in the guise of furniture for his lodge, and he had assembled it himself. Since then it had been kept fully fueled and ready to go—his emergency escape route.

Wasting no time, since he had performed the movements many times in memory, he started the engine and checked the gauges. While the engine was warming up, Jordan unlocked and opened the wide garage doors and checked the long stretch of road leading to the lodge. It was empty.

He taxied easily down the sloping driveway and swung the plane around to face the straight length of road. Braking the plane, he revved up the motor, and then released the brake. The plane moved down the road, skidding a little from the slippery, packed snow, but building up speed. He eased back on the stick and felt the sudden smoothness that told him the wheels had left the ground.

He was airborne.

Jordan climbed quickly to 600 feet. He wanted to stay under the radar and yet go as high as he could in case a border patrol spotted him and fired on him. Thirty miles, he said to himself, just thirty miles. He opened the small plane up to its top speed.

Time seemed to move with agonizing slowness. He scanned the countryside beneath him, snow-covered land and frozen lakes, and tiny cars crawling slowly on the small white roads.

He was almost at the border when he saw the patrol beneath him, about a hundred yards to his right. They were waving and shouting. He saw them raise their rifles, and undeterred by the Red Cross markings on the plane, they began to fire at him, but they were too far away to do any damage. Now the danger was that they would radio for a fast pursuit plane.

He didn't think reaching the border would stop pursuit, but if he could get far enough over it, closer to the small Finnish city of Lappeenranta, he had a chance. The Russians couldn't risk creating an international incident, not when they had just tossed *glasnost* out the window and sealed the country.

He crossed the border. Five minutes passed and there was no sign of pursuit. He switched his radio to the international distress frequency.

Just a few more minutes, he thought, a few more.

Finally, in the distance ahead, he could see the outlying buildings of Lappeenranta and began to broadcast in French: *"M'aidez . . . m'aidez . . . m'aidez . . . Je suis Amèricain. C'est un cas d'urgence. Y a-t-il quelqu'un là qui parle anglais? . . ."*

In English, a heavily accented voice responded: "This is the Lappeenranta control tower. We have you on radar. . . . What is the nature of your emergency?"

He took a deep breath of relief. His hands were trembling now, but his voice was still firm and sure. "I am an American citizen escaping from Russia. I request temporary asylum in your country."

The reply was immediate.

"This is Lappeenranta control. Continue on your present course. You are cleared for landing."

REUTERS, GENEVA —

A SPOKESMAN FOR THE GENEVA-BASED WORLD HEALTH ORGANIZATION (WHO) SAID THEY ARE BEING FLOODED WITH REPORTS OF DEATHS FROM THE CANCER IMMUNIZATIONS BEING GIVEN WORLDWIDE.

AUTHORITIES REPORT DEATHS IN THE MILLIONS WITH MANY MORE MILLIONS INFECTED. THEY ADVISE THAT IMMUNIZATIONS BE STOPPED AND SUPPLIES OF THE VACCINE DESTROYED. "THIS SYNDROME IS NOW A WORLDWIDE HEALTH THREAT," WHO DIRECTOR-GENERAL JEO GARLEM DIENDTLAND SAID IN AN OFFICIAL STATEMENT.

Chapter 17

Washington, D.C.

THE CIA SERVED as a focal point for the interpretation and dissemination of political and military intelligence, and the channels for handing priority information within the CIA itself were well defined. When the report from Jordan—coded with the highest priority—came in, Taggert was alerted immediately.

He went to the decoding room and waited impatiently while the report was run through the computer equipment, which would decode it automatically.

Taggert knew that Jordan was under deep cover in Russia, and the fact that he had broken out into Finland to make this report signified a degree of urgency that was serious. Anxiously, he read the report and his face paled.

"Call an emergency session of the Operations Coordinating board," he ordered tersely. "Have the wire photos come in yet?"

"No, sir," his assistant replied.

"As soon as they do, bring them to me. I'll be in my office. And arrange for one of our fast jets in Europe to pick Jordan up and bring him over for debriefing as soon as possible."

He left the decoding room and went quickly to his office. It had finally happened. His mind almost refused to accept the words on the paper. But Jordan would never have made an error of this magnitude . . . would never have sacrificed his deep cover without sufficient cause. . . . Intuitively, Taggert knew the report was genuine, but he had to have it corroborated.

He picked up the phone and issued concise orders. "I want the most recent satellite data on the Russian Federation analyzed for anything we can get on population density and shifts in energy output. Also request an immediate high-altitude reconnaissance flight over Moscow and Leningrad for those same parameters. . . ."

Taggert put down the phone and sighed heavily. There was one more thing he had to do . . . even at this early stage of appraising a possible threat to national security, and he dreaded it.

He picked up the red telephone that would connect him directly with the president.

AT THE STRATEGIC Air Command in Omaha, a high-flying SR-72 reconnaissance jet screamed its way into the upper reaches of sky. The Lockheed-built plane had a ceiling of 120,000 feet; it could fly above ninety-seven percent of the earth's atmosphere at a speed of over 2000 miles per hour. A top-secret method was used to mask the SR-72's heat emission to confuse Russian infrared tracking, and it was equipped with sophisticated radar-jamming gear and heat-sensing devices.

The Russians were unaware of the silent intruder penetrating their iron curtain: it passed undetected over the Leningrad industrial complex and the sprawling Moscow Oblast.

AT THE WHITE HOUSE, President Harland, accompanied by Blair, stepped into an elevator that plunged them 400 feet downward to a bombproof War Room.

"Is the Chinese translator standing by?" Harland asked.

"Yes, Mr. President."

The doors snapped open. The two men entered a spacious room, which held desks and computer consoles facing a large screen that covered an entire wall. The president nodded to the people in the room, glanced briefly at the screen, and went into a small office. It held a few chairs and a single desk on which stood a group of telephones—one of them was the hot wire to Peking.

The president sat down behind the desk, and Blair took a chair opposite him. Blair glanced at his watch.

"It's almost time," he said.

Harland nodded and did not speak. His gaze was on the bulky, dual phone that was the hot link with Peking. His patience was strained to the limit. The phone rang—a sharp and unbroken ring. Harland picked up the phone and motioned for Blair to pick up the other receiver.

It was the Communist Chinese Prime Minister Ling En-huai. He spoke in English.

"We have confirmed the information you provided, Mr. President," he said. The Russian Federation sent us the vaccine knowing it was deadly. This is an act of war." His voice was quiet, with a fatalistic acceptance of the disaster to come.

Harland felt a surge of satisfaction. "What are you going to do, Prime Minister?"

"My people are dying, Mr. President. We will not wait for the Russians to walk across our borders. While we still have the strength, we will fight. . . ." He paused and continued, and sorrow covered the anger in his words. "My advisors urge me to appeal to the United Nations for justice," he said slowly. "They say we will be utterly destroyed in a war with Russia, . . . but either way we will die."

"The United Nations cannot help you." Harland knew that the undeclared and totally informal alliance that had existed between China and the United States since the Nixon and Ford administrations in the seventies was foremost in the mind of the prime minister.

"What do your advisors tell you, Mr. President?" Ling En-huai asked.

"Much the same as yours." Harland's voice was bitter. "They say there has been enough death, that the world will condemn the Russian Federation, that nuclear war is not the answer."

"My world, my country, is dying. . . ." Ling En-huai's voice was calm, flat, emotionless. "I'm trapped, Mr. President."

Harland nodded, and then said aloud, "Yes. Our scientists are trying to find a cure, but it will take time, probably a long time."

There was silence on the line, and then Ling En-huai spoke: "There is an ancient saying you have probably heard: 'The enemy of my enemy is my friend.' What will you do when the Russians land on your shores?"

Harland did not hesitate. "I will not wait for them to land, Prime Minister," he said in a hard voice. "When your first missile leaves its silo, I will give the order to attack."

There was a tired despair in the prime minister's voice. "Then we are agreed?" he asked.

"Yes, we are agreed." Harland replied quietly.

"There is little time," Ling En-huai said softly. "Good-bye, my friend."

The line clicked and went dead. Harland replaced his phone and looked at Blair, "Order a Condition Red," he said. "And I want the effort to bring all known or suspected Russian agents in the country into custody beefed up immediately."

When Blair left the small room, Harland leaned back in the chair and smiled slowly. He was pleased with the Prime Minister's decision, had counted on it, in fact. If the Russians had sent just one vial of the vaccine to the United States, he would not have had to depend on the Chinese to make the first move.

No one could accuse him now of using the situation as a pretext for launching a preemptive nuclear attack—the informal alliance with the Chinese must be honored.

Harland thought of the men in Moscow and a cold hate closed over him. He could see Vassilov's utter ruthlessness behind the gambit—for sheer audacity it was unequaled. He felt a mixture of hate and envy for the man. He envied Vassilov's power, his control of the SVR and FSB—the vast clandestine forces he used to preserve his power within the Russian Federation and to expand it outside his country.

CIA RECORDING OF TELEPHONE CALL TO CNN FROM THE WHITE HOUSE—

Harland: "This is the president speaking, Mr. Patterson. This call must be kept confidential."

Patterson: "Yes, Mr. President. No problem, sir."

Harland: "I want you to assemble a news team as well as any equipment you need to broadcast worldwide and bring it to the White House. Immediately. Is this possible?"

Patterson: "Yes, sir. It certainly is."

Harland: "You'll be the only news team allowed in. You'll have to share what you see with the other media. I want this news blasted out worldwide. Do you agree to these conditions?"

Patterson: "Yes, sir. You can count on CNN. Can you give me any idea of what we'll be covering, Mr. President?"

Harland: "All I can say right now is that you'll be broadcasting from the underground War Room. And I need you here right away."

Patterson: "We're on the way, sir."

Chapter 18

Survival Six Underground Shelter, Nevada

RESA WAS SURE they were on the right track now. The certainty, that intuitive right feeling, was there deep inside her. Her voice was strong and confident as she spoke to the staff of scientists assembled in the data processing area for an urgent review of the photomicrograph analyses she had ordered earlier.

"Cancer," she said, "is an aberration of normal cell growth; it is cell regeneration gone wild. The synthetic virus in the Stanford vaccine altered that wild growth by interacting with the cancer virus. It cured cancer victims. But when there was no cancer virus present in the body, when the recipient of the vaccine was healthy, the synthetic virus proceeded to overcome the body's *normal* cell regeneration processes.

"The adult human body," she went on, "is estimated to contain some 60,000 billion cells. Every second some 50 million of those cells in the body die, but during that same period of time 50 million infant cells are born to take the place of the dying cells. In fact, our skin replaces itself every two weeks. It takes longer for our bones to be replaced; this happens roughly every seven years.

"The Stanford vaccine suppresses this normal regeneration of cells . . . and the result is the syndrome we are seeing today. We've been using cancer drugs like Gleevac for leukemia that works by blocking the chemical signal that tells the cancer to grow, hoping that it will block the synthetic virus or at least slow it down. Along with this we're using immune boosters to help the immune system fight the virus. And, of course, we're using antivirals.

"It's not enough. We know what the synthetic virus molecule looks like. We have to block it."

Resa motioned to Mark Ashton who sat at the master computer console. "Let's reconstruct exactly what happened. On the screen we have the standard DNA pattern—with which we are all familiar—of the synthetic virus interacting with a cancer virus. Now we'll compare this structure with the mutation pattern seen in the syndrome."

The screen changed. "This is the mutated virus attacking a normal cell. All of the cell studies on victims of the syndrome show this pattern. And now we know that, in addition, all of the cancer patients who received a series of *maximum doses* of the synthetic virus also show the existence of the mutated virus in their cells. A smaller dose would have cured the cancer only. It's the excess amount that produced the mutation that attacked the normal cell generation processes.

"As you can see, the mutated virus is very similar to the synthetic virus except for one small portion of the chain that would normally be reacting with a cancer cell, if one were present." She nodded to Ashton who increased the magnification on that critical portion of the chain. "When there is no cancer present to react with this one portion of the chain," Resa said slowly, "the mutation appears." She paused, and could see understanding spread over the faces of her team. The key to stopping the syndrome is with this one small portion of the chain that doesn't have a cancer cell to react with. It doesn't have a cancer cell that in fact turns it off, stops it from reacting with other healthy cells."

"Then, to put it bluntly," one of the scientists said, "we can stop the syndrome only by providing the missing strand of RNA . . . by giving the patient the disease before he dies of the cure."

"Yes." Resa smiled and said, "That's it exactly. We need to synthesize a blocker comprising the missing part of the pattern. And that missing part will be a composite of the codes that control the wild cell growth in cancer viruses. If I'm right, it will be a portion of the cancer virus model from which we derived the synthetic virus originally."

Resa could feel the excitement that flashed through the room, the relief that, finally, here was something concrete to work on. Ashton began passing out the assignments he and Resa had drawn up just before the meeting.

Across the room, Resa saw Paul and she went over to him. "Resa," he said, gripping both of her hands. "Does this mean you've found a cure? I couldn't follow all of your talk, but you sounded so—"

"Yes," she said. "Now we have to synthesize it, but the worst part is over."

"Excuse me, ma'am," said a security guard who had come up beside Resa said. "I'm here to escort Mr. Linder to another level."

"What for?" Resa asked, annoyed at the interruption.

"He doesn't have a security clearance for this level, ma'am. It just came out on a routine computer check. He'll have to be moved immediately."

Paul looked sharply at the guard and rose.

Resa said angrily, "He's not being moved anywhere. You get Swenson down here—now."

The guard hesitated, and then pressed a button on an electronic paging device he wore on his belt.

Within a few minutes, Swenson came into the room followed by three more guards. "What's the trouble here?" he asked sharply, looking at the guard.

"Mr. Linder is not cleared for this level, sir," the guard replied quickly. "I was attempting to move him, but they objected." He motioned toward Resa and Paul.

Swenson glanced at Resa then back to the guard. "I gave no such order," he said impatiently. "Clear out and let these people get back to their work."

"But, sir. The computer check—"

"Sergeant—Mr. Linder is handling the computer work for these researchers. I don't give a damn what your order says. I give the orders around here. Now move out," he said angrily. "Don't you realize people are dying while you're standing here delaying this whole group?" He turned to the other guards who had accompanied him. "Dismissed," he said curtly. The guards left and the tension in the room eased.

"Mr. Linder, please accept my apologies. This won't happen again," Swenson said quietly to Paul. He turned to Resa. "Is there anything I can do for you while I'm here, Dr. Myles?" he asked.

Resa had not expected Swenson to react the way he did, and she felt an enormous relief. For a few moments, she had thought the situation would lead to open conflict, but Swenson's quick intervention had prevented that. "As a matter of fact, there is, but first I want to thank you for handling this problem the way you did."

Swenson shook his head. "It shouldn't have happened," he said. "What can I do for you?"

"We'll need some volunteers who are willing to have a new antidote tested on them—about fifty people who have had the vaccine."

Swenson stared at Resa in surprise. "You've found an antidote?" he asked, a mixture of joy and relief in his voice.

"Yes," Resa said. "I'm sure we have it now."

"Thank God," Swenson said.

Myles looked at him, puzzled. Why was Swenson reacting so strongly to the news? He had shown little interest in the researchers when they first arrived, and, in fact, had acted as if they were an annoying disruption to the rigidly supervised functions of the shelter. But now . . .

"My wife . . . ," Swenson said. "She took the vaccine on a shopping trip outside the shelter. I didn't know about it. She didn't even tell me when she started feeling ill, and now the doctors say she's dying. . . . Without an antidote . . ." He shook his head. "There's no hope."

So that's it, Resa thought. She felt a rush of pity for this man, who had had his life so well organized, so secure, everything so neatly compartmented.

"It's not ready, yet," Resa said. "As soon as we have some, I'll certainly give it to your wife. But you understand it will be on a volunteer basis. . . . I am personally sure it will be effective. However, we have to test it. It's because I *am* so sure it will work that I've asked for human volunteers instead of using test animals for the first stage of testing. . . . Every minute counts. Too many people are dying all over the world."

Swenson's face had become pale and strained while Resa spoke. "When will it be ready?" he asked.

"It will probably take somewhere between twenty-four and forty-eight hours," Resa said.

A look of pain spread over Swenson's face. "That's too late," he said in a low voice. "She's dying now. . . ."

"Where is she?"

"In the hospital wing on Level 4," Swenson said slowly.

"Take me up there," Resa said. "Let's see how much time we have." There had been so much death. Here was a patient she could fight for. She was determined to do everything she could to save this woman.

Resa looked at the young woman lying in the hospital bed. The shelter physician had put her in the intensive care unit of the hospital wing, and Resa saw that the latest monitoring equipment was being used to track her condition.

A nurse standing by Resa's side handed her a chart containing a record of the woman's treatment and results of laboratory tests. It was a classic case of the syndrome in its final stages.

The doctors had been keeping her alive by treating the symptoms the virus produced in the body. Blood transfusions had been given liberally in an attempt to dilute the virus in her blood stream.

Resa examined her carefully. She was in a deep comatose state, and all of the vital processes were depressed markedly. She estimated the patient couldn't last more than about eight hours.

She stepped back from the bed and stared at the monitors on the wall that were recording the woman's vital parameters. Her mind was racing. Time. Just one more day.

There was only one way to wash enough of the toxic virus out of her blood stream to give her the time she needed—a total blood replacement. In medical terminology it was called an asanguineous hypothermic total body perfusion.

The procedure was a dangerous one; it required that the body be cooled to as low as 25 degrees Centigrade, and for a period of time the patient became clinically dead—with no heartbeat, no apparent brain activity. But without the blood replacement she didn't have a chance.

She turned to Swenson, who had been watching her with anxious eyes during the examination. "Can anything be done to help her?" he asked quietly.

"The only way we can keep her alive until the antidote is ready is to remove all her blood, wash out the circulatory system, and replace her blood with fresh whole blood. It's dangerous." Resa explained the details of the procedure to Swenson in simple terms. "It's a controversial procedure that was developed from cryonics studies. Dr. Schiller on my staff has done this type of replacement before. . . . I think she has a chance to make it, but it will have to be done immediately—she's getting weaker every minute."

Swenson looked once at the still figure lying on the bed, and then met Resa's steady gaze. He nodded. "Do it," he said in a low, choked voice.

Resa turned to the nurse. "Notify Dr. Schiller to prepare for a stat total blood replacement, and then get the patient ready for surgery. . . . We'll need a lot of blood."

"I'll check the supply of her type in the blood bank, Dr. Myles—if it's short we can use the computer files to locate donors in the shelter immediately." The nurse left, and Swenson turned to Resa. "Could I stay with her? I mean, during the surgery?"

"Yes, of course. I'm sure there's a gallery in the operating theater here."

The nurse nodded at Resa's unspoken question. "One of the nurses will take you over there, and I'll join you as soon as I can."

RESA WENT TO the communications room and had a call put through to Blair in Washington. The lack of her own telephone and the privacy in which to use it annoyed her, but there was nothing she could do about it—at least not for the present.

"Your call is ready, ma'am," the technician said.

Resa took the phone. "Dave?"

"Yes, Resa. Is anything wrong?" Blair's voice came clearly over the line.

"No," Resa replied. "Just the opposite. We've licked the problem, and are synthesizing the first batch of the antidote now."

"Thank God!" Blair said. "When will it be ready?"

"At least one full day, maybe two."

"I'll pass the news along to the president. . . . Resa, I can't tell you how glad I am about this. We're in the middle of a crisis here. I don't know how it will turn out, but your news may be an important factor in the decision. I'll get back to you as soon as I can, but it may be a while."

Resa could hear a note of strain in Blair's voice.

Now what's going on? she thought. "Do you want me there in Washington? I could leave here now, . . . everything is under control."

"No!" Blair's reply was sharp. "Sorry, Resa. I can't explain, but it's very important that you do *not* leave the shelter until you hear from me—personally. Only on my word, Resa, no messages."

Resa replied slowly, cursing the lack of privacy that prevented open conversation. "All right, Dave. I understand."

But she didn't.

She handed the phone back to the technician, who had pointedly made a show of not listening to the conversation. The whole damn thing is probably recorded, Resa thought.

She left the room in an uneasy frame of mind, and it was only with effort that she put this new worry aside as she went back to the research area to check on the synthesizing in process.

WHEN RESA JOINED Swenson and the other observers in the gallery, the surgical team was already on the floor and working on the patient. Myles saw that Swenson's hands were gripped together rigidly, his knuckles white from the tense pressure. Resa began to speak to him quietly, explaining the precise, efficient movements of the surgical team, which she knew were confusing, even frightening to an uninitiated observer, and especially so when it was a loved one's life that was dependent on the skill of others. Resa knew well the frustration of that helpless feeling and could sympathize with it.

"The anesthesiologist," Resa said, "has inserted an intratracheal tube into your wife's windpipe through which he can control her breathing should it become necessary." Resa saw that the bag on the anesthetic machine was filling and emptying at an even rate. "He'll be giving her oxygen right now because, since she's in a deep coma, a general anesthetic won't be needed."

"Won't she feel the surgery?" Swenson asked.

"No. The surgeon will inject a local anesthetic before he inserts the catheters that get hooked up to the heart-lung machine. Right now the team is inserting the electronic devices to measure her vital parameters. Look at the monitors on the wall," Myles said. "Those small catheters in her arm are measuring the blood gases and pressure you see on the monitors. The anesthesiologist has already inserted an electronic thermometer into her esophagus to measure temperature; usually, there's a small microphone with it that picks up the heart sounds. They'll probably turn up the volume when surgery starts. Those lines on the monitors are the standard electroencephalograph and electrocardiograph tracings that are used to measure brain and heart activity."

The surgical team was draping the patient with sterile sheets until she was completely covered, except for the two small windows at the neck and groin where the surgery would be performed to connect the catheters necessary for the total blood replacement.

"I think they're ready to start now," Resa said. "This whole procedure was developed from cryogenic studies and, believe it or not, longevity studies. In fact, the Lackland Air Force Medical Center has a total-body washout machine, or at least they used to."

The volume on the cardioscope was turned up and the familiar sound of a heartbeat echoed from its speakers throughout the operating theater and gallery. Working through the window openings in the drapes covering the woman, Schiller injected xylocaine into her lower neck and groin. Then he made about a small incision in the groin, laying open the skin and subcutaneous tissue to expose the femoral artery that lay beside the vein.

An assistant surgeon that Resa could not recognize beneath the mask and gown, had moved to the head of the table and was exposing the jugular vein which would also be connected to one of the catheters from the heart-lung pump.

The assistant nodded. "Ready here."

Schiller threaded the two catheters into the femoral artery and vein and then clamped them off while the assistant performed the same procedure on the jugular vein; then the three catheters were quickly connected to the heart-lung pump. Schiller looked at the monitor on the wall, making a final check on the patient's condition before starting the replacement.

Resa, too, glanced at the monitors. "You'll see a drastic change in the parameters when they start the procedure," she said to Swenson.

On the operating floor, Schiller spoke: "We're good to go. Start the pump."

A technician switched on the special heart-lung pump and the patient's virus-laden blood began to fill the empty reservoir in the machine—on the monitors, the blood pressure readings began to drop.

The special heart-lung pump used for a total blood replacement was a variation of the standard heart-lung pump used in open-heart surgery. In addition to the empty reservoir into which the patient's blood was being drained, the pump contained two other reservoirs encased in heavily insulated, temperature-controlled units.

One contained an oxygen-carrying solution to which small amounts of heparin and dicumerol had been added to prevent blood clotting, the other held the donor's blood. The clear solution would actually serve as a substitute for the patient's blood during the washing-out phase of the procedure. The temperature of the solution was held at around 5 degrees Centigrade—very close to freezing.

This ice-cold liquid was now flowing into the patient's body through the catheter in the femoral artery while her own toxic blood was pouring out through the catheters in the jugular and femoral veins.

On the monitors, Resa saw the body temperature reading begin to fall, and at the same time the pulse and ECG readings bounded ahead. "Her heart is beating very rapidly now," she explained, "trying to pump more oxygen to the cells, but the refrigerated solution is slowing the metabolism and oxygen use by the cells to as close to zero as possible. This deep hypothermia is important so that no cell damage results from lack of oxygen—especially in the brain cells— while the circulatory system is being washed out."

Resa noted that the woman's esophageal temperature was at 25 degrees Centigrade. "Very soon now you'll see that her heart will stop. This is the most critical stage of the procedure," she said. "The washout and replenishment of blood must be completed quickly then because there is a limit to the time the body can be without oxygen, even at this low temperature."

"How long?" asked Swenson, his face pale and strained.

"Nine minutes is the maximum limit known to be safe at these low temperatures, so far," Resa replied. She looked at the monitors: esophageal temperature, 20° C; rectal, 22°C. The solution leaving the body was almost clear, which meant that as much of the circulating blood as possible had been removed.

The anesthesiologist announced calmly, "Patient is asystolic."

On the monitor screen, the EEG and ECG tracings were flat. The patient was clinically dead.

"Increase the pump rate," Schiller ordered.

Resa watched the counter on the wall; it was recording the elapsed time since asystole. The minutes moved by slowly, tensely. In the quiet room, the hum of the pump seemed overloud. It had taken over the heart's function and was pumping the almost clear, ice-cold solution through the patient's body.

Swenson put his head in his hands and drew a deep breath.

"Dr. Schiller is trying to give her the best chance by washing out the largest possible amount of the toxic blood," Resa explained.

"Five minutes since asystole," the anesthesiologist announced.

Schiller looked at the solution flowing out of the catheter from the jugular and femoral veins: it was now clear. "Lower pump rate," he said. "Start blood replacement."

The technician monitoring the complex heart-lung pump turned the bypass valve that sent heated blood and packed red cells though the catheter inserted in the woman's femoral artery.

"This fresh blood has been warmed, relatively speaking," Resa said to Swenson, "and you'll see that the temperature readings on the monitors start to reflect the rise in body temperature very quickly. The blood is being oxygenated by the pump, and also some carbon dioxide has been added to the oxygen concentration to stimulate spontaneous respiration."

"Carbon dioxide?" Swenson asked.

"Yes. It's a respiratory stimulant." Resa smiled. Many people found that difficult to understand, because most laymen knew that one exhaled carbon dioxide in breathing, and they couldn't make the association between that process and respiratory stimulation.

"Adjust flow rate to 2400 milliliters per minute," Schiller said. "Close the system."

Swenson looked at Resa. "Why is he slowing it down?"

"That's the flow that is closest to the normal output of the heart," she explained. "They'll leave it at that rate now. All of the clear solution has been pumped out. You can see that blood is in the catheters carrying the flow back to the heart-lung pump. The system is closed and the machine is acting in place of your wife's heart and lungs."

"But how will they get her heart beating again?" Swenson asked in an unsteady voice.

"It should be spontaneous," Resa said. "Any time now." She was watching the ECG monitor on the wall, as was everyone else in the room.

"Six minutes since asystole," the anesthesiologist said.

"Step up the heating rate a little," Schiller ordered.

Resa kept her eyes on the ECG monitor that still showed only a tiny point of light moving across the screen. The EEG showed no sign yet of brain waves.

"Look!" Resa said to Swenson. On the ECG monitor, a small P-wave appeared indicating the start of a beat within the heart as the electrical pulses spread through the cells of the atria, or collecting chambers of the heart. "Her heart is trying to start."

"Stand by with the pacemaker," Schiller said.

"That's a precaution in case the heart doesn't start beating properly of its own accord," Resa explained. "They'll use it to apply an electrical stimulation."

"Seven minutes since asystole," the anesthesiologist said, and then added: "Spontaneous respiration established. Arterial pO_2 rising."

The monitors came to life. The EEG monitor showed the slow brain waves of a patient in coma; and on the ECG screen, the high spike of the QRS-wave that meant the ventricles of the heart were pumping appeared, followed by a normal, small T-wave.

"She made it," Resa said. She looked at the counter on the wall. "Seven minutes and ten seconds," she said, "that's well under the nine-minute maximum."

"Then she'll be all right?" Swenson asked, his voice filled with relief.

"From the blood replacement, absolutely. But we haven't stopped the toxic effects of the virus. It's still in her cells. We've just bought time for her with this fresh blood supply to help her body fight the virus," Resa said. "Now we need to get the antidote into her as soon as it's ready.

Swenson nodded and looked back down at the operating theater. He saw that the two surgeons were removing the catheters and closing the incisions. Glancing at the monitors, he was reassured that they were all registering some kind of readings, even though he couldn't interpret them. She was alive now and she had been dead for seven minutes. He remembered the helpless terror he had felt during that time, and turned to thank Resa for standing by, for helping him through those long minutes, but she had already left the gallery.

THE WASHINGTON POST—

VICE PRESIDENT'S FAMILY
SUCCUMBS TO DEADLY SYNDROME

Diana Grayson, age 37, wife of Vice President Theodore Grayson, and Jeffery Grayson, age 12, son of the vice president, died early this morning from complications caused by Project Immunity cancer immunizations.

Theodore Grayson is listed as in critical condition at the Walter Reed Army Hospital. He, too, was a recipient of the cancer immunizations.

Chapter 19

Washington, D.C.

CONDITION RED.

At Strategic Air Command bases, long-range B2 Stealth bombers streaked into the air and headed toward preselected fail-safe points, their bomb bays loaded with Peacekeeper missiles.

All of the Peacekeeper ICBMs were MIRVed, that is, they contained multiple independently targeted reentry vehicles, which made it possible for each single missile to drop many bombs at different targets.

Deep under the oceans, Ohio-class ballistic missile submarines made their way to predetermined points. Each of the submarines carried sixteen Trident III nuclear missiles. These missiles, too, were

216

tipped with MIRVed warheads; each missile carried up to fourteen individually targeted nuclear bombs.

While closer to home, all along the U.S. coastline, warships carrying the U.S. Navy's Aegis system moved to predetermined locations. The Aegis anti-missile defense systems featured the highly successful Standard Missile-6, and warships were deployed to protect Hawaii and Alaska as well as the mainland.

BLAIR STARED AT the large screen in the White House War Room. It was linked directly to the War Rooms in Omaha and the National Command Center in Washington. The entire defense system was controlled by a network of data processing units which, taken together, was the equivalent of several thousand of the largest commercial computers. The system was designed to handle simultaneously the myriad tasks required. It had to intercept radar signals; track incoming objects and eliminate false targets by distinguishing between warheads and decoys; predict trajectories; allocate and guide interceptor missiles, and arm and fire them if they got within range of a target; reject signals from earlier nuclear explosions; and coordinate the firing of defense missiles so they did not attack any of the Peacekeeper or Minuteman III missiles fired off at the enemy.

When the president had ordered a Condition Red, the offensive and defensive forces of the system had been triggered into a final state of readiness, awaiting only his go-ahead signal to attack.

Harland sat at one of the desks—with a red telephone before him—facing the large screen, and Blair stood a few paces behind him to one side. Although it was not outwardly apparent, Blair was too tense to sit quietly at one of the small desks. He had to be free to release some of that tension in movement, if only by walking a few paces. He was appalled that Harland had made no move to stop the upcoming war when he was told of the antidote being prepared at Survival Six.

On the screen was projected a large map of China. Blair's atten-

217

tion was focused on the central Asian mountain ranges, for it was there that the Chinese had excavated silos out of the rock in remote ravines to house their heavy nuclear missiles. They didn't have many—only about fifty or so ICBMs in the megaton range and a much larger number of smaller twenty-kiloton atomic bombs.

There was a brief sound of sharply in-drawn breaths in the silent room when the first wave of missiles appeared on the screen. Notations on the blips showed that the missiles were Chinese long range CSS-4 Mod 2s and the newer solid-fueled DF-31s.

The president picked up the red telephone and spoke to the commanding officer of the War Room. "This is the president, General Rogan. Start the attack." He put the phone back on the cradle and watched the screen.

Blair glanced at a CNN monitor and saw the words: America at War.

The rising Peacekeeper missiles were pinpoints of light, but Blair could picture the flaming boosters on the missiles. The most powerful of the stages in each rocket, the boosters burn for the shortest period of time but provide the most thrust. As the other stages ignited, burned, and dropped off, the missiles dispersed toward their preselected targets. Finally, the last stages dropped off and the reentry vehicles were flying in outer space, where they would be drawn back into the atmosphere by gravity toward their targets, . . . and the next wave of missiles appeared.

The map on the screen dissolved and an extended view of the Russian Federation and China appeared. The Russians had launched their antimissile missiles. The small blips of light rose swiftly toward the approaching Chinese missiles

An excited murmur ran through the group and low conversation broke out among some of the men.

"What is it?" Harland asked sharply.

One of the men pointed at the screen. "It's the Chinese missiles, Mr. President! Two of the ICBMs have burst at about fifty kilometers up."

Harland looked at the swollen blips on the screen. "Your point?"

"The Chinese have done it deliberately, sir. The bursting of a bomb in the megaton range at that height causes superheated temperatures from the nuclear explosion. It will disrupt the radar signals in the Russians' defense system—their ABM system will leak like a sieve. We call it a 'blackout,' sir. It will last about twenty minutes. By then, our first wave of missiles will be there."

Harland nodded and looked back at the screen. The swollen blips had appeared over Leningrad and Moscow.

"Enemy missiles picked up by PAR," one of the men seated at a computer console said sharply.

The screen dissolved and a projection of the North American continent appeared.

Now, Blair thought, the United States' ABM system would be tested. An updated version of the Nixon Safeguard ABM system was currently in use—its major components were a highly sophisticated radar system and the long- and short-range interceptor missiles. The sensitive perimeter acquisition radar (PAR) had picked up the enemy missile while it was still about 2,000 miles away from its target. And now the information had been fed into a bank of computers. In split seconds the computers calculated the speed, the trajectory, and the likely landing point of the enemy warhead. Immediately, this information was fed into a long-range ABM missile, which was fired off in the direction of the enemy missile.

"Target, Omaha," a technician announced. "Speed, two miles per second . . . Interceptor fired."

Blair watched the small blip blasting its way to meet the incoming enemy missile on the screen. The interceptor would explode in the face of the enemy ICBM and release a cloud of high-energy neutrons that would mess up the physics of the bomb inside the enemy missile. The enemy missile would be defused by the neutron bombardment and therefore would not explode . . . theoretically.

If the interceptor missed, smaller, short-range interceptors would be fired automatically by the defense system. The short-range missile could blast its way up at incredibly high speed toward enemy missiles that had been missed.

Blair began to lose track of the blips on the screen and the running commentary from the men at the consoles. Only the massive computer system could encompass the overall destruction without flinching.

"Moscow is out," one of the men commented. The computer eliminated Moscow as a potential target: it had ceased to exist as a parameter. And Blair knew the system would just as unfeelingly eliminate American cities or missile sites that no longer needed protection because of direct hits from enemy missiles.

Moscow is out—over seven million people. Blair thought of the chess players in Gorki Park, the students at the stately Tomonosov University, the museums, the theaters, the cathedrals . . .

THE WAR WAS over in a matter of hours after it started. The United States received only two hits, neither in a heavily populated area. Two of the Russian fractional orbital bombs had entered U.S. territory at an angle that the radar couldn't detect until it was too late. China had taken the brunt of the Russian retaliation: for all practical purposes it had ceased to exist. It was a radioactive wasteland.

The Russian Federation had sustained the equivalent of 1,200 one-megaton warheads: total population fatalities were 109 million, about 44 percent; industrial capacity destroyed was 77 percent. An assistant explained to the president that only one-third that amount of warheads—400-one-megaton equivalents—would have produced about the same result by destroying 76 percent of Russia's industrial capacity, which was only 1 percent less. And then there would have been only 30 percent instead of the 44 percent fatalities in the Soviet population—a difference of about 35 million people.

"It's an 'over kill', sir," the assistant said.

Harland listened impassively to the explanation. Then he rose and studied the huge screen for a moment longer before signaling Blair to accompany him from the room.

CNN NEWS SPECIAL— AMERICA AT WAR

The United States joined with China today in a brief but devastating attack on the Russian Federation. The Russians have known for some time that the cancer vaccine being distributed worldwide was deadly. They kept this secret from the rest of the world.

The vaccine that they had been stockpiling was sent to China as a deliberate act of war; it was sent to destroy that country. The immunizations the Russian people were given were just sterile water.

As Commander-in-Chief of the armed forces, President Harland reacted to this aggressive act by joining China in launching a retalia- tory strike against the Russian Federation. That country has ceased to exist. And China has ceased to exist. The U.S. sustained only two mi- nor hits in the action, one in the mid-west, the other in the south.

Chapter 20

Survival Six Underground Shelter, Nevada

AT SURVIVAL SIX, Resa's scientific staff had synthesized the new antidote in just over twenty hours. They had been told of the brief, violent war that for a few hours had raged through the skies, but the incredulous shock had passed quickly. Inside the shelter, they were deep within the earth, shielded by a massive range of mountains, cut off from the outside world. Here, the insanity above them was ignored.

In the intensive care unit of the hospital wing, Resa stood at the bedside of Swenson's wife. She was by far the most critically ill of the fifty-odd volunteers on whom the new vaccine was being tested. Swenson looked up when Resa and one of the nurses came in.

"There doesn't seem to be any change," he said quietly.

Resa nodded. She hadn't expected any apparent change yet; it had only been an hour since the woman had received the injection. "It's too early," she assured him. "I'm going to take a blood sample. That will tell us what's going on."

She strapped a tourniquet around the patients arm above the elbow, and then stroked her forearm upward from the wrist to raise the blood vessels. Anchoring the vein with her thumb so that it would not roll, she slid the needle deftly into the vein and drew out a small amount of blood. Then she released the tourniquet and withdrew the needle, pressing firmly on the vein with a cotton ball to stop any bleeding. She handed the blood sample to the nurse. "Mark this for a stat analysis," she said.

She took the patient's chart and compared the readings of her vital signs taken over the last hour with the current readings on the wall monitors. "Her fever is starting to drop a little. . . . Give it some time," she said to Swenson. "She has a good chance."

Swenson looked at her and smiled. "You were right before—about the blood replacement."

Resa nodded, remembering Swenson's joyous relief when his wife had emerged from the deep coma about eight hours after the total blood replacement. But since then the virus in her cells had slowly overcome her new resistance, and she was once more deep in coma.

"I'll check back later," Resa said as she turned toward the door. "Now I want to see what the blood studies show."

"Dr. Myles." Swenson's voice stopped Resa at the door.

"Yes?"

"Thank you," Swenson said quietly, "for everything."

Resa nodded and closed the door behind her. She was always a little embarrassed when patients or their relatives expressed gratitude to her, but she tried not to show it. She could remember her own dismay, when as a young student she had thanked a professor who had given her a great deal of his own time helping with a project, and the man had protested vigorously that it was nothing. In retrospect, she understood the professor's reaction.

THE MOLECULAR STRUCTURES of the DNA and RNA viruses in the blood cells taken from Swenson's wife were projected by the computer on a large wall screen in the shelter's electron microscopy lab. Resa and Mark Ashton studied the glowing structures carefully: molecules of simple sugars and phosphates formed the twisting spirals of the helix, which were connected with rungs formed by different combinations of the nitrogen compounds—adenine, thymine, guanine, cytosine, . . . and in the single-strand RNA molecules, the uracil base stood in place of the thymine. Resa began enlarging specific areas of the molecules for closer study.

"Look there," she said. "The benign virus has formed. It's working, Mark!"

"You're damned right it's working!" Ashton gloated. "That's it!" He grinned broadly. "Full production on the antidote?"

"The sooner the better," Resa replied with a wide smile.

Several hours later, she was collecting the lunch dishes from the dining table in her quarters moving carefully so that she didn't step on Isis, who was twining her way between Resa's legs. She dropped the dishes into the disposal chute with a small frown. "I'm just not cut out for this style of future living," she said to Paul. "One standard menu with no variations . . ." She shook her head, and then laughed. "I mentioned it to Swenson, in passing, and he's so elated over his wife's recovery he said he'd have whatever dishes we'd like added to the menu."

"Is she all right, then?" Paul asked, referring to Swenson's wife.

"She came out of the coma a few hours ago." Resa replied, "and in a week or two she'll be up and around."

"That's good. I've never seen such a change in a man before. He was as hard as nails, and a stickler for—"

A sharp knock on the door cut him off. Resa opened it and saw

Blair and Carlson standing in the corridor.

"Dave!" Resa stared at the two men in surprise, and then said, "Come on in. When did you two get here?"

"Just now," Blair replied. "Carlson flew me in from Washington in a military jet. I think he set a new speed record."

"You know Paul Linder, my brother-in-law," Resa said.

Blair shook hands with Paul. "Good to see you again, Paul."

"Please, sit down," Resa said.

Resa noticed that Blair was dressed in a suit and Carlson in uniform. Somehow they had bypassed the standard entry procedures, but she didn't question them about it. Blair's face looked tired and strained, and Resa knew that whatever had brought the two men to the shelter was too important to waste time on trivial questions.

"I'm glad you're both here," Blair said, including Paul in his glance. "It will save a little time . . . and we don't have much left." He took a deep breath. "I don't know where to start. There's so much to talk about, so many decisions to make.

"You heard about the nuclear war," he said.

Resa nodded. "What happened there, Dave?"

"The Russians found out somehow that the Stanford vaccine was deadly for healthy people. They sat on the information and sent their supply of the vaccine to China. For their own people, they used shots of sterile water. . . . They gambled and lost," he said heavily. "And millions of people have paid for it."

There was silence in the room, and then Resa spoke: "We have the antidote, Dave."

"I know. I told Harland, thinking it might stop him from going to all-out war, but I couldn't sway him one inch." Blair frowned, remembering Harland's brusque refusal to consider any other course of action, his outright lies to the Chinese prime minister. "Well, that's done and can't be changed. It's where we go from here that has me worried." Blair looked at Resa soberly.

"Resa," he said. "President Harland has you on his enemies list.

. . . I've seen the list. Everyone who has ever opposed him is on it. He's using the CIA to track these people."

Resa was silent.

"It sounds insane," Paul said quietly, a thread of anger in his voice.

Blair nodded. "I've had the same thought. But it is true . . . and it's what we have to deal with."

"What do we do, Dave?" Resa asked, a cold anger underlying her words.

"Now that the antidote is ready, we'll have to get you out of here. Harland won't need you when the tests on the volunteers are completed. I'm here now with his sanction, checking on the progress of the tests. . . . I mentioned casually that if this antidote didn't work, a crash program would have to be instituted to find another one that would work. So, until the tests are judged successful, you should be safe."

"But we know they're successful," Resa said.

Blair nodded. "Swenson told me on the way in. I asked him to leave that information out of any reports for the present. I'm not worried about getting you out of the shelter itself. There's some risk involved, but the greater problem is finding somewhere to send you that's safe—both of you. Can you think of a place?"

"It should be somewhere isolated," Carlson put in.

"The cabin," Paul said promptly. "Mac's cabin up near Lake Tahoe."

"Yes, that would be perfect," Resa said. "There's a food supply for months there, and the place has its own generator and water supply." Resa thought hard for a minute. "Mac always hired someone to plow out the private road to the place, but the whole area will be deserted now. Everyone has headed to the cities for medical help. We wouldn't be able to get in to the cabin now."

"Is there room for a helicopter to land?" Carlson asked.

"Yes. There's room at the Squaw Valley ski resort just over the mountain. But where are we going to get a helicopter?"

"You're going to steal one," Carlson replied. "And Paul is going to fly it."

"Well, I can fly one," Paul said dryly. "And I won't even ask how you knew."

Carlson laughed softly. "No mystery," he said. "Schaeffer mentioned it. You let it slip when you two were discussing flying."

"All right, it's settled," Blair said. "Now for the next problem. Resa, is there enough information in the computer here about how to make this antidote? Did your people keep records of some kind?"

"Well, there's some information entered into the computer but not really enough for anyone to synthesize the new protein blockers."

Blair leaned forward, "Could you put that information in?"

"Certainly . . . I would probably do it sooner or later anyway. When all of the research centers were tied into the CCA line, it was done routinely." She frowned. "What are you getting at, Dave? As soon as the news of the antidote is released, every laboratory in the country will have to start synthesizing the vaccine. Time is critical. The Stanford vaccine went out on a worldwide scale, don't forget. By now, a significant percent of the world's population is dead, and that will keep mounting. Risk or no risk—it has to be announced."

"I know, Resa," Blair said quietly. "I know." He met her angry eyes. "It will be announced. I promise you that. I'm just trying to find the best way to let the whole world know about it."

"I don't understand the problem," Resa said.

"Harland is the problem," Blair said heavily. "He's created a special group that he calls the National Security Force. They're responsible to him only, and have powers that supersede all existing civil and military authority. They are Harland's special police force, to put it simply. He has indicated that they will handle the dispersal of the new vaccine. You can be sure his enemies—real or imagined—will not get any, and neither will the old, the handicapped, those who oppose his regime, nor other countries that refuse to meet his demands."

"He must be stopped," Resa said angrily. "You've just described a tyrant, Dave!"

"Obviously, he's insane," Paul said coldly. "Have him removed from office. For God's sake, the country's in enough of a mess without this."

"It's not that easy," Blair said slowly.

"You're forgetting one thing," Carlson said to Resa and Paul. "We're still under martial law. We can't touch Harland. Also, he's moved people that are loyal to him into key positions. Dave has been giving you the inside information. Harland presents a sane, controlled, strong appearance in public. The steps he has taken so far, on the surface, are not alarming to those who don't look ahead. For example, the National Security Force has been played down to sound like a National Guard group. . . . The sick are concerned only with staying alive, right now. And those who are still healthy are doing the work of many to keep things going. Politics is the furthest thing from their minds." He shook his head. "Harland is only taking the preliminary steps for complete control now. This new vaccine will be an important weapon for him."

"When the people know of the cure, no damned Security Force will be able to keep it from them," Resa asserted.

"I agree," said Blair. "That's why we have to make sure the news does get out—worldwide—plus the technical information necessary to synthesize the antidote. Harland's group isn't strong enough to control all the laboratories in the country, or the whole world, for that matter. I thought of trying to use the research centers in some way, but that's really not on a broad enough scale."

"What about radio and television?" Resa asked. "And at the very least, scientists. In fact, I'm sure my people have a number of key contacts in the scientific world, and we should e-mail the information to all of them as well. Let's do everything."

"The communication networks were the first things he secured." Blair said "It was done under the guise of censoring news that would proliferate the riots and panic."

"Oh, my God," Resa murmured.

"I'll find a way to stop him. It will take time to organize some responsible government officials. I've already started that, but I need a week or two more. And the sick can't wait that long."

The room grew quiet. Paul had been listening intently to the conversation . . . and a man listening could think far faster than one engaged in talking. "I have a solution to your problem," he said quietly. The others gave him their full attention while he outlined his plan. "We'll just bypass the standard communication methods and use the satellite network. Resa will prepare a presentation of the information, and I'll use it to program the satellite network to broadcast her message worldwide at fixed intervals. All of the equipment I need is at the lab in Los Gatos. I worked there on the design for Echostar 14, and I'm sure I can program the satellite to relay the message to Intelsat. That's still the biggest worldwide satellite communication network, and I'll relay to some of the European and private satellites as well. Also, I think I know of a way to fix it so that no one can stop the broadcast from Echostar—at least not for a week or so."

"You mean that no one will be able to cancel it?" Blair asked, a broad smile on his face. This was more than he had hoped to achieve.

"That's right," Paul said. "I can foul up the command module enough so it will take a week or so to sort it out, unless they blast all the satellites out of the sky."

"I don't think Harland will go that far," Blair said. "He'll need the satellite network himself, but I'll try to steer his thinking away from the idea."

"If you have to get in the lab at Los Gatos, we should try to pick up the helicopter we need somewhere near there," Resa said thoughtfully.

"How about the San Jose airport?" Paul asked.

Resa shook her head. "That will be heavily guarded; it's an international airport." Then she smiled. "The Research Center," she

229

said. "There's the heliport on the roof. . . . Some of our people are bound to be there, and we can leave a supply of the vaccine with them so they can start administering it right away."

She turned to Blair. "Dave, the vaccine has to go out."

"Didn't you use all you had on the volunteers for the tests?" Blair asked in a shocked voice.

"No, only a small amount of the first batch was used, and we're in mass production right now. The equipment here is top of the line." She glanced at her watch. "In about eighteen hours there will be new batches ready about every four hours. We're putting the new stuff through on a staggered production rate."

"You'll be leaving here before then," Blair said. "Give me part of what you have right now. It's urgent. The vice president is in critical condition and he's one of those officials I told you I'm counting on."

"Right," Resa said. She picked up the phone. "Page Mark Ashton, please."

The reply came quickly. "Ashton, here."

"Mark, this is Resa. How are the latest cell studies on the volunteers holding?"

"They're excellent."

"Good. Listen, package up the vaccine we have on hand as fast as you can. I'll send someone over. Keep it quiet, if any of the guards are around."

As she finished speaking, Paul rose and went to the door. "I'll get it," he said.

While Resa was on the phone, Blair had been conversing in low tones with Carlson. "Resa, Carlson will fly the vaccine to Washington—the vice president is in the Walter Reed Army Hospital—then he'll come back here and pick me up."

Resa nodded. "Do you have a contact there you can trust?'

"Yes, the Chief of Surgery."

"While the supply is limited," Resa said, "only those that are critical should be given the injections."

"We'll have to make that clear, but it would be safer not to put anything in writing," Blair remarked.

"Safe isn't an option. It doesn't matter now. I can explain to Carlson how the antidote should be given and he can pass it along, but written instructions should also be included," she suggested. Blair nodded and Resa turned to Carlson. "You'll have five 100-cc vials. That's enough for 1,000 injections; the dose is 0.5 cc. If your man at Walter Reed has any contacts with other hospitals in the area, tell him to send some of the vials out. It's important that the patients who are on the critical list get the vaccine first."

"I'm sure he'll agree with that," Carlson said. "No problem."

Paul returned, carrying a small package. Resa scribbling instructions rapidly on a piece of paper, folded it into the package and handed it to Carlson. "Here. Good luck."

"Wait," Blair said. "Are you giving him all of it?"

"Yes." Her voice was firm. "I'm waiting for the next batch. We can't leave right now anyway, Dave. I have to prepare the presentation and we have to get foreign language subtitles added to it—at least key languages like French, Spanish, Japanese. And I want to take as large an amount of the antidote as I can out with me."

"I don't like it. Harland could put an order out for your arrest at any time. He's unpredictable." But Resa wasn't budging, Blair thought, recognizing the stubborn set to her jaw.

"Dave, we have to arrive in the Los Gatos area in the evening, after normal working hours, so Paul can get into the lab and use the equipment without being stopped. The evening hours are the only plausible time. We really have no choice in the matter. I'm not sure exactly where we are, but it will take some time to get back to Los Gatos." She glanced at her watch. "It's too late to make it by this evening—and the vaccine we have here is needed now."

"Well," Blair said slowly, "You're quite right. My feeling of urgency is overwhelming my good sense. You've put the problem in perspective very neatly. By the way, you're in Nevada. An ideal place for the shelter. The state has a small population yet it's fairly near

231

the heavily populated California area. Carlson will give Paul exact directions tomorrow." He nodded to Carlson, who took the small, precious package containing the antidote and left. "See you in about eight hours or less," Carlson said.

"Now," Resa said, "we have to get busy. I'll get started on the presentation."

"We'll need a digital camera," Paul said. "I'll round one up, and then I'll get over to data processing and get some of the crew started on entering the vaccine data into the computer. Do you want to be able to trigger printout at the research centers from here instead of having it accessed?" Paul asked Blair.

"Yes. That would be excellent. I'll have to see Swenson and bring him up to date on what's going on," Blair said. "Let's split up now and we'll get together in the morning and see where we stand."

AT WALTER REED Army Hospital, the young vice president stirred restlessly and opened his eyes. He had some difficulty focusing on the white-coated figure bending over his bed, and then his vision cleared and he recognized the doctor, who was swabbing his arm with something cold. A sharp sting . . . the doctor was saying something. He couldn't understand him. It didn't matter. They always said the same thing: "This will help you." But he knew he was dying, . . . and he felt regret for all the bright plans there would never be enough time to accomplish. Harland wouldn't have to worry now, he thought. How the president had hated his interference. . . .

REUTERS, GENEVA—

A SPOKESMAN FOR THE GENEVA-BASED WORLD HEALTH ORGANIZATION (WHO) ISSUED A WARNING TODAY THAT DANGEROUS LEVELS OF RADIATION ARE SWEEPING ACROSS EUROPE FROM THE NUCLEAR DEVASTATION IN RUSSIA AND ACROSS THE PACIFIC RIM FROM FALLOUT IN CHINA.

AUTHORITIES WERE URGED TO WARN CITIZENS IN DANGER AREAS TO KEEP INSIDE THEIR HOMES. THE RED CROSS AND OTHER ORGANIZATIONS ARE SENDING TEAMS INTO THE AREA TO ASSIST SURVIVORS.

Chapter 21

Survival Six Underground Shelter, Nevada

ROSTOV HAD LOST sight of Resa Myles for a short time when she disappeared into the Moffet Field Naval Base, but soon tracked her to the underground facility in Nevada. He was camped nearby, his plans complete. He was ready to infiltrate the heavily guarded shelter when word reached him about the war that had devastated Russia.

That blow had almost unnerved him.

There was no purpose to his mission now. He had failed. For the first time he was cut off completely from his superiors. Only with great difficulty could he control his emotions; the hate, the anger, the bitterness threatened to overcome him. Revenge was the only option available to him now. But how to take it?

It didn't matter anymore if Myles found an antidote to the Project Immunity syndrome. He had underestimated her more than once. An image of her fighting her way through the mob at the Research Center flashed through his mind. He almost smiled. She had been a worthy opponent. She was not weak as he had first surmised. I think she would have made a good Russian, he thought. Intelligent, resourceful, strong. He allowed a small trickle of respect for the woman to enter his mind. But if he killed her, he would be stopping any aid she would give to her country. She was a resource whose loss would be devastating to America.

And then his thoughts went to the man who had instigated the war that destroyed Russia—President Harland. He did not deserve to live. The idea of Harland enjoying his victory was abhorrent to Rostov. Harland had to pay for what he did. Harland must die. There was no doubt of that.

He felt calmer now. The only decision left for him to make was whether to kill Harland alone. Or whether it would be better to kill both of them, Myles in addition to Harland.

THERE WAS NO warm morning sunlight to awaken her. We're like moles, Resa thought as she reached to shut off the alarm clock before it rang. She knew it was morning only because the hands of the clock told her it was—the room was dark and silent. She had never before realized the variety of muted sounds that had penetrated the walls of her house.

Here, in the shelter, the soundproofing was complete, the silence total, the darkness absolute. It was deeply comforting to have Isis leap up beside her and focus those beautiful leaf green eyes on her face. Isis broadcast a deep rumbling purr the minute Resa's hand touched her pale gray fur.

She had worked on the antidote speech until the late hours of the evening, and when she finally went to bed, she was exhausted.

She switched on the lights in the living room, adjusting the knob to the "daylight" setting, and winced at the blaze of artificial light that flooded the room. She reminded herself that this was her last day in the shelter: it helped stem the rising irritation she felt toward the place.

She decided that the presentation sounded good, as she listened critically to the technical descriptions. Paul had advised her to keep the message as brief as possible—about 30 minutes long, and it had taken some careful condensing to pack all the necessary information into it. She had had to presuppose a large degree of job knowledge on the part of those who would use the instructions. But that's all right, too, she thought. Anyone with lesser knowledge would be incapable of synthesizing the vaccine.

I think we're in business, she told herself. She went to the kitchen and fed Isis, and then made her breakfast selection. The meal was not leisurely. Uppermost in her mind was the escape planned for that afternoon, and she tended to eat hurriedly, almost distractedly. Isis would have to stay here at the shelter with Mac. Fortunately, the cat knew him well and liked him.

Now that the presentation was ready, she went to get some notes written to go with the vaccine they were taking out. She glanced at her watch. The new batch should be ready in a few hours.

Before she had finished with the instructions, Paul arrived, carrying a map. "Carlson is back from Washington," he said, "and we've worked out a flight plan that will keep us over isolated areas as much as possible." He took the coffee Resa handed him. "Thanks," he said. "I guess I forgot about breakfast."

"Well, that's not enough." Resa eyed the coffee she had given him. "You know better, Paul," she admonished mildly, and busied herself with ordering what she considered a proper breakfast, while Paul explained the flight plan to her.

"Yes," Resa said, studying the map. "I think the Reid-Hillview airport in San Jose is a good idea. It's never very busy out there—it may even be deserted now—and it's fairly close to Los Gatos. I can head to Stanford by taking 101 and then 280 for a straight shot up there."

"And I'll stick to the side roads to the lab. I know this area well, so if any of the streets are blocked I can figure out a detour quite easily," Paul said.

He looked at the steaming dishes Resa was placing in front of him and smiled his thanks. "It's good, big sister," he said, tasting a large forkful of the scrambled eggs and minced ham. "The only problem we may have is getting a couple of decent cars without wasting a lot of time. I mentioned that to Blair and he said he'd see what he could do—"

A knock at the door cut him off. "That should be Blair and Carlson now," he said. "They said they'd meet us here."

Resa went to the door.

"Is the disk ready?" Paul asked.

"Yes. It might be a good idea if you listened to it," she said. "Then if you notice anything that should be changed, we can burn another one. We ended up repeating my presentation with voice-overs in the different languages. We've got a regular United Nations' kind of staff here. And I think it works better."

Paul nodded. "Sounds good. I'll listen to it.

Blair and Carlson sat down at the table, and Resa drew up an extra chair to join them.

"We have to leave shortly," Blair said. "I must be back in Washington when you make your escape so that Harland doesn't get suspicious." He paused. "Resa," he said slowly, "when Harland finds out you've slipped through his fingers, there'll be hell to pay. I'll have to go along with any orders he gives about recapturing you. . . . God knows what he'll do."

He sighed heavily. "The only way I have a chance to stop him is to stay in his favor. Then I'm free to use what authority I have to organize some official opposition to what he's doing. Otherwise, I'd have to go underground. And then it would take a lot longer." His eyes were pained as he made his careful explanation.

Resa knew that the deviousness Blair was describing was foreign to his basically straightforward nature, knew what it was costing him to work against a man he had once respected. "I understand, Dave," she said. "Do whatever you have to do. I can watch out for myself."

Her eyes locked with Blair's. "I've been thinking about the problem," she said carefully in a cold, determined voice. "I'll stay under cover for a few days—but that's all. That's time enough for the broadcasts to spread the news. And then I'm coming out." Her firm words brooked no argument. She had had her fill of hiding, of being ordered around, and this was as far as she would go to cooperate with Blair's plans.

For a moment, she thought Blair would continue to argue with her.

"All right," Blair said quietly.

BLAIR SIGHED IN defeat as Resa outlined her stance. This meant he would have to warn her about Rostov. He had hesitated to bring it up. It was an extra burden, and Blair knew it would revive the painful memories of her sister's violent death . . . but he had no choice now. Resa had to be warned. She'd be out in the open.

"Could you do anything about the cars we need?" Paul asked.

"Yes," Blair said. "Carlson explained your flight plan to me. Two cars will be waiting for you when you land at the Reid-Hillview airport. Agent Robert Martinez will meet you. He'll flash a light on and off, three times. Don't move out of the plane until you see the signal. He'll take the plane south and leave it at some out-of-the-way airport. I've left that up to him. It may buy some extra time for you."

"And danger for him," Resa objected.

Blair smiles. "He's used to that; he's one of our better CIA agents." He paused, and then said seriously, "A lot more lives depend on your getting the vaccine to the Research Center. And your own lives depend on getting the helicopter you need to reach the cabin at Tahoe."

Resa could not disagree with that point, and nodded her acquiescence.

"With Carlson's help," Blair went on quietly, "I've arranged for the vaccine produced here to be flown out by jet to hospitals in the larger cities. Carlson has a number of friends who say they have to get in their flying time. Swenson will cover for us at this end, but I don't know how long we'll be able to get away with it. Swenson isn't sure he can trust all the military staff here, so he'll be bluffing it out all the way."

"Whatever we can get out will help," Carlson said. "But the real necessity is to get production started all over the world." He looked at Resa. "And that is where you come in. With your reputation, the scientific community will listen to you. I'm sure we'll see some action when that video is broadcast."

"I hope you're right," Resa said. "That's what I'm counting on"

"Before we leave, there's something I have to tell you." Blair said. He thought for a moment. There was really no way to play down the danger Resa was in. He hated to bring this up. But she had to be warned. "When the trouble with Russia started, the CIA pulled in all known or suspected Russian agents, and they got some important information out of one of them. The agent confirmed that the Russians had landed Nicolai Rostov on the California coast—his mission was to stop you from either disrupting the immunization program or finding an antidote afterward."

Resa's jaw hardened. "Rostov," she said softly. "The name itself doesn't mean anything to me." But there was a plot to kill her, and that meant that Detective Brennan had been right after all. Resa looked quickly at Paul. His face had gone white.

"Where is he?" Paul's voice was cold and hollow.

Blair shook his head. "I don't know. There's been no trace of him. Taggert is sure he's still in the country, so until the news about the antidote gets out, we have to assume that Resa is still Rostov's target." He reached inside his jacket and drew out a photograph. "This is the best of the few photos we have of him. He has avoided having his picture taken and probably doesn't even know we have these."

Resa reached out for the picture and looked at it. "My God," she said softly. "There's no mistaking the cold eyes, the big-boned face, the hair thick and low on his forehead. It's Allan Sutherland. It's the man that was at Catherine's party," she whispered.

Paul took the picture with a trembling hand and stared at it; his face was white and rigid.

Blair looked in amazement at their reactions. "You know this man?" he asked incredulously.

Resa nodded, and remained silent for a moment. "We know him as Allan Sutherland," she said slowly. "A man named . . ." She wrinkled her brow, searching her memory for the name. "Shaughnessy. Jim Shaughnessy brought him to the party. They were both supposed to be writers. . . . I think Shaughnessy really is one—I've read some of his articles."

"Thank you, my dear," Blair said.

Paul stood up abruptly and left the room.

Blair moved to go after him, but Resa stopped him. "Let him go, Dave. He needs a few minutes alone. He'll be all right. . . . This Rostov alias Sutherland is the man Paul's been looking for."

"I'm sorry, Resa," Blair said quietly. "You had to be warned."

"I know that, Dave. I'm glad you told us." Now the enemy has a face. He's real. He's flesh and blood. No longer an intangible, nebulous threat. "Despite the danger, I'm relieved. It's always easier to know what you were fighting."

"I'll pass the information you gave me along to Taggert. Maybe it will help the CIA pick Rostov up," Blair said.

"It's worth a try," she said, and then smiled sardonically. "But if we meet him first, the CIA won't have to bother."

Blair studied the grim, determined look on Resa's face and thought, she means it. Even in the most civilized person, the veneer could be penetrated. Blair knew that Resa could kill this man who had made chaos of her life, without a qualm.

"When I talk to Taggert, I'll ask him to assign Steve Sheldon to help you and Paul. You know him and trust him."

"Yes. That would be wonderful, Dave. I've been worried about Steve. We haven't heard from him."

"Taggert has him tracking down Russian agents. The FBI can't handle all of it; a lot of their agents had the inoculations, so the CIA is pitching in domestically." He gripped her hand. "We have to leave now," he said quietly. "I'll try to have Steve connect with you at the Research Center. That's probably the best place. Good luck, Resa, and be careful. For God's sake, please be careful. We need you alive and well. On top of this deadly syndrome we have massive nuclear fallout over Europe and the Pacific Rim. We desperately need all of our scientists."

Resa nodded. "I know," she said softly. "I *will* try to be careful, but you know we're all in danger."

LATER THAT AFTERNOON, Paul went to Resa's quarters. "It's almost time to leave," he said quietly. "Swenson will be here in a few minutes. I've checked the disk, and I have it with me. And I talked to Mac. He's going to pick Isis up right after his shift is over so he can spend some time with her."

She nodded and closed the case containing the vaccine, which she had been giving a final check. "I'm ready here." She picked up Isis and cuddled her, scratching behind her pale gray ears. The cat's grass-green eyes closed in pleasure as she rumbled into a loud purr. "I have to leave, sweet girl," she whispered, "But I'll be back for you."

Paul met her gaze. "I'll fly you to the resort," he said firmly. "And then I'm leaving. . . . I want Rostov, Resa."

"I do too, Paul," Resa hedged, torn between her promise to Blair and her desire to go with Paul. "All right," she said heavily. It didn't matter whether she agreed or didn't agree. She knew Paul's

241

resolve was unyielding. She put Isis down on the couch.

Paul sensed the struggle in her mind. In a gentler tone he said, "I'll find a way to keep in touch with you. It may take a long time to find Rostov. I don't even know where to start looking . . . but I just can't wait." His eyes asked for understanding.

"I know, Paul." Resa gripped his shoulder. "I know the feeling well."

"Yes, and I'm glad to hear that. If anything happens to me before I get to Rostov, you'll have to do it, big sister."

"I promise. You can count on it." She held out her arms and hugged Paul tightly for a moment. "For Cathy," she whispered, her eyes filling with unshed tears.

Swenson knocked at the door and asked if they were ready to leave.

"We're ready." Resa blinked and pulled herself together with a deep breath. She took the case from the table and gave Isis one final loving stroke.

Swenson led them to the elevators and as they stepped in he said, "We're going directly to Level 1." He pressed a metal disk against a plate on the wall of the elevator. "This bypasses the locking mechanism that usually keeps the elevator from going above Level 2," he explained, while the elevator rose swiftly.

The doors snapped open and they stepped out into a suite of rooms similar to the living quarters on the lower levels, but more spacious. Resa saw two small piles of clothing, neatly stacked on a table.

"I decided hospital whites would be the best choice for you, Dr. Myles," Swenson said, "and for Mr. Linder there is a set of casual sportswear, since he will ostensibly be going into work. Everything you might need is there, including sets of fake identification cards." He turned to Paul. "Your wallet and genuine identification cards are there, as well. I thought you might need them to get into the laboratory."

"I will. Thanks," Paul said.

Resa took her clothes and went into the bedroom to change, but left the door open so she could hear Swenson. Paul dressed in the living room while Swenson continued his explanation. "Yesterday," he said, "I scheduled a flight out for two civilians. I'll take you to the plane so you won't be stopped and asked for passes. That way there's less chance that someone will recognize you. Don't worry about flight clearance—ask for it in the standard way. The flight controllers are with us. We were lucky there. It will make it a lot easier to get the vaccine out when Carlson's friends show up."

Resa came back into the room. "When is the first pickup?" she asked.

"In about three hours," Swenson said. "A Lieutenant named Schaeffer is supposed to pick it up."

"He'll be here," Paul said with a smile. "We've met him."

Swenson went to a closet and took out two coats—a deep blue fleece for Resa and a brown overcoat for Paul. "Put these on," he said. "It'll be cold on the outside. I'll take the case. We're going to retrace the same path we took when you came in."

He led them to the underground train. On the short, lightning-fast ride through the tunnel, they studied their new identity cards. Resa saw that Swenson had taken much of the information from their original papers, which would make it easier for them to remember their new identities.

"Don't rely too heavily on these fake papers," Swenson said. "When your broadcasts start, our brave-new-world president will send his hounds after you. They'll have your pictures and descriptions—a fake name won't deter them."

"We'll remember that," Resa said grimly. Running from the authorities was a new role for her, but she learned fast. What was fair, what was right, didn't really matter. She'd fight any way she had to in order to win.

The train stopped and they got into an electric car. Swenson drove them to the large hangar where they had first arrived. No one paid much attention to them. Casual looks were directed their way, but Swenson's familiar figure in the group lulled any suspicion before it was born. He drove directly to the small, single-engine plane, which stood on the platform that would raise them to the hangar above, and stopped the electric car.

Paul climbed into the plane, and Swenson handed him the case of vaccine, which Paul stowed carefully behind the seat. Then Swenson turned to assist Resa into the plane.

"Thank you for everything you've done to help us, Mr. Swenson," she said as he took her arm.

Swenson smiled. "It's my pleasure, Dr. Myles, believe me," he said. They shook hands and Resa climbed into the plane. Swenson held the door for a moment. "Take care," he said softly. "We have a whole world to rebuild." He shut the door and signaled to a technician at the control panel.

Resa looked out the window at Swenson as the plane rose slowly. His parting words, she thought, might have sounded emotional, even trite, from someone else's lips, but Swenson had spoken them as a quiet statement of fact. She raised her hand in an easy salute.

The lift stopped; the hangar doors were open and the afternoon sunlight poured through them. Paul put on the headset, started the engine, and called the shelter flight controller. "This is Alpha Charlie Six Niner Three, requesting clearance," he said.

"You are cleared for takeoff, Alpha Charlie," a deep voice replied promptly.

Paul taxied to the runway.

The plane seemed to lift into the air almost eagerly. Or is that just my imagination? Resa thought, as they climbed swiftly over the desert floor and left the small cluster of buildings behind.

IT WAS DARK when they reached the San Jose area. Paul circled the small Reid-Hillview airfield once and made his landing approach from the south. The airport seemed deserted. There were no lights on the field, but he had landed there before, and the nearby scattered lights would help guide him. He came in slowly over the large, dark shopping mall adjacent to the field.

Keep over the tall trees in the mall parking lot, he reminded himself. He saw their dark shapes rising in front of him and cleared their tops easily. Then he throttled back further as they went over the highway and dropped smoothly onto the runway.

Paul taxied toward the control tower and stopped. He left the engine running.

"There it is," Resa said as she saw a light flash three times.

Paul cut the engines. Quickly, they left the plane and went toward the man who had stepped out of the shadows of the building to meet them.

"Dr. Myles?" the man asked quietly as they approached.

"Yes."

"I'm Agent Robert Martinez. You better hurry. Someone may have heard the plane and decide to check on it. The two cars are here." He pointed to two late model cars parked next to the building. "The registrations under your assumed names are in the glove compartments. Keys are in the ignition," he said quickly.

Paul handed him the keys to the plane.

"Thanks," said Martinez. "I'll get that plane out of here now. Any questions?"

"No," Resa said. "We'll move right out after you take off."

"Good luck," Martinez said, and went quickly to the plane.

They watched him taxi down the runway and lift the small plane into a fast, steep climb.

"He can handle a plane," Paul commented, watching in admiration.

Resa turned to him. "Let's meet at the parking lot near the Medical Center, just to play it safe. I don't want to go into the Research Center without you," she said.

Paul nodded. "Absolutely. I'll be there. Wait for me. I don't know what I'll run into when I program the satellite. It may take a little longer than I've estimated."

They got into their cars and left the airport. Resa followed Paul the short distance to the Highway 101 entrance, and then flashed her headlights as she turned onto the freeway and headed north toward the 280 interchange.

I'll take it fairly slow up to Stanford, she thought. That will give Paul a little extra time to catch up with me and also lessen the chance of my being stopped. She took a deep breath, trying to relax.

Paul's mission was critical. The information had to get out to all the laboratories capable of creating the antidote, every minute counted. It would be next to impossible for her to actually relax until he rejoined her.

RADIO STATION KGSH (Palo Alto, CA)

"Mariah Mauney reporting live. This just in. We interrupt programming for a special announcement.

"Red Cross officials are asking for emergency supplies of food, water, and warm clothing, which will be airlifted to Red Cross centers being set up in civilian areas of the Russian Federation and China to aid survivors of the nuclear devastation.

"Please call this station for the location of drop-off centers."

Chapter 22

Los Gatos and Palo Alto, California

PAUL WALKED BRISKLY up the wide, paved walk to the double doors at the front of the long low building. Only the front doors were used after normal working hours, and through the heavy glass he could see the familiar figure of the security guard, Mike Conklin, sitting in one of the padded leather chairs, leafing through a magazine. He felt relieved. At least Mike hadn't been put out of action. In fact, the entire laboratory seemed unchanged.

The mercury vapor lamps illuminated the outside area brightly. The lawns were clipped and well-tended, and, in the distance, he could hear the automatic sprinklers watering the shrubs on the spacious grounds around the laboratory complex.

Paul stopped at the glass double doors and pressed the night bell. Conklin looked up and tossed his magazine aside. The elderly, white-haired man with his severely tailored gray uniform, his gleaming security badge, his holstered gun, looked incongruous in the flamboyant décor of the lobby, Paul mused. Here the decorator had gone all out to impress the visitors who rarely ventured into the clinic-like laboratories beyond the reception area, but frequently congregated in the front offices.

Paul pressed his badge against the door and Conklin, although he knew the younger man by sight and had passed him into the building many evenings, scrutinized the identity card carefully, nodded, and unlocked the doors.

"Hello, Mike." Paul smiled. "Has it been quiet around here?" he asked, as he signed the in/out sheet and carefully noted the exact time of his arrival. He knew Conklin always checked such minute details.

"Yeah. Been quiet. The trouble's out there," the guard replied laconically, nodding toward the doors. "They roam like packs of animals. . . . But I'm ready for them." He patted the holstered gun at his side. "You won't be bothered by them in here, sir. I'll see to that. Have to watch out for our best consultant." He grinned.

"Thanks. That's good to know, Mike," murmured Paul as he left the reception area, anxious to avoid a lengthy conversation the guard.

His footsteps echoed hollowly in the silent building as he walked down the brightly lit corridor toward the communications center. The room was empty. He let out his breath with a sigh of relief—unaware that he had been holding it, and opened the door. The countless hours he had spent here were paying off now, everything was in its familiar place, and he wasted no time locating what he needed. Moving quickly, he switched on the equipment: computer, transmitter, modulator, and then signed on with his system user's sign-on code:

M8SX42

He had hardly withdrawn his fingers from the keys when the system was actuated by the satellite's reply.

ON LINE AND READY FOR DATA

Paul smiled and typed:

ACTIVATE DIGITAL RECORDERS 1 AND 2
RECORD PROGRAM DATA
FILE NAME: ANTIDOTE PROJECT IMMUNITY

The answer appeared immediately.

READY TO RECEIVE DATA

Paul placed Resa's disk in the computer drive. He checked his watch and tried to still his impatience while the signals sped from the ground station to Echostar 14. The satellite was positioned over the Pacific Ocean some 22,300 miles deep in space where it remained "stationary," always over the same spot on the earth, rotating as the earth rotated . . . drawing power for its solar batteries directly from the sun.

PROGRAM DATA RECORDED

The message jarred Paul out of his reverie and into action. Quickly, he typed the words:

DEACTIVATE RECORDERS
ACTIVATE MEMORY FOR COMMAND DATA

On the screen, he saw:

MESSAGE ACKNOWLEDGED

He glanced at his watch. Resa had suggested having the broadcasts start at ten o'clock this evening if at all possible.

TRANSMIT RECORDED MESSAGE VIA AM/FM AND TELEVISION TRANSMITTERS STARTING 2200 AND REPEAT AT 0001 INTERVALS

The satellite replied:

MESSAGE ACKNOWLEDGED

"Now," Paul murmured. "Let's expand."

RELAY DATA AND COMMANDS TO INTELSAT 900 THROUGH 1000 NETWORK, IRIDIUM 99, MILSTAR FLT-9, ASTRA 6a, JCSAT-12, NSS-9, DIRECTV-31, GALAXY 7C,

STELLAT 7, NSTAR D, HOT BIRD 9 – 12, HISPASAT ID, EUTELSAT W8, TDRS 11 (L), STENTOR, NSS-17

On the screen appeared:

RELAY COMPLETE

Paul signed off: the satellite responded routinely:

FILE CLOSED 1806

He took a deep breath. Now came the critical part of his plan. He signed on again, but this time he used a maintenance access code:

Z99Z99

The response was immediate:

CAUTION—NOW IN MAINTENANCE MODE—

COMMAND SAFETY CHECKING DISABLED

Paul grinned. With the satellite in a maintenance mode, he could now give illegal commands that would ordinarily be rejected in the standard user mode. Quickly, he began typing a series of instructions that would confuse the satellite's command decode logic. He finished sending the codes and tried to sign off. The satellite did not respond.

It worked, Paul thought jubilantly. The satellite was hung up. It would probably take the analysts a good week to get it back into a state where it would respond to normal commands. And the record of Resa's presentation remained safe in the satellite's command storage matrix from where it would be relayed as planned.

The machines stayed silent. Grinning, Paul took the disk from the drive and stuffed it into his pocket. He switched off the equipment, and after a quick look around the room to see if he had forgotten anything, slipped hurriedly into the hall.

Time was running out. It was after eight o'clock; in less than two hours the satellite would start transmitting. The whole area would be a hornet's nest. Paul knew he had to rejoin Resa quickly, and they had to be well out of the area by then.

Halfway down the corridor to the reception area he hesitated. It had taken about half an hour to program the satellite. Never before had he stayed such a short time when working in the evening—he dared not call attention to himself.

He turned right, went down a short hall, and into his office. Quickly, he crumpled some old notes from one of his files and tossed them in the wastebasket—a few pencils and folders left on the desk, his chair pushed back, the desk lamp on (he often forgot and left it that way). That should do it, he thought. Now to get out of here. Earlier, he could not have gotten in through the rear entrance, but it was no problem to get out that way, because it was always un-locked from the inside.

The night air felt cold on his face as he hurried to the car. Now he was glad he had automatically parked in the rear lot. Conklin wouldn't hear the car or see him leave. Even though it was against regulations, Paul had forgotten to sign out often enough in the past that, if noticed, it wouldn't be unusual. By morning it wouldn't matter anyway.

He kept the lights off until the car left the driveway and turned onto the main road. Then his foot pressed heavily on the accelerator, his concentration undivided as he took the winding curves as fast as he dared. The minutes seemed to be flying. Up ahead he could see the freeway entrance. He relaxed a little: now he could make good time up to the Research Center.

Are you watching, Cathy darling? We showed them a thing or two. . . . He glanced at the speedometer: it crept past ninety, and then he held his gaze to the road, a half-smile on his lips.

BOLDLY, RESA DROVE onto the Stanford campus and parked the car at the Medical Center, choosing a spot adjacent to the west parking lot of the Research Center. From here she could see that military guards were on duty in front of the Center, which, judging from the huge banner stretched above the entrance, had been turned into a Red Cross shelter. She looked toward the top of the building and could see the outline of at least one helicopter.

She decided to take a quick look around the Center and try to figure out the best way to get in. It didn't look too good. There were guards milling about the front entrance.

She glanced around the spacious parking area and saw only a little activity: a few people walking to their cars, and the occasional gleam of headlights closer to the adjacent Medical Center itself. But it was quiet near her. She had parked on the outer fringe of the lot, next to a divider strip planted thick with tall shrubs.

She left the car, and, using the shrubs as a shield, moved cautiously south, following a line parallel to the side of the nearby Research Center so that she could cut over and check the back of the building without being seen by the guards in front.

She lucked out. The back of the building looked deserted: no guards, no cars, no pedestrians strolling around. She straightened and walked casually across the street to the rear of the building; if anyone watched, she didn't want to call attention to herself by moving furtively while out in the open. She felt exposed, vulnerable, as if unseen eyes were stabbing at her, and had to force herself to move slowly.

In the dark shadow of the building, she moved more easily, and then halted, her heart sinking as she saw that the back entrance had been barricaded shut. I'll never be able to break through that, she thought, not without being detected.

"Damn," she muttered under her breath. Now what? The only other way in was through the front lobby. And that meant some diversion was needed to get the guards away from the front of the building. Unless—briefly, she considered a bold approach: just walk in past the guards. No, she decided, that's too risky. She could be stopped and asked for identification, or the guards might recognize her.

Resa made her way back to the car carefully, and got in. The way the back was barricaded so tightly, she needed to think of a diversion around the front to distract the guards. She looked at her watch. She had to think of something fast. She had been here fifteen minutes already, and Paul wouldn't be much more than half an hour behind her.

Resa thought hard. "A fire," she said aloud, "I need a fire."

That would be a good attention-getter, and the parking toward the front of the Research Center would do nicely. She rummaged through the glove compartment and found nothing useful. "Damn it all," she murmured and looked again. But she couldn't find anything sharp or burnable. Then she thought to check the trunk of the car.

"Jackpot!" she whispered. She found a small tool kit that included a box of safety matches and a small packet of flares. She dumped the tools out and selected the heaviest flat-edged screwdriver she could find.

She decided to make her way around to the back of the Research Center and up along the divider strip of the other side of the building. She didn't want to draw attention to this side, because Paul would be pulling in here.

She planned to use the screwdriver blade to cut the gas lines on some of the cars at the far end of the lot, where the ground sloped toward the Research Center. Some of the gas would run down the side of the building into the gutter. She'd be able to fire it out of sight of the guards, but she'd wait until she saw Paul drive up before she did that.

If all went well, she'd just have time to run around the back of the building and up the other side a bit, before the first car went up. Then she could join Paul and both of them could go in from that side of the building together.

She thought hard for a minute, searching for any flaws in her plan. Paul might come before I'm finished, she thought. I'll have to hurry.

She put the case with the antidote in the car for safekeeping. Then she moved quickly along the line of shrubs and crossed to the rear of the Center where she broke into a cautious run. Time was short.

She reached the far side of the building and crossed the driveway to the divider strip that ran up along the east side of the parking lot. Counting on the dense shrubs to conceal her, she moved quickly toward the end of the lot—a good hundred yards. At the end of the strip, she moved out carefully, crouched down, and looked over toward the entrance of the building to check the guards. They were moving about casually, unaware of her presence.

Resa ducked back and went to the first car in the line behind the bank of shrubbery. She dared not risk opening the hood of the car to try to get at the gas line, nor to show a light by which to locate the line, for that matter. In fact, she wasn't too sure the gas line could be reached from under the hood of the car. My best bet, she thought, is to go for the gas tank. At least she knew where that was. Her hands groped underneath the car and felt the outline of the tank. She took up the heavy screwdriver. It would take too long, she decided, to pry a hole in the tank.

She looked around and located a heavy rounded stone lying under the shrubs and wrapped it in her handkerchief to cushion any noise. She used the stone to ram the blade of the screwdriver into the gas tank. It was easier than she had thought it would be—the blade punctured the tank smoothly, and as she withdrew it with a twisting motion, the pungent odor of gasoline filled the air.

Resa moved back from the car. She looked out into the darkness toward the road at the edge of the complex, the road that Paul would be taking to the Medical Center—there were no headlights in sight.

Swiftly, she went down the line of cars, stopping along the way to punch open a few other tanks. There were about thirty cars in the row. Four or five cars should do it, she thought, watching the gasoline trickle along the gutter formed where the curb of the divider strip joined the street. Moving ahead, she punctured the tank of the last car in the row, and then left the shrubbery and crossed to the shadowed safety behind the Research Center.

She looked across the back of the building toward the Medical Center. Nothing yet . . . She looked at her watch; thirty-five minutes had passed since she had arrived. Paul should be coming.

Could I have missed him? Resa thought.

She moved out a little from the back of the building and looked at the street. The gasoline had spread down along the side of the building as she had planned, leaving a dark stain on the roadway. The air filled with the odor of the volatile liquid. She looked again at her watch. She couldn't wait much longer. One of the guards could wander down near the end of the building and smell the gasoline.

And then she saw a car moving slowly along the edge of the nearby Medical Center's parking area. Paul had arrived.

I'll give him two minutes, Resa thought. She checked the time. Impatiently, she counted the seconds. It was time. She took out a book of matches, lit one, and dropped it in the middle of a small puddle of gasoline in the street.

The match went out. It sank harmlessly to the bottom of the puddle.

Resa caught her breath, stunned for a moment. "It's not supposed to do that," she whispered to herself. "Damn!" It always worked on television and in the movies. She decided not to bother with the matches. She took out one of the flares, broke it in half and tossed the sputtering pieces into the gasoline soaked roadway.

The gasoline ignited in a sudden burst of flame that flashed out of her sight around the side of the building.

She turned and ran hard across the back of the Center and around the far corner of the building. She saw Paul approaching and ran to join him. "The case is in the car." Resa pointed the way and they quickly retrieved the case.

"Did you program the satellite?"

"We're good to go at ten o'clock."

A blast rocked the air and flames lit the sky as one of the cars exploded.

They came in view of the parking lot in front of the Research Center. "Nice show," Paul murmured.

Another explosion shook the ground and blasted hot air and

flames into the sky. The whole row of cars seemed to be burning and a wall of flame moved toward the front entrance of the Research Center where the gasoline had seeped over. The guards were fanning out around the burning part of the lot; people were running out of the lobby, trying to move cars that had not yet been endangered by the flames, while the guards shouted at them to stay back, to no avail. Pandemonium reigned. In the distance, they could hear the shrill whine of a fire siren growing louder.

They moved quickly along the front of the building, watching the fire with what Resa hoped was a natural curiosity. Another car exploded. Paul took the case from Resa and, his hand on her arm, ushered her quickly through the front entrance.

Resa walked straight into the lobby and saw a guard rise and step toward them. In the same instant, she saw Marge Bryson, her secretary, standing next to the information desk. She wore a gray and white uniform with a Red Cross emblem on her sleeve.

Marge froze for an instant, and then moved quickly toward Resa, cutting off the guard.

"You're late, young lady," she admonished in a loud voice. "Both of you are. Bring that case along now. I'll show you where I want it. Follow me."

She turned toward the elevator and halted, almost tripping over the guard who had come up close behind her.

"I'll take care of this, George," she snapped. "Why don't you do something about that confusion out there before someone gets hurt?"

She pointed toward the flaming parking lot, and as she finished speaking the roar of another explosion lent emphasis to her words. "George, you better go clear an area for the fire trucks and make it quick; I can hear them!"

"Yes, ma'am." The guard raced through the front doors.

Marge took a key and unlocked the elevator door. They stepped inside and the doors closed. She turned quickly to Resa. "I thought you were dead," she said intensely.

"Far from it," Resa said. "Thanks, Marge, that was fast thinking. You saved our skins out there. You remember my brother-in-law, Paul Linder, don't you?"

"Of course I do." Marge snorted. "Dr. Myles, you shouldn't have to sneak into your own building."

"Is my old office empty?"

"Yes." She pressed a button on the elevator panel. "You've got to get out of here. Both of you—it's not safe. I'll find a place—"

Resa stopped her with the pressure of her hand on the woman's arm. "We'll be leaving by helicopter, but I need your help with something first."

"Anything," Marge said as the elevator stopped and the doors slide open. She glanced down the hall. "It's clear," she whispered, and led them to Resa's old office suite where she unlocked the door and waved them in.

Paul took up a position near the door so he could hear anyone approaching.

Resa turned and faced Marge. "There's not much time." She took the case from Paul and held it out to her. "This is the antidote."

Marge took the case carefully in both hands. "Thank God," she murmured.

"We can use it right here. The Research Center has been turned into a Red Cross shelter. Basically, it's a hospital for victims of the syndrome. You can imagine how desperately we need this antidote."

"It's the only supply in the area that I'm sure Harland doesn't have control of. He's setting up a dictatorship, Marge, and only those on his approved list will get the antidote."

Marge winced. "Mother of God, what's happened to us?"

"We can stop him," Resa insisted. "And we can lick the syndrome. You must see that the antidote is given to as many people as possible by ten o'clock tonight. Give critical patients priority. We have to save as many lives as we can." She checked her watch. "It's nine-twenty—you'll have to move fast. Instructions are in the case."

"What happens at ten o'clock?"

Resa glanced at Paul, who smiled and said, "There'll be a very special thirty-minute broadcast."

"Paul has set up a broadcast of a digital recording I made that will give out all of the information on how to make the antidote. We hope that laboratories worldwide will start turning it out. Also, Marge, I included the fact that a supply of the antidote has been left here for critically ill people."

Marge looked startled.

"It's the only way. The people have to know it exists and that it works. They have to know there's hope for their critically ill loved ones. Only mass resistance will win us back our freedom. That's why you have to give as many serious cases the antidote before the broadcast—Harland will try to confiscate your supply. It'll be dangerous, Marge."

Marge brushed the thought aside with a wave of her hand. "I'll attend to it, Dr. Myles. . . . Now, you must leave. There's a guard on the roof. I'll call and have him report to the lobby. You two use the stairwell. Here, take this master key—the doors are all locked. Now go . . . hurry."

Marge picked up the phone as Resa opened the door and checked the hall. "Come on," she said to Paul, moving quickly down the corridor. She unlocked the stairwell door and they raced up the short flight of stairs to the roof.

Resa signaled for quiet and then unlocked the door to the roof and slowly eased it open. She heard elevator doors close. The guard was on his way down.

"Let's go."

Paul moved out ahead of her and they both spotted the tall figure leaning against the helicopter at the same time.

"Steve!" Resa ran ahead of Paul and threw herself into Steve's waiting arms.

"Glad you could make it," Paul said

"So am I. I've been tracking down Russians and worried sick about what was going on here. When Blair got hold of me, I was more than ready to go."

"I'm so glad you're here," Resa whispered, her lips close to his ear.

She pulled his head down and kissed him hard.

Paul laughed. "Come on you lovebirds. Let's get airborne. That guard could be coming back at any time."

"No problem," Steve said, even as he moved to climb into the helicopter. "He's on our side."

"Good," Resa said. "Marge will need all the help she can get."

Paul gave the helicopter an approving look. It was a Sikorsky Firehawk. In addition to being used for medical evacuations, it was a high-performance, multimission helicopter that could also be used for firefighting and high-altitude rescues. He climbed into the pilot's seat, put on the headset that had been left on the seat, and scanned the instrument panel. He located the gauges: altimeter, fuel, tachometer. On his left was the pilot's cyclic control stick; on his right, the pilot's collective pitch lever ringed with a twist-grip throttle. His hands moved quickly over the controls.

"Can you fly it, Paul?" asked Resa from the back.

"It's a Sikorsky," he replied.

Resa looked at Steve questioningly. "Is that a yes or no?" Steve smiled and nodded, "Definitely a yes."

Paul started the motor; the rotor blades moved sluggishly, and then burst into power. The cabin shuddered as he built up power, and the rotor blades tore through the air. He moved the controls, and the helicopter ascended in a smooth fast vertical climb: the towering Research Center, with flame and smoke billowing from its base, dwindled from view as Paul swung the chopper north.

"Lake Tahoe, here we come," he said with a grin.

IN RESA'S OLD office, Marge Bryson briskly organized a crash program to administer the antidote. As evening supervisor, she was in a unique position of control over the nurses and technicians under her, but she knew that pressure wouldn't be necessary—they were almost all from Resa's old staff and fiercely loyal to her.

She had just ordered a call to go out over the paging system for all floor supervisors to report to her immediately, and while she waited, she read the instructions Resa had enclosed in the case. Separately wrapped packages for other hospitals in the area were also included in the case, and Marge knew she would have to see that those packages left the building before the military found out what was going on.

The nurses began to file into her office; she put down the papers and rose.

"Quiet, please. I have urgent instructions for you and little time to explain any details."

She paused and looked around the group of familiar faces. "I rely on your confidence," she said slowly, clearly. "Dr. Myles has just delivered a supply of a new antidote for the Stanford virus to us—the *only* supply in our area that is not under government control."

The group stirred, but remained quiet, listening intently. "We have until ten o'clock to administer the antidote without interference. At that time, a broadcast arranged by Dr. Myles will go out worldwide and the news of the antidote will be common knowledge. The broadcast will include specific instructions to laboratories on how to synthesize the antidote. That's the good news. The bad news is that we are still under martial law, and president Harland will move to stop us. He wants total control over who gets the antidote, total 'worldwide' control.

"There will be more of the antidote available, but how much and how soon is up for grabs. So you must act quickly and quietly—the military must not know what we're doing. Choose the most critical cases first. Every patient is to be injected with 0.5 cc of the antidote. . . . Are there any objections to these orders? If so, you need not participate; it will be dangerous if we're caught. I ask only that you keep the secret." She looked at the nurses; no one spoke.

"Let's get busy." Tammy Fournier, the niece of the Nobel laureate Mark Fournier, spoke.

"Good," Marge said briskly. She began to hand out the 100-cc vials to the nurses. "One more thing, we have extra vials that could go to the emergency field hospitals—they'll just be confiscated if they're found here. But I'll need volunteers to take them out and try to talk someone into giving the shots. You'll have to be very careful because the military are running the field hospitals."

"I'll go," Tammy Fournier said immediately. "I have some friends doing volunteer work at two of the field hospitals over on the east side." The other nurses in the room echoed her words.

"Report back to me after you've given instructions to the ward nurses on your floors. . . . We have to move fast now."

The nurses left quickly and Marge picked up the phone and dialed the switchboard. "How many couriers do we have in the building? Only three . . . well, have them report to me stat." She hung up the phone and sorted the wrapped packages.

When the couriers arrived she gave them terse instructions. "These packages of emergency drugs are to be delivered to the area hospitals noted on the covers at once. You are to *hand deliver* the drugs only to the person whose name is written on the outside cover. If he or she is not on duty you will deliver the package to that person's home. You'll each have to make a number of stops. I'm sorry but we're shorthanded, and it's an emergency. You're to leave immediately. If you're stopped for speeding," she added—and the eyes of the young couriers lit up with excitement—"request a police escort. Tell them it's a medical emergency."

Hard on the heels of the departing couriers, the floor nurses began filing back to get the extra vials slated for the field hospitals. "Get these vials divided among you," Marge said. "I think I know a way to get them given out quickly."

She checked her personnel roster to see who had been assigned to the shelter as the military duty officer, and then picked up the phone. "Connect me with Lieutenant Simpson right away, please."

"Lieutenant Simpson, here."

"This is Mrs. Bryson, Lieutenant, the evening supervisor. We have an emergency situation here and I need your help."

"Yes, ma'am. What's the trouble?"

"We've had an outbreak of cholera on one of the wards. The shelter will probably be put under quarantine by health officials in the morning, but we must take emergency measures at once."

"Cholera! What do you want me to do?"

"The shelter must be sealed off, isolated—as if we were already quarantined. No one must be allowed to pass in or out."

"Yes, ma'am," he said firmly, "you leave that to me!"

"Now, there is one more thing, Lieutenant."

"Yes?"

"We must distribute the anticholera serum we have here to all the field hospitals at once. The sick must be inoculated, or they won't have a chance; and, as you know, the field hospitals have no serum on hand. I have some nurses who have already been inoculated and have volunteered to help administer the serum. I will need military escorts for them, Lieutenant, about eight cars."

"Yes, ma'am. Right away."

"Thank you, Lieutenant," she said gratefully. "I knew we could count on the military in this emergency."

"No trouble at all."

"And you *will* see that *no one* enters the building? We cannot risk an epidemic, or," she lowered her voice confidentially, "a panic."

"Yes, ma'am!" he said emphatically. "No one will get by us!"

"Thank you, again, Lieutenant. My nurses are on the way down." She hung up the phone, and saw broad smiles on the faces of the nurses waiting to leave.

She signaled them to go, calling "Good luck" as they left. Then she went to the window and looked down on the parking area. The fire engines had gone; only the blackened row of cars testified to the brief holocaust. A line of military police cars drew up to the front entrance and the nurses came out of the building, each escorted to a car by an armed guard. She smiled as the cars drove off with sirens blaring.

It was nine-forty. She had time for a quick check on each floor to see if any of the wards was falling behind schedule. But the pressure had eased off—she knew they would make it. The artificial quarantine she had maneuvered would buy them any extra minutes they might need.

THE FIRST MILITARY car pulled up at an emergency field hospital in the East Palo Alto area and the driver jumped out to open the back door. The Red Cross nurse, Tammy Fournier, got out and strode briskly into the field hospital, the entrance to which was flanked by two military guards. A corpsman rose as she entered.

"Who's in charge here?" she asked peremptorily.

"Captain Enzo Gutierrez, ma'am."

"Take me to him at once, please. This is an emergency."

The corpsman ushered her into a small cubicle where the Captain sat at a littered desk, poring over a pile of papers, and then left. The Captain looked up and rose.

"Captain," she said, "we have an emergency. There's been an outbreak of cholera at the Stanford Red Cross Shelter. I've brought you some anticholera serum." She opened the small case and took out a large vial. "It must be given at once."

"Cholera! But I haven't been told of—"

"You're being told now," she said coolly, and then looked around. "And keep your voice down, please. Do you want to cause a panic?" she snapped. "The serum is in short supply right now. You're lucky we had some to spare for the field hospitals. . . . But then," she went on in a persuasive tone, "I'm sure you know what a supply problem we're all having."

Mollified, he said, "Yes, ma'am, I sure do. Don't worry; I'll take care of it." He took the vial and looked at it. "There's no label," he objected.

Her heart leaped, but she replied with disdain. "Of course there's no label. Do you want the whole city to know about it? We'd be mobbed! There'd be a panic!"

"Oh, of course. I didn't realize . . ."

"It must be given immediately, and only to the sickest patients," she stressed. "The dose is 0.5 cc. Those who are up and around can wait for the next batch."

"I'll see to it . . . Miss . . ."

"Fournier, Tammy Fournier." She gave him a dazzling smile, and he escorted her to the hospital entrance personally. With relief, she noticed that the waiting military escort seemed to impress him with the importance of her visit.

As he turned back into the hospital, she heard him call out sharply, "Corpsman!"

20:00 HOURS: RADIO AND TELEVISION WORLDWIDE—
"Hello everyone. My name is Dr. Resa Myles. I was formerly the Director of the Control of Cancer Agency at Stanford University in Palo Alto, California. Some of you will remember that I was relieved of that position by President Harland because I spoke out against his premature launching of Project Immunity. What I have to say now is urgent. Please listen carefully.

"The CCA scientists here have created an antidote to the Project Immunity syndrome that has been decimating our population worldwide. It is critically important that you record the balance of this presentation, because in it I will show your scientists how to create the antidote in their own laboratories. Time is critical. Minutes count if we are to save as many lives as possible.

"First, a warning. If you are in the United States, you know we are under martial law. The president, as commander-in chief of the armed forces, is running the country. He wants to control the antidote. He will not *give it to everyone. Take whatever precautions are*

necessary to get the antidote out to as many people as possible.
"Now, here are the instructions for making the antidote . . ."

Chapter 23

Washington, D.C., and
Lake Tahoe area, California

WITHIN FIVE MINUTES after the satellite network broadcasted Resa's message for the first time, President Harland was notified—and the cool control that typified his public appearances snapped.

"I want those broadcasts stopped!" he shouted, his face livid with rage. "How dare she bad-mouth me. I'm the president!" Urgent orders poured out from the White House at a frantic rate as Harland issued his demands. Confiscate immediately any vaccine at the old CCA Research Centers. Apprehend Dr. Resa Myles and her companions and place them under arrest immediately.

Harland sent for Blair and paced up and down in his office,

waiting impatiently for his chief of staff to arrive. He cursed the empty room and poured himself a drink with hands that trembled from violent anger. That woman was giving the antidote away to the whole damned world. He could have been in complete control! He was sure she led a conspiracy against him. And by God, she'd pay for it, Harland promised himself.

Blair came into the room.

"Have you heard?" Harland asked angrily.

"Yes, Mr. President," Blair replied quietly. "It's hard to believe Dr. Myles would do this."

"Well, she damn well has! And where have you been? I needed you!"

"I've been following up on the orders you sent out, sir. The Red Cross officials at the former Stanford Research Center report an outbreak of cholera and deny any knowledge of the vaccine."

Harland was taken aback for a moment. Cholera? he thought. No, it's a trick. And even if it wasn't a trick—so what. "I want that vaccine," he said coldly. "I don't give a damn what outbreak they claim to have there." His voice rose. "I don't care if it's a plague!"

"Yes, sir," Blair said, and nodded to an aide who stood at the door waiting to relay Harland's orders.

"What about Dr. Myles?" Harland asked. "Where is she?"

"Security at Survival Six cannot locate her, sir. They're sure she couldn't get out of the shelter and they think the other scientists there may be hiding her. Security is searching all levels for her now."

Harland's eyes narrowed and he frowned. "She's not there," he said slowly, and met Blair's steady gaze. "I know she's not there. . . ."

"I'm inclined to agree with you, sir," Blair said. "In my opinion she must have broken out somehow. That's the only way she could have set up the broadcast. If she could get control of the satellite network, she could probably quite easily fool the computer system at the shelter. When I was there, I noticed the security force seemed to rely quite heavily on the computer for control. . . . But I may be wrong. The system is supposed to be infallible."

"No. No, you're not wrong. I know." Harland sat down behind his desk. "I'm glad you agree with me, Blair." He studied his assistant carefully. "Where do you think she is?"

Blair thought for a minute, frowning. "I'd say she would have headed right for the CCA Research Center at Stanford, and then . . . the Canadian border."

"Why there?" Harland looked at Blair sharply.

"Well, she has to get out of the country or she risks getting picked up quickly. Her face will be well known by the general public."

Harland nodded. "Go on."

"I think she would decide against the Mexican border—she knows that *I know* she has gone down there around Baja on occasion. . . . And that leaves the Canadian border," Blair said simply.

Harland smiled. "Your logic is very interesting, Blair—except for one thing," he said.

"Yes, sir?"

"She would expect you to keep that information about Baja secret, to remain a loyal friend," Harland said, a hint of cunning in his voice.

Blair replied slowly, "You may be right, sir. . . . I have regarded her as a friend and respected her for many years." He looked directly at Harland, meeting his eyes, apparently without a qualm. "But when one turns against one's country and seeks to destroy it, then loyalty must be forgotten." There was a curious sadness in Blair's eyes as he spoke.

Harland wondered about that look of sadness for a moment, but he felt the truth in Blair's words. Resa had betrayed his friendship. Satisfied, he smiled.

"She will expect you to keep your knowledge secret. Order the search concentrated in southern California, especially the area near the Mexico border," Harland said softly. "I want Dr. Myles and everyone with her shot on sight."

"Yes, Mr. President." Blair rose and then stopped. "There is one other matter, sir. I recommend that the antidote being made in the Survival Shelters be airlifted to all military bases as soon as possible for the military personnel and their families."

"Shouldn't we do just the military first? Let the families wait?"

"I strongly recommend against that sir. Morale is an important issue. Our military people must know their families are safe."

"All right, Blair, we'll do it your way. You handle it."

"Thank you, sir. I'll take care of it." Blair left the Oval Office, hiding his concern at the danger Resa and Paul had to face. He forced his thoughts to more constructive essentials, and as he walked down the hallway to his office he promised himself that at least half of the antidote in question would go to civilian medical facilities, not just the military."

ONLY THE GLOW from the instrument panel lit the cabin of the helicopter. The throb of the twin turbine GE engines was loud, making conversation difficult. Exhausted, Resa sat with her head resting on Steve's shoulder, eyes closed.

Paul flew the chopper low, following the contour of the land to avoid detection by radar. There was no traffic on the roads below, which were heavily blocked with snow and looked as if they hadn't been plowed out for weeks. It was not surprising. There were too many people sick or dying.

"We're almost to Tahoe," he said loudly, over the roar of the engines.

Steve nodded. He had been watching the mountains beneath them, covered with snow that glistened in the moonlight and thick with stately trees that rose dark and deep. They passed over Lake Tahoe and rose to clear the mountains beyond it.

Suddenly, a shock wave and the roar of a jet engine rocked the helicopter.

"Damn!" Paul shouted. "It's a fighter jet!"

"Did he spot us?" Steve asked.

"Probably . . . he must have seen something on his radar." Paul's spoke urgently. "He'll be checking out our ID. Steve, Squaw Valley is just ahead. I'm going to drop you two off—you can find skis and make it to the cabin from there. I'll try to draw the fighter away and ditch the chopper."

"No! Let's stay together," Resa shouted.

"Don't argue—damn it! We don't have a chance if I just land the damned thing. I'll try to ditch it in the lake. Maybe they'll think we went down. And three of us can't jump while I'm aiming this crate for the lake. . . . So get ready!"

Wide-awake, her pulse pounding, she recognized the logic in Paul's argument, but her heart ached at the danger he was placing himself in.

Steve shouted instructions in her ear. "We're going to jump. . . . Try to roll when you hit."

"Don't wait for me, Resa! Get to cover. I'll move out fast, ditch the chopper, and head for the south shore. . . ." Paul slowed the helicopter and hovered about twenty feet over a high snow bank.

"Now!" he shouted.

Steve forced the door open. "Jump!" he yelled to Resa.

Her hands braced on the edges of the opening, Resa struggled to keep her balance against the buffeting wind. She hesitated at the open doorway and turned to the pilot's seat. "Paul . . ." There was so much she wanted to say, and only seconds were left.

"I know, big sister." Paul reached over the back of the seat and gripped her hand once, hard and brief. "It'll be all right. Go! You know Cathy would want you safe!"

She jumped blindly out into the whirling snow and fell through the frigid air, the blue coat she wore from the Survival Shelter worthless in the freezing weather. When she hit the top of the snow, she drew up her knees and curled her body over them, and rolled down the bank. She looked up and caught only a glimpse of Steve falling into the snow somewhere off to her right. The helicopter re-ceded rapidly toward the south as Paul went to full throttle and the rotor blades bit viciously into the thin air.

"Steve!" she shouted. "Where are you?"

"I'm here," his muffled reply drifted to her. Looking toward the sound, she saw a dark blur moving toward her.

Steve came up to her. "Are you all right?" He brushed the loose snow from her face.

"Yes, I'm fine. Just so cold," she said a little breathlessly, and then she heard the roar of the jet approaching.

"Get down," he shouted, shielding her with his body.

Steve's weight pressed her down, deeper into the snow bank, but she heard the jet make its pass, flying slower than the first time it had gone over them—slower and quite a bit lower.

She knew then that the pilot had spotted the helicopter. Get out, Paul, she thought urgently, get out.

The helicopter was out of sight when she eased out from beneath Steve and saw the jet make a tight turn and start another run. Damn him, Resa thought, he's going to circle the area where he first spotted us.

And then she saw the flash of an air-to-air missile streaking from the plane—and an explosion lit the sky far to the south of tem. She struggled to get to her feet.

"Paul!" she screamed. "Steve—was that the helicopter?"

"I think so," he said grimly. "But even if it was, Paul probably already ditched it. I just don't know, darling." He pulled her to him.

"Oh, Steve," she sobbed. "Not Paul, too. Damn them! Damn them all! Not Paul."

"I hope not," he said softly, holding her tight, soothing her with quiet words. He watched the sky: there was still a glow toward the south, but the fighter jet had gone. "It's all right now. We have to get moving, darling. . . . Come. We can't stay here." He helped her to her feet and led her toward the dark, deserted buildings of the ski resort.

He was grateful now, for the number of times he had skied at Squaw Valley; it would help him locate the equipment they would need to get to Mac's cabin. He looked at the summit, rising tall and forbidding in the darkness. At first light they would have to be up there, ready to start the long, difficult run to the cabin.

Resa leaned heavily against his arm and he knew she needed rest. She shivered in the bitter cold, and her clothing was wet from lying in the snow. He led her up the steps of the main lodge to a long, narrow wooden porch on which the doors of the hotel rooms opened. He forced the lock on the first unit they came to, and guided her into the room.

She collapsed onto a chair. "Oh, damn, I'm so cold," she said, shivering uncontrollably, her teeth chattering. "Have to watch out for hypothermia." But she knew her reaction was from shock as well as the cold. She wasn't used to being hunted by armed military, and she was, literally, worried sick about Paul. He was all she had left of what she considered her family.

"I'll get some heat on. Start getting out of those wet clothes." Steve drew the heavy drapes across the wide picture window and turned on a small table lamp so he could locate the thermostat that controlled the electric wall heaters. "The room will be warm soon," he said, as he turned up the thermostat.

He pulled the linen back on the bed. "These sheets feel like ice," he commented.

"Use blankets," Resa mumbled. "Need hot shower." She headed toward the bathroom.

"While you're in the shower, I'm going to see if I can find something hot for us to drink," he said. "I won't be long."

"Okay. Thanks."

STEVE WENT TO the main kitchen off the large dining room that served the motel units and rummaged through the shelves. He found some individual serving packets of cocoa and coffee, and an unopened box of saltine crackers and jar of strawberry jam.

It's better than nothing, he thought, as he looked through the cabinets. He located a hot plate, a small pot, some mugs, and silver-ware, and piled everything into a large paper sack. On his way out, he noticed a flashlight on one of the counters and pocketed it, thinking it would come in handy when he went to the larger build-ing where the ski equipment was kept.

He went back to the hotel room, calling out to Resa as she ap-proached the door, so he wouldn't startle her.

"I hit the jackpot," he said. "How about some hot cocoa, crack-ers, and jam?"

"Oh, I'd love some." Her voice sounded tired. She had draped her wet clothes over a chair in front of the wall heaters and was sit-ting up in the bed, wrapped in blankets and leaning on the head-board.

"Stay there. I'll fix our dinner and you can tell me about Mac's cabin."

"Thank you," she said, and talked quietly of what they would find when they reached the cabin. She wanted to take her mind off the danger they were in, the concern for Paul, and the fighter plane that could still return.

"You'll like it. It's a real log cabin, nestled between two huge mountains—you can ski down to it from the summit here. It's a long run, but I've done it before." She took the mug he offered along with some crackers spread liberally with jam.

Between bites, she continued. "Inside, the cabin looks like a rustic ranch house, with bright colors, a huge stone fireplace, and a modern kitchen. But—no telephone, no doorbell."

He smiled at her last remark. "But what about emergencies?"

"There's a ham radio, if you really need to get some help, and a four-wheel drive jeep in a garage attached to the cabin."

"Good thinking on Mac's part."

"I like it there best at night, when I can hear the wind blowing through the tall pine trees all around the cabin, and it's warm and cozy inside with a roaring fire going."

"Will we stay there long?"

273

"No," she said firmly. "I promised Blair to hide out for two days only. There's so much to do. But right now I need to get some sleep while my clothes dry. Then we can pick up some ski equipment and heavier clothes for both of us so we'll be all set to leave at dawn."

He nodded. "Good idea. I'll join you." He took her empty mug and put it on the dresser, and then got some extra blankets out of the closet, stripped his damp clothes, and dropped them over a chair near the heaters, and wrapped a blanket around himself. He eased into the bed next to her and draped another blanket and the bed-spread over both of them. Slipping his arm beneath Resa, he pulled her to him and held her tightly.

Resa put her arms around him and snuggled as close as she could get. Her last thoughts before drifting into an uneasy sleep were of Paul. Was he tramping through the heavy snow to the resort area at the south shore? Or did he delay too long getting out of the helicopter?

IT WAS STILL dark when they had rested enough to gather the supplies they would need in the morning.

"You get the ski stuff, and I'll find the clothes," Resa suggested.

Steve had to smash a window to get into the heavily locked building where the ski equipment was kept, but the small ski shop near the rental equipment area had been left unlocked.

"Sounds good to me. We'll need parkas, ski pants, gloves, and heavy socks." He located another flashlight in the shop and gave it to Resa.

He used the flashlight he had found earlier in the kitchens to guide him through the rooms. The lights, he decided, would be too difficult to shield with all the windows in the place. It was cold and damp, and his footsteps echoed hollowly in the emptiness.

How strange, he thought, to see this busy place deserted; he had noticed earlier that the main road leading to the lodge had not been plowed for some time. The resort was probably inaccessible now.

That meant the only threat to them would come by air.

He flashed the light over the stacks of skis lining the wall and chose two pairs of metal skis that were about his height and Resa's. We'll sacrifice the extra speed of longer skis for control on that difficult run, he thought. He selected poles and ski boots, mentally congratulating himself that he had remembered Resa's shoe size.

While he adjusted the step-in bindings on the skis to fit the boots he had selected, he went over his mental list of other things they would need: snowshoes and a harness on which to strap them and food and drink would be a problem.

It took them two trips to get everything back to their room.

Sorting through the supplies, Steve noted that Resa had included headbands and sunglasses. They'd be blinded by the bright glare on the snow in the morning without them. And best of all, she'd found some candy bars, snacks, and soft drinks. "Where did you find the grub?" he asked.

I smashed open a dispensing machine."

He grinned. "What would I do without you?"

"You'll never know, my love. I've decided to keep you."

"Well, that's good to hear. I'll hold you to it, but let's get what sleep we can before morning."

CNN— BREAKING NEWS
LIVE FROM WASHINGTON CORRESPONDENT
ALICE ROBERTA JENNINGS

"Americans are rising in protest against President Harland. Martial Law notwithstanding, people are lining up all across the nation picketing federal buildings with signs protesting the brief war waged by President Harland and, even more angrily, protesting Harland's attempts to control the distribution of the antidote to the deadly Project Immunity syndrome. Shouts as well as signs of 'Impeach Harland' are sprinkled liberally among the marchers.

"Military troops charged with breaking up the demonstrations

275

are for the most part just watching the nonviolent picketers. In some areas, there are reports that the military have actually joined the people protesting Harland's policies.

"Although the protests have been mainly nonviolent, there have been reports of citizens firing upon the military who are barring access to Red Cross shelters across the country.

"Here in Washington, a White House spokesman said that steps are being taken to bring order to the country, and that the president will be addressing the nation in a special broadcast later today."

Chapter 24

Washington, D.C.

DAVID BLAIR SAT behind his desk, staring blankly at the papers in front of him, his mind filled with pain and anger.

Pain for the loss of a friend.

Anger at the waste of a brilliant mind destroyed by power politics.

In the early hours of the morning a report had come in from the West Coast that a fighter jet had intercepted and shot down the helicopter Resa had taken from the Stanford Research Center, and Blair could not stop brooding about it, could not put it from his mind.

At least Harland wasn't there with me when the report came in,

Blair thought.

He knew he never could have hidden his reaction to the news, and even now he delayed a confrontation with Harland. The president had called and told him to be at a nine o'clock meeting in the War Room with the officers of the newly formed National Security Force—about one hundred men would be there and Blair was to record Harland's speech to his elite corps. Harland would introduce them to the country via selected members of the press. The sound of the president's voice on the telephone, his air of supreme disdain and utter confidence, had infuriated Blair.

There was a quiet knock on the door and Taggert came in.

Blair looked up and said, "Did you hear about the report?" His voice was bitter and angry.

"I heard about the preliminary report," Taggert said. He glanced at his watch. "It's still too early for the follow-up; it's not daylight yet in California. They'll be sending out a reconnaissance helicopter to verify the identity of the occupants in the wrecked chopper."

"But you and I already know their identities," Blair said heavily. "Resa Myles is dead."

"Maybe . . . ," Taggert said quietly.

"What do you mean?" Blair frowned. He had no patience for false hope. No patience for much of anything with the country falling apart around him.

"The helicopter was heading south, not north, when it was shot down," Taggert explained. "I think the pilot may have dropped Dr. Myles and Sheldon off already and was heading south back toward the Center at Stanford when he was shot down. I sent Phil Jordan out to the West Coast to try to get on that reconnaissance chopper just in case Myles was not in the crash. He has orders to protect her at all cost. Jordan is the agent that was under deep cover in Russia. He was flown here from Finland for debriefing. I trust him fully. He'll keep her safe if it's at all possible."

"Then she might still be alive," Blair said slowly. But the pilot wouldn't be, he thought. Paul. . . . It would have been Paul who had gone down in the helicopter. Unless he managed to get out somehow. But how could one bail out of a helicopter? Maybe into the water . . ."

"At least the satellite network is still broadcasting worldwide," Taggert said quietly, interrupting his thoughts. "Apparently, no one can figure out how to stop it. The CIA could really use Paul Linder."

Blair smiled. "Paul knew what he was doing," he said softly, and then made an effort to shake off his depression. "The world lost a brilliant computer systems analyst when he gave up computers to start his own air freight line."

"Maybe we can convince him otherwise. If he comes through this alive." Taggert shook his head and sighed. "So many good people lost. And that reminds me. How is the vice president?"

The meeting with him is set for tonight. He's recovering rapidly, and we've managed to keep it from Harland. Everyone thinks he's still on the critical list."

"Good," Taggert said. "I'll be there. . . . Are you going to Harland's special meeting this morning in the War Room?"

"Yes. I have to. Orders." Blair's face and his voice reflected his distaste.

"I've just finished setting up a special screening process—hidden, of course—no arms are allowed in the room."

"Harland's become paranoid about conspiracies," Blair commented. "But I didn't think the suspicion extended to his new, hand-picked National Security Force."

"He doesn't trust anyone," Taggert said. "And that includes the CIA. I expect to be removed from the directorship any day now. I never know what the president's going to do next. We'll have to be very careful about getting him removed from office."

He turned to leave and hesitated.

"By the way, the antidote is still going out from Survival Six. And telegrams have started to pour into the White House about Dr. Myles's broadcast. I think every doctor and scientist in the country

279

has heard that speech."

"Good. You'll let me know what Jordan finds?"

"You bet. As soon as I have any news, you'll hear it, too."

So there is some good news, Blair thought, as the door closed behind Taggert.

A little easier in mind, he put a new tape in his recorder and prepared to go down to the War Room.

A NUMBER OF the National Security Force officers in their severely tailored, royal blue uniforms had begun to drift into the War Room. Blair sat in his usual place, on the far side of the platform from which the president would speak, near the private entrance, facing the audience. His face expressionless, Blair watched the men come into the room.

Who are the simple dupes? He wondered. And who are the power hungry, the sadists, the misfits?

His eyes wandered carelessly over the men, and then a tall, heavily muscled figure caught his attention. Only a lifetime of practice at masking his emotions kept Blair from showing the shock that ran through him. The man looked exactly like the Russian agent, Rostov.

But it can't be, Blair thought, not here in the White House, and certainly not with Harland's special force.

The eyes of the audience and the eyes of the television cameras turned to the presidential entranceway. Blair glanced back and saw Harland pausing to speak to an assistant, and then he heard a voice at his elbow. "Sir, Taggert has an urgent report for you."

Quickly Blair turned the recorder over to the man sitting next to him and followed the young aide out of the room. Taggert, grim-faced, waited in the hall outside the doors, which were flanked by armed guards. He took Blair's arm. "Come with me. Hurry."

"What's going on?" Blair asked as Taggert led him briskly to the elevator and up several floors to a small room.

"Wait," Taggert said, ushering Blair into the room.

"You got him out," one of the men watching a group of closed-circuit television sets said in relief, as they came in.

"Yes," Taggert replied. He looked at the screens. "Has he made any move?"

"No."

Blair saw that the screens showed different views of the War Room. Hidden cameras, he thought. That must be it—there had been no cameras set up in the open. "Will someone please tell me what is going on here?" he asked quietly.

"Sorry, Dave," Taggert said. "We spotted Rostov when he went through the screen, and I wanted to get you out of there."

"So it *was* Rostov," Blair said slowly.

"You recognized him?"

"I thought I did."

Taggert's question was sharp and quick: "Did he know that you spotted him?"

Blair smiled. "No," he said with quiet certainty. "But why are you letting him stay in there? What's going on, Taggert?"

"We're watching him," Taggert said, his eyes on the screens. "He's wired, Dave," he added slowly.

"Wired? How do you know?"

Taggert nodded toward the banks of equipment lining the walls. "Modified body scans and computer analysis," Taggert said crisply. "He's carrying plastic explosive and a detonator. He can blow up himself and everyone else in that room.

"My God," Blair said slowly.

"I think he's after Harland, now," Taggert went on. "I don't know if he just switched targets after Dr. Myles was sent to the Survival Six shelter or if he's striking out on his own. But I'm inclined to think the latter. . . . He wants revenge. He can't go home to Russia. Basically, there's no Russia left for him to go to. Between them, Harland and Ling En-huai took care of that."

"And the Chinese Prime Minister is dead, but Harland is

alive," Blair finished for him.

Taggert remained silent, his eyes still on the screens.

"Are you asking me to approve letting this man assassinate the president and everyone else in that room?" Blair asked.

"No, . . . I'm not." Taggert's voice was calm, controlled. "I'm explaining why I used a ruse to get you out of there. We can't touch Rostov. At the first sign of opposition he'd detonate that explosive." He met Blair's gaze. "I'm taking a calculated risk that he has some other plan than assassination in mind. . . . And it's my decision." Taggert turned back to the screens.

But Blair knew that Taggert didn't want Rostov stopped. In his own way Taggert was just as ruthless as Rostov. And as soon as the thought formed, he was ashamed of it. If Harland was stopped now, how many lives would be saved? What decision would I have made, Blair asked himself, if the choice had arisen yesterday, before Harland's order had gone out to shoot Resa and her companions on sight? He sat down beside Taggert and watched the screens.

Taggert glanced at him briefly. "Rostov has the detonator is in his pocket. . . . Let's hear what Harland's saying." He turned on the speaker.

Harland's voice, deep and vibrant and imperious, flooded the room. ". . . nothing can stop us from getting down to the task of rebuilding our country into this position of world leadership. We have the antidote to the deadly syndrome sweeping the world. The People's Republic of China and the Russian Federation have been destroyed. They've destroyed each other. The role of the United States in this was mainly defensive. But the fact remains that the Russian Federation showed itself to be our enemy. And our enemy, fellow Americans, can no longer harm us. We will—"

Rostov rose to his feet. "But Mr. President, what about Russian retaliation?" He spoke in flawless American English.

Harland laughed. "There's no one capable of retaliating. Russia is dead."

"That's not quite true. This Russian is alive and well." Rostov smiled.

"Good-bye Mr. President."

Blair held his breath as he saw Rostov's hand slide into his pocket.

The blast destroyed the hidden cameras, . . . and everything and everyone else in the room.

No one spoke for a long moment, and then Taggert turned to Blair. "The vice president must be notified at once," he said quietly. "I'll get an order to call the military off Dr. Myles." He glanced at his watch. "I hope it's not too late."

NATIONAL SECURITY AGENCY
URGENT ORDER FROM DIRECTOR
CEASE ALL HOSTILITIES TOWARD DR. RESA MYLES IMMEDIATELY. ORDER ALL LOCAL AND MILITARY AUTHORITIES TO GIVE THE FULL SUPPORT NEEDED TO ENSURE HER SAFETY.

Chapter 25

Squaw Valley Ski Resort, California

RESA AWOKE JUST before dawn. She looked out the window and saw a faint lightening of the dark sky toward the east. False dawn.

"Steve," she called softly. "Wake up, darling. We have to leave."

"I'm awake, Resa." He rolled over and kissed her gently. "Let's do it."

They dressed quickly in their ski clothes, and then made hot cocoa—which Resa insisted on instead of coffee, saying it was more nourishing—and ate some more of the saltine crackers and jam.

"When we get to Mac's cabin, I promise to cook you a superb meal. Steak and all the trimmings. And you can help."

Steve laughed. "I'll gladly help in the kitchen if it means getting some solid food."

Outside, it had grown brighter, and as they left the motel the sun came up, warm and golden, in a cloudless sky. Their boots crunched on the snow as they trudged, skis hoisted over their shoulders and snowshoes strapped to their backs, to the building housing the cable car that would take them to the summit.

"We're in luck," Resa said, as she tried the door to the building and found it unlocked. Someone left here in a hurry, she thought.

They went to the loading platform and Steve said, "You load our gear on the car and I'll see if I can get this thing running."

In the control room Steve examined the motor and gears. "It looks pretty straightforward," he called. "Are you ready?"

"Yes," she called back. "But this car isn't out on the main cable."

"That's okay. We can move it easily." Steve started the motor and threw the lever that started the cable moving.

"Get in," he called to Resa, as he guided the car out of its siding. Then he stepped into it and slammed the door shut. "We're on our way," he said with a smile.

Resa returned his smile, but the strain still showed on her face. The empty ski slopes all around them were a constant reminder that it was not a normal day.

The ground fell away as the car rose slowly toward the snowy peaks ahead. There was no wind today to make the car lurch sickeningly, and Resa was grateful for that. Her stomach was still tied in knots. Every time she wondered about Paul's fate, she actually felt a physical pain shoot through her. "It will take us about half an hour to reach the summit," she said. "We'll have to switch to a chair lift at the receiving station."

"I vaguely remember that," Steve said. "It's been years since I've skied the expert runs."

Long before they reached the summit Resa began to feel a sense of urgency. They had transferred quickly to the chair lift, and Steve had remembered to stop the cable so nothing would appear amiss should a plane come back, searching for them. But the chair seemed to be moving in slow motion, and it was far colder out here in the open than inside the cable car. She shivered occasionally, unable to suppress her body's reaction.

"There's the ramp just ahead of us," Steve said, moving the bar across the front of them out of the way so they would be able to stand up and ski off the chair lift.

Smoothly, they let their skis touch the head of the ramp, stood up, and skied down the gentle incline while the chair was raised over their heads by the moving cable.

"I'll turn off the chair lift," Steve said.

When he came out of the control shed, Resa was looking out over the vista of snow and mountains and trees. "It's so beautiful," she said softly, with a note of sadness in her voice. "Why have we made such a mess of the world?"

He knew she didn't expect an answer, but he caught something of her feeling as he looked at the far-flung beauty spread before him.

"We're barbarians," he said quietly.

She turned to him and reached for his hand. "Not all of us." she said tenderly. "Not you or Paul or Mac or Marge or Dave . . . I could go on for quite a while."

Steve took her hand, slid back the glove, and kissed her palm.

UPI NEWS SPECIAL—
PRESIDENT HARLAND KILLED

Washington, D.C.—President Matthew Harland and the entire leaders of the newly formed National Security Force were killed today when an explosion rocked the White House. A spokesman stated officials have determined that a Russian agent infiltrated the president's National Security Force and acted as a suicide bomber. The explosion took place in the bombproof underground War Room minimizing any damage to the White House itself. Vice president Grayson has been notified and is expected to assume command of the nation.

Chapter 26

Northern California

THE RECONNAISSANCE HELICOPTER had left Beale Air Force Base just before dawn, and as the sun came up, the Lieutenant sitting in the copilot's seat spotted the charred wreckage of the Sikorsky Firehawk.

"There it is," he said to the pilot. "Can you land there?"

The pilot, Phil Jordan, nodded and set the chopper down in a small clearing about thirty yards from the crash site.

The two men walked quickly to the wreck, passing chunks of metal that were scattered all over the place. The Lieutenant looked inside the smashed cabin and fought down the nausea that welled up inside him. "Only one body," he said. "It's still strapped into the pilot's seat."

"Then it's probably not Dr. Myles."

"No, . . . it must be Paul Linder," the Lieutenant said looking at the burned figure. There wasn't much left of the body to identify the man. "He must have dropped the other two somewhere."

The pilot nodded in agreement.

"Well," the Lieutenant said heavily, "my orders were to backtrack and search for the others, if they weren't all in the helicopter."

"And shoot on sight," the pilot added.

"Yes."

The two men went back to their helicopter, and the pilot started the motor.

"Head north," the Lieutenant said. "He was going south when the fighter got him. Stay low so we can watch for any tracks in the snow."

The pilot swung the helicopter north and the Lieutenant took out a pair of binoculars and scanned the mountainside beneath them. "They'd probably head right for some kind of shelter. It's damn cold up here at night," he commented, thinking of the sub-freezing temperatures in the Sierras at this time of year.

"You don't seem too keen about this mission," the pilot observed. "What did this woman do, anyway?"

"I wish I knew," the Lieutenant replied heavily. "There's something screwy here, all right. First the orders were to arrest her, and then they were changed to shoot her on sight." He turned and looked at the pilot. "I'll follow my orders," he said sharply. "But I don't have to like it. . . ."

"I'm with you, buddy," the pilot said equably. "I just couldn't help wondering what in hell's going on. Did you hear those broadcasts? They're running continuously. I don't know what to think. I heard some scuttlebutt that this new antidote really works. . . . And here we are trying to shoot down the doctor who made it." He shrugged, "I just follow orders, too. . . ."

The Lieutenant stemmed a rising annoyance. This guy Jordan

talks too much, he thought. He turned in his seat and concentrated on watching the land below. And except for the throb of the motor, it was quiet in the cabin.

"There's Squaw Valley up ahead. Let's check it out," the Lieutenant said, a few minutes later. The helicopter hovered over the group of buildings. "Take it down. I see some tracks between the buildings."

The pilot landed and shut off the motor. "They'd have heard us coming," he said. "They won't be here now."

"We better check anyway." The Lieutenant picked up his machine gun and stepped out of the chopper.

They checked the buildings carefully, but quickly. "They were here all right. And there's only one place they could have gone." The pilot looked at the cables strung toward the high peaks.

"Let's get on with it," the Lieutenant said in irritation. "I have to report in, and I want to be able to tell them something concrete."

"Then we'd better move." The pilot looked at the sky. "It's perfectly clear right now, but the forecast said we're supposed to have more snow up here today. If it comes down heavy, we won't be able to see a thing."

"Head for the summit," the Lieutenant ordered, as the helicopter rose slowly above the ski resort.

The pilot began to crisscross the slopes in a mechanical search pattern. As the search slowly continued, clouds started to gather.

Balancing the machine gun on his knees, the Lieutenant searched the slopes carefully. "There!" he said, as they cleared the pinnacle of a mountain. "Ski tracks—follow them."

As the pilot swung the helicopter along the path marked clear and sharp in the virgin snow, the first few flakes of new snow began to fall.

"Up ahead," the Lieutenant said, "about five hundred yards to the right."

"I see them," the pilot replied, and his hand dropped to the holstered gun at his side.

The Lieutenant watched the fleeing figures through the binoculars. They had heard the helicopter and were skiing fast toward the shelter of a stand of trees at the base of the slope. His hand gripped the machine gun. He knew they'd never make it when the smaller figure—it must be the woman—fell, and the man stopped and went back to her. He'd never shot a woman before. The helicopter was closing on the couple. He had to raise the machine gun and fire . . . but he couldn't make himself do it.

He turned to the pilot who watched him with cold eyes, a revolver in his hand.

Startled, the Lieutenant blurted, "What are you doing? Whose side are you on?"

"I'm on their side." Jordan nodded toward the fleeing couple.

"Well, you won't get an argument from me so put your gun away," the Lieutenant said angrily. "As far as I'm concerned someone else can have *this* job." He jerked his head toward the couple below.

The pilot smiled and put away his revolver. "Doctor Myles can't go far. The roads are blocked. There are no open airfields nearby. If she *has* done anything that means she should be shot, she'll be found." His words were clipped and precise.

The Lieutenant stared at him in surprise. The man's easy, off-hand manner had changed completely in the last few minutes.

"It's just as well we couldn't locate Dr. Myles," the pilot said quietly. "Our report will indicate a fruitless search." He met the Lieutenant's gaze. "I think that's best, don't you?"

A curious blend of relief and confusion appeared on the young officer's face. He nodded in agreement, and then looked away.

The pilot smiled and turned the helicopter south.

Outside, the snow began to fall more heavily.

FROM THE SHELTER of the trees, Resa and Steve watched the helicopter move away from them.

"Why are they leaving?" Resa asked, her voice still breathless from the exhausting run down the slope.

"I don't know," Steve said slowly. "It's a military helicopter . . . and I know they saw us." He shook his head. "They were almost right on top of us."

"Maybe they weren't really searching for us, Steve. Maybe Paul did ditch the helicopter in the lake. . . . Those men could just have been on a routine patrol."

"Maybe . . . ," Steve said. "But we better get out of here while we can."

"We'll have to use the snowshoes for a bit."

They strapped their snowshoes on, and moved quickly through the trees toward the next open slope on which they could ski.

Resa's precise mind examined and rejected the possible explanations for their encounter with the military helicopter as she led Steve through the deep snow. It didn't make any sense, she decided. She knew Paul hadn't made it to the lake because she'd seen the explosion when the missile hit. She could only hope he had been able to jump in time.

They came out of the trees at the top of a wide rolling slope. "We can ski now," she said to Steve. "We'll take it slow. This thin air takes some getting used to."

Steve helped her put on her skis and then quickly stepped into his own. "You lead off. Just take it easy, darling," he said, concern in his voice.

She smiled. "I'm all right. Just a little tired."

Steve set the edges of his skis and pushed off in an easy traverse across the hill as he followed her.

The snow fell heavily now, making it difficult to see where she was going. But it will cover our tracks, Resa thought. Well worth the extra effort they would have to expend to reach the cabin. She concentrated on choosing the best path around the moguls on the steep slope.

"We're almost there," Resa called to him as she turned and

stopped after about twenty minutes of hard skiing.

He came up beside her. "Where to?"

"It's a straight run now," she said. "At the bottom of this hill we only have a short hike through those trees to the cabin."

Steve nodded, and Resa pushed off down the hill.

When they reached the bottom, Steve took her skis and hefted them onto his shoulder along with his own and motioned to Resa to head out.

She led the way through the trees. Two days, she thought to herself. That was what she had promised Blair. Then they would head for the Palo Alto area. She was concerned about dragging Steve into danger. But what he did for a living was incredibly danger-ous—it wouldn't be anything new to him.

How vulnerable love makes one, she thought. . . . And how alive . . .

They topped a small rise and saw the shadowed outline of the cabin through the falling snow.

Steve turned to Resa. Her face was pale and strained; she was exhausted.

"We're here," she said in relief.

The catch in her voice tore at his heart. He put his arm around her slender shoulders and drew her closer to him. "Yes, darling," he whispered. "We're safe now."

Snow blocked shut the door of the cabin; Steve used his snow-shoes as a scoop to clear it. The cold damp air had pervaded the cabin, but just to have shelter from the snow and the rising wind was a relief.

Steve started the generator Mac had installed at the cabin and turned the electric heaters in the rooms on full. While Resa watched from the couch, he started a roaring fire in the large stone fireplace that filled an entire wall in the cozy living room.

"Are you hungry?" Steve asked, eyeing Resa's pale face with concern. She shook her head. "I'm too tired to eat a thing right now. Maybe later . . ."

Steve helped her take off the heavy parka and ski boots and then discarded his own heavy clothing and joined her on the couch in front of the crackling fire. They fell asleep there, entwined in each other's arms.

Exhausted, they slept through the entire night and most of the morning, until a pounding on the door and Schaeffer's voice awakened them.

Resa jumped up and opened the cabin door quickly, her fears dispelled the moment she saw the broad grin on Schaeffer's face.

"This is Phil Jordan," Schaeffer said, nodding toward the man standing beside him. "He's with us. It's okay. Blair sent word to us to bring both of you out. Harland and his special corps aren't with us anymore."

"What happened?" Resa asked.

"The Russian spy, Rostov, took them all out with a bomb, himself included."

"Damn," Resa muttered. "I wanted the bastard myself."

CNN—BREAKING NEWS
LIVE FROM WASHINGTON CORRESPONDENT
ALICE ROBERTA JENNINGS

"Former Vice President Theodore Grayson has assumed the office of president of the United States. One of his first acts was to grant full amnesty to all members of the scientific community who were charged with treason under President Harland's presidency.

"At a brief press conference, the president said steps would be taken to get the antidote to Project Immunity manufactured and dispersed to the public and to international groups, such as the World Health Organization and the Red Cross as soon as possible. He briefly addressed the need to provide food and shelter to those left devastated by the chaos resulting in the aftermath of Project Immunity."

Chapter 27

Los Gatos, California

RESA LINGERED ALONE for a few moments at the freshly dug gravesite in the small cemetery in the Los Gatos foothills, her heart heavy with grief. Paul was with Cathy now. At least she hoped that was what happened. They had been all she had left of her family. And her pain was too raw to feel any comfort from the thought that Paul and Cathy were together. She wanted them back. She wanted them with her.

"Paul," she said quietly. "I would have kept my promise to you to get the man responsible for Cathy's death, but someone else already took care of that." She thought back to the long talk she'd had with Dave Blair. Rostov had been the one who set the steps into motion that had ended with the attack on her and Cathy. But he'd been following orders from the chief of state of the Russian Federation, President Aleksandr Ivanovich Vassilov. And he was killed along with millions of innocents in Moscow.

So the vendetta was finished, but not the repercussions. Blair had pleaded with her to help the government make amends with the scientific community. He was deeply concerned about the amount of radiation released in the short, violent war. "There is so much to be done, Resa, so much damage to repair, so much healing needed." And, of course, she had agreed to do all she could.

Finally, she turned away and looked for Steve among the throng of people who had stayed after the brief memorial services for Paul. She saw him standing beside Blair, and his eyes, warm with love and compassion, met hers and lingered for a moment. Her heart was full with love as she returned his warm gaze. He was her family now.

She walked toward him and then stopped as a man detached himself from the crowd and came forward to her.

Resa recognized those much-publicized features at once. It was the former vice president, Theodore Grayson, who was now the new president of the United States. She watched Grayson approach with mixed feelings. The man was as unlike Harland as night and day, but he was still a politician, and Resa felt an almost automatic distrust and dislike of all of them. David Blair was the one exception, the only one.

The two studied each other, and Resa met the president's steady gaze with more than a little cold challenge in her eyes.

"I wanted to meet you," Grayson said simply. Then he looked toward the mound of newly turned earth behind her. "And I wanted to pay my respects to him," he added quietly.

Resa saw a fleeting look of pain cloud Grayson's candid, level gaze and she remembered with a twinge of shame that the new president had lost his wife and son to the Project Immunity syndrome.

"Thank you, Mr. President," Resa said gently. "He would have appreciated it."

Grayson nodded. "I've authorized a posthumous award of the Presidential Medal of Freedom With Distinction to Paul. And if we had a functioning Congress to act he would also be awarded a Congressional Gold Medal. Both are the highest civilian awards we have. But he deserves so much more. . . ."

"Will you walk with me?" Grayson motioned toward the empty paths in the main area of the cemetery.

Resa nodded and fell in step as the president moved away from the onlookers. Behind them, at a discreet distance, two secret service men followed.

Grayson began to speak in a quiet, earnest tone. "I know you're too intelligent to blame me for Harland's mistakes, but you've suffered a great deal at his hands and I wanted to dispel any doubts you might have about me by meeting you in person."

Resa didn't speak for a few moments. "Mistakes is a pretty weak word to describe what Harland did," she said shortly.

Grayson sighed and nodded. "Toward the end, he was a sick man, Dr. Myles. And he misused the power he had." The president paused and faced her. "I give you my word it won't happen again," he said steadily, his eyes meeting Resa's wary gaze. "At least, not on my watch."

"Well," Resa responded slowly, her tone dry, "I'm glad it's still going to be a free country."

Grayson laughed softly and placed his hand on her shoulder. "I guarantee it. Please trust me."

"I do, but—well, Mr. President, let me spell it out," she admonished gently. "Your goals are too small. . . . The syndrome caused *worldwide disaster.*

"I think we've lost at least half of the world's population. Something good should come out of all that pain and suffering. Maybe something like a free planet. You could help to make that happen."

Startled, Grayson looked at the bittersweet smile on Resa's face. He was silent for a few minutes, lost in thought.

"Sir, I know it will be a tremendous undertaking after all the deaths, all the destruction. . . . But I know you've probably heard words like: *If not now, when? If not us, who?*"

Then Resa saw him smile, a smile that touched those steady, determined eyes, and she felt his personal charisma that had catapulted him from a relatively unknown young senator to the vice presidency in his first campaign for that office.

"Worldwide freedom is not an easy goal, but I'm willing to try, if you're willing to help."

She returned his smile and yielded to the urgings of her instincts that here was a man worthy of trust.

"I'm with you, Mr. President," Resa said with a smile. "A free planet . . ."

Grayson nodded, his pleasure reflected openly in the look he gave her.

"Then we'd better get busy," he said, and folding her arm in his, turned back to the small group at the far end of the cemetery and began to walk briskly toward them "We have one hell of a lot of work to do."

"We do indeed." She looked ahead and saw Steve walking to meet them. She waited until she made eye contact with him, and then smiled to let him know that all was well.

TWO YEARS LATER

CNN NEWS Bulletin—

The Nobel Foundation announced today that Dr. Resa Myles has been awarded two international prizes. She has been unanimously voted as the recipient of the Nobel Prize for medicine for her leadership in developing an antidote to the Project Immunity syndrome.

She has also been awarded the Nobel Prize for the promotion of world peace. The latter prize is bestowed on her for her efforts in disseminating the antidote on a worldwide basis, for her efforts to rally the worldwide scientific community to deal with the nuclear contamination in Russia and China, and for her role in working with governments worldwide to set up safeguards against any future nuclear disasters.

When interviewed, Dr. Myles said the skill and knowledge of her late brother-in-law, Paul Linder, made it possible for her to broadcast the information about the antidote to the world.

"If they had a Nobel prize for saving the world," she stated, "my brother-in-law would definitely have been a recipient."

About the Author

Arline Todd is the former owner of Todd Advertising, a Silicon Valley, California agency that specialized in advertising and sales promotion for a variety of high-tech companies. She has an eclectic educational background that includes nursing, engineering science, technical journalism, and fine art and graphic design. She received a BS from Cal Poly, San Luis Obispo, and an MS from San Jose State University.

Currently, Arline is working on a futuristic series and a romantic suspense novel. She has lived in many places, including New York, North Carolina, Alabama, Pennsylvania, California, and England. Today she lives in a small suburb of Dallas, Texas close to her daughter and four grandchildren.

Arline enjoys hearing from readers. Feel free to contact her via e-mail at arline.todd@gmail.com or on Facebook.

ARLINE TODD